OVERTURN

Overturn

HARRY HAINES

Harry Haines
12/16/14

Colonial Publishing, Inc.

This novel does not depict any actual person or event.

Colonial Publishing, Inc.
2576 Oak Valley Drive
Vienna, VA 22181

COVER DESIGN: Steven L. Mayes
Library of Congress Control Number: 2014913296
First Edition—First Printing 2014
ISBN: 978-0-9834537-4-1
Printed in Canada

To the memory of Shirley . . .
. . . my first reader.
I miss her more than words can say.

Prologue

In April, during a presidential election year, the Texas Legislature delivered the prize. They passed House Bill 27, making all abortions illegal throughout the state. The country's leading political journalists were virtually unanimous on two points: (1) it couldn't have happened at a worse time, and (2) this action would eventually lead to a confrontation that would overturn *Roe v. Wade*.

Part I

MAY

1

At home, 1109 Westbrook Terrace, Amarillo, Texas

The day they took my daughter . . .

The day I would later regard as the worst day of my life . . .

The day, like a thousand others, started with mundane, commonplace routine. I remember sitting at the breakfast table annoyed by two simple irritants—a morning paper with bad news and an empty coffee cup. My wife hovered with her carafe, offering to fix the latter.

"More?" Jenny asked.

I nodded. "Just a half."

Then, as she attempted to pour, our seventeen-year-old son Brent brushed through the kitchen with his trombone. "I'm late," he said as he snatched a piece of toast and ran out the door. Seconds later we heard the roar of his old jalopy.

"I'm going to take his keys if he doesn't get that muffler fixed," I groused.

"Why so grumpy this morning?" Jenny asked as she poured.

"McCormack." I pointed to the headline story in this morning's *Amarillo Globe-News*. It featured an oversized photograph of presidential candidate Reginald Q. McCormack standing in front of the West Texas Abortion Clinic—which had been located in Lubbock.

Past tense.

The clinic was now closed because of House Bill 27—legislation passed almost a month ago—which made it illegal for any woman to have an abortion in the state of Texas. The newspaper article recounted details that now led to a McCormack visit.

Jenny pushed the paper back toward me. "I don't see why you're so upset. You don't do abortions."

I took the paper. "Rarely."

Her eyes blazed at me. I knew that look—the glare of confrontation—as she took the chair opposite me. "What do you mean—rarely?"

"Just what I said. I *rarely* do abortions."

"My God, Joe. You never told me."

Our eyes met, and I felt suddenly overwhelmed by the importance of standing my ground. "Remember doctor/patient privilege? You know I can't tell you a lot of things, even if I want to."

"How many?" Apparently my wife felt the need to stand her ground, too.

"Jenny, don't go there."

"I have a right to know how many babies my husband has killed."

I looked away and sighed. "Jenny, I really don't want to talk about this."

"My God, Joe, have you forgotten we're Catholic? What would all our friends at St. Mary's think if they knew?"

Sometimes a pause helps, so I took a moment to study Jenny before my next words escalated into something we might both regret. I thought about how lucky I was to have such an attractive spouse. Her tall narrow frame, long graceful neck, beautiful brown hair with just a touch of gray—always neatly groomed—belied her forty-six years. Even at breakfast, in robe and slippers, she exuded a photogenic elegance.

The phone rang. Normally I would have dreaded it, since early-morning calls at a doctor's house almost always bring bad news. That morning, for obvious reasons, I welcomed the interruption.

"Hello." I answered before the second ring.

"Dr. Wright, this is Caitlin."

I recognized the voice of my daughter's twenty-three-year-old roommate, Caitlin Rogers. Both were seniors at Canyon State University.

"Bretta's missing."

At the sound of my daughter's name, I gripped the phone tighter. "Say again?"

"This is finals week," Caitlin continued in a rush. "Bretta went to the library to study last night. Before she left, she told me not to wait up for her. When I awoke this morning, she wasn't here, and her bed hasn't been slept in."

I fought the dread as I tried to be logical. "Have you called her cell? Maybe she spent the night somewhere else. What about her boyfriend?"

"No way," Caitlin balked. "Our *Forms and Analysis* final is at ten o'clock this morning, and it's the biggest and toughest of all our tests. We'd planned to go out for breakfast together and cram for the exam."

"I'll be right there." I hesitated. "Maybe you'd better call campus police."

"I already have. They're on the way." She hung up.

"What about Bretta?" Jenny asked, a worried look on her face as I hung up the phone.

I tried to put a better face on it as I related the conversation and collected my keys. "Maybe Caitlin's upset about nothing. There's probably some plausible explanation."

"I'm going with you," Jenny said, her voice filled with anxiety. She quickly dressed, and together we rushed for the door.

On the way I called the hospital and arranged for my medical partner, Melvin Campbell, to take rounds for me. Then, in silence, we drove fifteen miles south to Bretta's small, campus apartment in record time.

My heart thudded in my chest when I saw red and blue lights flashing—a university police cruiser parked at the curb. We hurried inside where we found Caitlin arguing with two campus cops.

There was no sign of our daughter.

2

Bretta's Apartment, 2016 Second Avenue, Canyon, Texas

I listened as Caitlin gave the officers grief about an APB, an all-points bulletin. She wanted the police to issue one immediately. They refused, saying their policy required a twenty-four-hour waiting period.

"Excuse me, Officer," I said, interrupting as I pulled out my smart phone. "I'm Bretta's father. I see your badge is number 121. Could I get your name?"

"Bobby Griffin."

"And yours, sir?" I turned to the second policeman and entered badge number 124.

"Tom Anderson," he said, shaking his head.

"We need action," I said, keeping my voice restrained, nonthreatening. "My daughter didn't come home last night, and nobody's seen her since late yesterday. I want an APB—"

Officer Griffin interrupted. "Sir, taking our badge numbers and calling headquarters isn't going to change things. We see situations like this over and over again with college kids."

"Like I was telling Miss Rogers," Anderson continued, "we've seen this too many times. College kids are notorious for disappearing overnight. They turn up sooner or later, full of apologies for worrying everyone when they've been partying or sleeping in someone's dorm room."

"Sir, my daughter isn't in the habit of—"

"I'm sorry," Officer Griffin cut in again. "There's simply nothing we can do until twenty-four hours have passed."

Griffin and Anderson got in their cruiser, turned off the flashing strobes, and started backing away from the curb.

I followed along, pleading with them, and finally, as they drove away, clenching my fist and yelling, "You can't value rules and procedures more than the life of my daughter." I knew Bretta would not do this on purpose.

Frustrated and defeated, Jenny, Caitlin, and I drove the four blocks to the library where Bretta had supposedly spent Sunday evening studying with friends. Caitlin found three of Bretta's study-buddies who confirmed that she had left a few minutes before midnight to walk home.

"Alone?" I asked.

They looked at one another, then back at me, three heads bobbing up and down in affirmation, a speechless reaction to the accusatory tone in my voice.

"Did she say anything as she was leaving—that perhaps she wasn't going back to her apartment?"

Then it came. A flood of chatter as all three reported that Bretta planned to get a good night's sleep, to be ready for the difficult test.

We left on foot to search the short distance between the library and the girls' apartment. Jenny and Caitlin started knocking on doors, checking every house.

My initial concern now turned into frantic worry. I hurriedly walked the path—intending to do it twice—first on one side of the street, again on the other. On the second pass I spotted an article of clothing in some Juniper bushes off to the side, less than a block from the girls' apartment. In my haste I'd almost missed it.

It was a maroon, CSU jacket. Bloodstains drenched the front, hem, and right sleeve.

In my lifetime I've occasionally felt fear, but never like that moment. As I reached into the green foliage, my heart raced with terror. Bretta had a coat just like this one. I hoped—I prayed—this one would have a name. Someone else's.

It didn't.

But in the pocket I found a cell phone. With trembling hands I tried to work it, to find a clue to ownership. Whether my nervous frustration, a dead battery, or damage to the phone was the cause, the result was exasperating failure. The damned gadget refused to give up its secret.

I called 911 on *my* cell phone and started running toward Jenny and Caitlin, back toward the library.

Within minutes two police cruisers answered our call—one from University PD, the other from the Randall County Sheriff's office. On the steps of the library, with teary eyes and trembling hands, Jenny and I showed four officers the bloody jacket and broken phone. Immediately, one of the officers took the cell phone and headed to the bi-county crime lab to have an electronics expert examine it. Another took the jacket to Northwest Texas Hospital where they had a sample of Bretta's blood work and could run tests to see if the jacket's bloodstains matched.

Amid all this activity, the CSU dean came to speak with the police.

Jenny and I stood nearby, anxious to hear if he had something to report.

"Bretta failed to show for her ten o'clock final," the dean said.

His words sucked all the breath from my lungs and left me paralyzed. I couldn't breathe. Instinctively I grabbed Jenny and held her tight. And, as air eased back into my lungs, I worried about my wife, about what I would do if she fainted.

As so often happens in life, I worried about the wrong thing. Instead of fainting, Jenny started babbling.

"Joe, we've got to call the relatives. We've got to *do* something. To notify them that Bretta's missing. Go to the high school and find Brent. We must tell Brent. What about the neighbors—maybe they'll help us. Joe, you've got to do something." She pulled away, her raving almost maniacal.

Gently, I put my arm around her, pulled her close again, and tried to calm her. "Yes, you're right. We need to go to the high school and get Brent."

One of the policemen stood nearby, watching, police radio in hand. "Want me to call for a doctor?" he asked.

"I *am* a doctor," I said. "She's breathing normally. She just needs some time to calm down a little. We're both in shock here. I'm sure you can understand that. I'm going to take my wife to Amarillo High and pick up our son."

"Leave me information where you can be reached," the officer said. "Cell and home phone numbers."

I quickly scribbled the information on his notepad. Then Jenny and I left.

After picking up Brent, we drove home and found the FBI waiting at the front door. Special Agent Willis Bernhardt wanted to use our house to coordinate the efforts of University Police, Canyon PD, Randall

County Sheriff, and the Texas Highway Patrol.

Once Brent had joined us, Jenny seemed calmer. The spurt of mania she'd exhibited earlier had all but disappeared. Cool now, and focused, she offered help in any way she could. Jenny gave Bernhardt a copy of Bretta's graduation photo.

The FBI agent studied the photo for a moment. "Beautiful girl," he said and held it where we both could see it.

As I looked at those enormous blue eyes, perky nose, beautiful-white even teeth, and high cheekbones—topped by silky, blonde hair—that projected an image of rampant femininity, her round, open face pulled at my heartstrings.

"I'll give this to the media," he said. "They'll make copies and distribute it."

Thirty minutes later, Bernhardt pulled me aside, into the kitchen. With a somber face he informed me, "The blood on the jacket matched your daughter's."

I put a fist through the wall.

When the FBI tells you it's your daughter, *your daughter's blood,* your thinking stops and you feel compelled to do something violent. I slammed the damn wall so hard it pulverized the sheetrock, creating a huge hole, debris falling everywhere.

"Hey. Hey man, take it easy," Bernhardt yelled. Two policemen rushed over and grabbed me by the arms.

The four of us stood there for a moment with me breathing hard. Then the cops led me to the sink, washed and bandaged my hand. Role reversal—police giving medical assistance to the doctor—another example of how our world had turned upside down.

In another half hour, Bernhardt announced that the cell phone was Bretta's. The two officers stood ready in case I went ballistic again. But they needn't have worried. Like Jenny had done earlier, my mania had passed.

As each bit of information compounded the bad news and inched toward an unthinkable tragedy, a cloak of naked fear fell over our home. Jenny cried continuously, her face swollen with grief, as I stood helplessly by, praying for a break in the case.

The six o'clock news opened with Bretta's photograph. "Bretta Jean Wright," a newscaster announced in voiceover, "has disappeared without a trace. The hunt for this twenty-three-year-old music major is area law enforcement's number one priority. Authorities report that . . . ."

Lead story and the reporter made it sound like a sales pitch—exploitation to build his market share. This was our daughter they were talking about. My beautiful, talented, warm, golden girl. My baby. Rare tears spilled onto my cheeks. I brushed them away with the back of my bandaged hand, feeling the rough stubble of a day's growth. Had it been a full day since we learned she was missing?

The TV blinked off. I looked at Jenny, the remote in her hand, face hard. "Let's eat," she said, heading for the kitchen

"I'm not hungry," Brent spoke as he started up the stairway toward his room.

I'd forgotten he was there. Forgotten nearly everything but Bretta.

"You have to eat," Jenny called back. But we all knew this was just a mother's words.

Brent paused, turned and his stare met mine. Raw pain glazed over his eyes, the muscles in his face taut. This seventeen-year-old kid hadn't shed a tear since kindergarten. But I knew that at that moment he wanted my reassurance, my calm, my strength. I tried. But the words wouldn't come. Silently, I went to him and we embraced, after which he retreated up the stairs to his room.

I found Jenny in the kitchen slapping sandwiches together like a factory worker. Bread. Meat. Mayo. Bread. Meat. Mayo.

"Two's enough," I said. "Brent's upstairs."

Jenny looked at me, lips quivering, more tears welling in red eyes.

I crossed the room to take her in my arms. She clung to me, weeping, trembling.

Was Bretta even alive? I winced at the question my traitorous heart was asking. Another part of me answered—yes, she was. She had to be.

The sandwiches remained on the kitchen counter, untouched, a sign of our despair.

No word came from police all evening. Finally, Jenny started running the vacuum sweeper like a madwoman. To get away, I climbed the stairs to Bretta's room. Maybe I'd find a clue there. Something that would hint at where she was.

Fading daylight cast eerie shadows over the once-happy room. I flipped on a light and gazed at the collection of dolls on the shelf. At the ruffles on her curtains. At the photos on the bulletin board. Bretta smiling with her friends. *Who would want to hurt her*?

I picked up a framed photo from the desk. Bretta and Brent at Disneyland. She wore braces.

My chest felt tight, and I wondered for a moment if I was having a heart attack. Then Brent came to the door. "Dad, can we talk?"

His presence caused me to relax, and the tightness eased. But, just as I opened my mouth to respond, the phone rang. Jenny answered downstairs.

Brent and I rushed to the master bedroom, and I picked up the extension in time to hear Agent Bernhardt's words.

"We've found Bretta."

3

At home, 1109 Westbrook Terrace

"Thank God," Jenny cried out on the extension.

"How is she?" I asked, fearing the answer.

"Alive," Bernhardt answered.

The FBI agent's one-word description of Bretta's condition hit me like a sledgehammer. Even a non-medical parent would read sinister implications. As a doctor, I dreaded the worst.

"She's in an ambulance in route to Northwest," he said.

"We're on our way." I slammed the receiver into its cradle.

The three of us jumped into my BMW, and I drove like an Indianapolis 500 racer through almost-deserted streets to Northwest Texas Hospital. Jenny, always an outspoken critic of any speeding, sat beside me in the front passenger seat, but didn't say a word. In the rearview mirror, I saw Brent in the back seat pull his seatbelt tighter.

At the hospital, we found four police cars, red and blue lights flashing. In the center of the light show was an ambulance—backed up to the loading ramp, its rear doors open. Instead of pulling into my usual spot in the reserved "doctors parking," I stopped at the emergency entrance and literally ran into the ER, Jenny and Brent struggling to keep up. There we found nurse Elsa Jennings, two EMTs, and a score of uniformed police.

Elsa recognized me. "She's in ER2. Dr. Young's with her."

I left Jenny and Brent with the police and entered examination room number two. Peter Young, MD—the hospital's ER chief—and two nurses huddled around the treatment table. Pete looked at me, and for a moment, our eyes locked. He was twenty years my junior, and I saw uncertainty in his face.

"Joe, I'm not sure you should be here," Young said. He didn't need to explain—we both knew the standard policy. Because emotional involvement can affect medical judgment, doctors typically refrain from surgical treatment of their own family.

"You're in charge," I assured him. "I'm only here to assist."

"I've already called Irwin and Olsen. They're on the way."

I recognized the names. Both were top-notch specialists—Irwin in anesthesiology, Olsen in orthopedics. A team composed of these three doctors guaranteed that my daughter would get the best in medical care. Young was right; they didn't need a fourth physician. But I wanted to do something . . . anything to care for my daughter.

"Pete, please. I'll stay out of your way."

He grimaced—an acknowledgement of our circumstances, there wasn't time to argue—and turned to the two nurses. "Vital signs," he ordered. "Get ready for multiple transfusions."

The nurses had anticipated his orders and were already busy attaching monitors and electronic leads. In a matter of seconds, they had IV tubes everywhere, trying to get blood going.

Then the doors flew open as Doctors Irwin and Olsen rushed into the room. The presence of so many MDs gathered around the small ER table escalated our feeling of crisis to a new level. This was Bretta. This was my daughter lying there and it scared me. With no movement, no signs of life, fear caused my heart to pound and, for a moment, my brain turned to mush. I didn't know what to do.

Others in the room moved with purpose. Irwin organized the anesthetic, Olsen examined the thigh area, Young directed the nurses with the IVs.

Finally, in the midst of all this feverish activity, I made a decision to work my way around to the far side of the table where I got my first full look at the patient's face. What I saw took my breath away.

I didn't recognize her as my daughter.

4

The ER, Northwest Texas Hospital, Amarillo

I stood there, paralyzed by revulsion, staring at the bloody, mangled face. How could this be my beautiful daughter? Then the team—three doctors and two nurses—turned her so as to address the bleeding in her leg, and I saw the birthmark.

Bretta was born with a small, discolored, almost square, pink patch of skin behind her left ear. When she was a child, we sometimes joked about it, about how it was hidden by her hair, about how we would keep the secret of her "pink freckle." This tiny, distinctive pinkness of the skin measured less than a half-inch across—but it was absolutely unique.

We all have memorable incidents in our lives that jar us, that pierce our souls with such force they become etched forever in the gray matter of our brains. Recognizing Bretta's birthmark, as she lay comatose on that ER table, was such a moment for me. I'll never forget the emotional jolt; it transformed me. Right then my persona changed from an apprehensive zombie into a medical machine. A calmness came over me, and my new self brought into sharp focus the complex problems that lay on the ER table. At that instant, it seemed as if my entire life—my medical training, my years of experience as a practicing physician—became nothing less than preparation for this time. It gave me super strength, a physical/mental prowess, and I reacted. Nothing else mattered. I had been given, by some unexplainable twist of fate, the opportunity—no, the responsibility—to save my daughter.

"Blood pressure thirty-five over fifteen," a nurse said.

"Pulse irregular, almost unreadable, probably less than ten," said another.

With fresh, razor-sharp, mental awareness, I analyzed the patient and the procedures now reported.

Heat.

The answer leaped out at me. Bretta needed heat.

"She's been out all night," I said. "She's hypothermic. We've got to warm her."

Dr. Young was the first to react.

"I agree," he said. "Get some blankets. And be sure those IVs are heated. We don't want cold fluids going into her."

Immediately, the team responded. For the next few minutes the room accelerated into a blur of physical motion. Blankets appeared out of nowhere. Multiple hands changed the infusion packets.

In the midst of these actions to warm our patient, a nurse wearing blue scrubs came to the table. I recognized her. And her different colored clothing identified her as a member of Northwest's special rape team.

"Rape kit?" this new nurse asked. "The EMTs reported bleeding and bruising in her pelvic area. They say she's obviously been attacked."

"Not now," I answered, my voice harsh, authoritative. "If we don't keep her alive, it's not going to matter."

“Pulse a bit stronger,” a nurse said. “We now have a reading of ten.”

A monitor’s slow, rhythmic beep filled the room—an impersonal, mechanical testimony confirming the nurse’s statement.

“Obviously, the left femur is fractured,” Dr. Olsen said. “And all that bleeding from her thigh indicates there must be damage to the femoral artery.”

“We need to prioritize,” I said. “First things first if we’re going to save this patient.”

“Blood pressure is improving,” a nurse said. “We’re fifty over twenty-five. And body temp has come up a degree.”

“Pulse is building. It just increased from ten to twelve.”

“Rape kit?” the nurse in blue scrubs repeated. “If we don’t do it now, we’ll lose the evidence needed for prosecution.”

Suddenly, the monitor emitted a high-pitched, steady tone—the dreaded signal of cardiac arrest.

“We’re losing her,” Dr. Irwin shouted.

5

The ER

The room erupted into a cacophony of loud voices.

"Increased bleeding from the femoral artery," Olsen shouted.

"Renal failure," Irwin barked, his volume even higher. "Kidneys are shutting down."

"Pete," I yelled, my voice the loudest of all, words in a jumbled rush, "she came in with low body temp that slowed the hemorrhaging. Now that her vitals are up, she's bleeding out."

Everyone in the room—the four doctors most of all—could see the abrupt reversal of circumstances. A moment ago, Bretta was improving, but warming had caused her to slip into cardiac arrhythmia—a death sentence.

Dr. Peter Young just stood there, staring at me, his face turning white, obviously thunderstruck by the turnaround.

As I looked into Young's face and our eyes locked, a subtle warning in the back of my brain grabbed me. Suddenly, like a flashing neon sign, it came to me that our loudness was wrong . . . that these frantic, emotional outbursts were creating confusion. Olsen and Irwin were communicating at the top of their lungs. And I was an even worse offender.

Instantly, I realized two things: we needed less bluster and immediate action.

In a quiet, well-modulated, normal tone of voice, I said, "Pete, you've got to shock her." I handed him the paddles.

Young nodded and then, apparently without thinking, he reacted. To his credit, he knew exactly what to do, and he did it quickly, decisively. First, he ripped away the blankets and what was left of Britta's clothing until her chest was bare. Then, with practiced skill, he placed the electrical paddles in perfect position and yelled, "Clear."

We all backed away. Everyone knew to avoid touching Bretta, the table, anything that might carry the electrical shock.

The nurse at the controls pressed the release switch, and we all heard the terrible, awful sound of cardiac stimulation—the medical treatment of last resort for a human whose heart has stopped.

As expected, the electricity caused Bretta to react. Though unconscious, her body visibly contracted.

"Clear," Pete yelled for the second time in as many minutes.

Again, we all backed away.

The room became deathly quiet. No one moved. And I had the sensation that no one even breathed.

The nurse at the controls pressed the switch.

I watched, I prayed, I willed my daughter to respond. The crackle of electricity permeated the room as Bretta's limp body stiffened, almost jumped from the table.

She's breathing," Irwin said, his voice, emulating mine, now calm.

"We have a pulse," the nurse at the monitor said.

"Pete," Olsen said, his voice returning to normal volume, "we've got to stop the hemorrhaging around the femur. She'll bleed out in minutes if we don't."

I said a silent prayer. I thanked God for the skill of these three doctors. Young had performed the shock treatment perfectly. Olsen knew exactly what to do to stop Bretta's bleeding from the femoral artery. And I saw Irwin assuming coordination as the anesthesiologist, carefully guarding Bretta's fragile cardio-pulmonary condition.

The monitor resumed its steady beep—giving the room a feeling of hope.

The ER came back to life. What had been, for the past two minutes, an assemblage of people who stood without movement, became a frenzy of medical activity.

Olsen and his nurse stopped the flow of blood from Bretta's thigh, the most immediate danger.

Irwin concentrated on vital signs and pronounced her pulse regular, an accomplishment I would have thought impossible just minutes ago.

Young again took over as ER chief and established the priority of treatment.

In the midst of all this carefully coordinated and unbelievably successful work, the nurse from the rape treatment center interrupted for the third time. "Rape kit?" she asked. "It has to be done before she's cleaned up. And we should include a test for pregnancy."

Young exploded with anger. In a voice so scathing it could peel paint off the wall, he shouted, "Hey, we're trying to keep this woman alive."

If looks could kill, Dr. Peter Young would now be dead. The nurse in blue scrubs turned and stomped out of the room.

I shifted my attention to Bretta's general, unclean condition. She reeked of urine; her fragments of clothing were soaked. The only plausible explanation was that her assailants, as a final act of degradation, had urinated on her. It made me sick. Who could do such a thing?

A nurse helped me, and we cut away the rest of Bretta's filthy, reeking clothing. Then, we used alcohol pads to clean her skin, being careful not to exacerbate her cuts.

Olsen's orthopedic team wheeled in a portable x-ray machine, and almost immediately, they had images on the florescent display. Using these pictures, Olsen set the femur, the large bone in her left thigh, and built a cast.

While all of this was happening, I did the sutures. Thank goodness my daughter was unconscious. I counted 163 stitches.

Irwin's careful management of Bretta's vital signs made it all possible. By the time we were finished and ready to send our patient to recovery, he had established a regular pulse and an almost normal blood pressure.

At noon, approximately twelve hours after her arrival at the hospital, we took Bretta from ER to RR, the recovery room.

As we were leaving, Peter Young placed his hand on my shoulder. "Glad you were here," he said.

6

Northwest Texas Hospital, Amarillo

Anyone familiar with ER patient protocol knows that the recovery room—the transitional site and time immediately following surgery—is the most critical. If anything goes wrong, if some unexpected problem develops, it most likely will happen in the RR.

All hospitals have strict rules and procedures to protect this vital process, one of them being that no visitors are allowed in the recovery room. Fortunately, there's a little thing called RHIP—rank has its privilege. At my request, Northwest Hospital brought in a cot, and I stayed with my daughter.

Obviously, the recovery room time schedule varies with the nature and seriousness of the treatment. Because of Bretta's fragile condition, her RR experience expanded to almost twenty-four hours. During that course of time, as Doctors Young, Irwin, and Olsen attended her, Bretta's horrific ordeal came tumbling into light.

Using fragments of evidence and snatches of Bretta's semiconscious ramblings, the police and EMTs reported that she had been raped by three young men who were probably high on methamphetamines. Brenda put up a good fight, but one of these thugs had a knife and cut her badly, especially her face. I recounted the treatment of those lacerations, thankful that I was there to do the stitches.

Bretta's most serious injury, however, was her broken leg, the result of an angry blow with a baseball bat. One of the many ways our daughter had fought off her attackers was by kicking, until the bat rendered her leg useless.

Bleeding, beaten, and unconscious, she had been left for dead on a lonely dirt road near Palo Duro Creek. Luckily, she'd been found in time by Randall County Sheriff Deputies and rushed to the emergency room.

After Bretta transferred from RR to ICU, Jenny and I took turns staying by her side for the next forty-eight hours. Then, when her recovery allowed her transfer to a regular hospital room, we arranged eight-hour shifts among our family. Jenny took the day watch. Brent arrived after school. I came at 11:00 p.m. and stayed until 7:00 a.m.

I still remember that first night—when Bretta and I were alone—as I sat on the edge of her bed and held her hand while she slept. It reminded me of a time when she was a little girl and, after we'd finished her bedtime story, I told her that I would watch over her so she could go to sleep. Those memories brought tears. And recrimination—I hadn't been there to protect her when she needed me most.

This led to an emotional rage that consumed me. I wanted to lead the search for the bastards who had done this and render a father's justice. Each day I made calls to law enforcement to check on their progress. Finally, Agent Will Bernhardt came to see me at the hospital. After a brief visit with Bretta, he asked that I go with him for a cup of coffee in the hospital cafeteria.

"How's the investigation?" I asked.

"We're doing all we can," he answered, his eyes reluctant to meet mine.

"In other words, you've got squat?"

"You know," he hedged, "when the semester ends, students leave campus."

"Hell, you've got names and addresses for the entire student body. Go after them."

"That's the problem. The entire student body numbers over 7,000."

"What about your leads?" I asked, my voice rising. "You told me you had suspects."

He slouched back in his chair, eyes down. I sensed his resignation as he exhaled a long, slow breath.

"You're giving up?" I stood, leaning forward across the cafeteria table, hands squeezed so tight my fingernails cut into my palms.

"Of course not," he said. Then he stood, and we faced off eye-to-eye. "I've come to ask your help."

Raised voices, two men standing, scowling at each other—I sensed that nearby cafeteria patrons were looking at us.

Anger had so gripped my emotions, all I could think about was lashing out. In the next few moments, as we stared at each other, and as I thought about his words, his asking for my help, I slowly realized he was not the person with whom to be angry.

Cooling my rage, I relaxed my tense muscles and slowly sat.

He, too, reclaimed his chair

"Sure, anything." I drew a breath. "Just tell me what you want me to do."

"We're all working double shifts," he said. "Your daily calls aren't helping."

For a moment, a silence hung between us. It hit me hard, harder than words, and it left me with no response.

"Back off," he said. "Give us a chance. We'll find these guys."

I broke our eye contact, turned, and looked out to the east. The hospital cafeteria's east wall was floor-to-ceiling glass. The panoramic view showed a beautifully landscaped area that sloped down to a nearby lake. As my eyes swept over the pastoral scene, my breathing slowed, and I weighed Bernhardt's words. Gradually a thought wormed its way out of my subconscious—this guy needed help rather than harassment.

"Okay," I answered after a long moment and then held out my hand.

He took it, and with his other hand, grasped my wrist for a two-handed handshake. "I understand your angst, your frustration, and I can't blame you. You'll be hearing from me."

We finished our coffee and stood. Then, together, we walked from the cafeteria to the hospital lobby, and we parted with a new feeling of mutual respect.

I stopped my daily calls about the rapists. It wasn't a conscious decision to back off—to care less about justice for what these vicious, evil men had done. I just narrowed the focus of my daily existence to Bretta's medical care.

We continued our twenty-four-hour family vigil.

Day by day my daughter began to recover.

7

Northwest Texas Hospital, Amarillo

In the next few days, as Bretta's recovery showed day-by-day improvement, I began to think about a test for pregnancy. But concern for Bretta's mental and emotional health dominated everything. It seemed crucial that we, the caregivers, give her positive support. We wanted good news. She needed good news. So I took the lead and did my best to make sure a "good news" environment prevailed.

But when I was alone with my thoughts, I weighed the alternatives.

If we were lucky, if Bretta was not pregnant, we could focus on her medical and emotional recovery. She would have an enormous challenge to face—dealing with gang-rape and all of its attendant psychological complications.

Among my old medical-school textbooks, I found a passage about treatment of rape victims. It stressed the need to deal with humiliation, that these feelings could escalate and destroy self-worth, that the worst part of rape is often the aftershock. Many women never recover and are unable to enter normal sexual relationships.

That was the good news.

The bad news, the possibility that Bretta might be pregnant, loomed as an abhorrent alternative. The new Texas law against abortion now made it illegal to consider a medical solution. I could see that, if Bretta were forced to endure a pregnancy as a result of this rape, it would be devastating.

It was a no-win situation.

We didn't talk about it.

When faced with two alternatives—one bad, the other worse—it seemed easy to "deal with it tomorrow" and let each day pass without confrontation.

Northwest Texas had an excellent rape-crisis counseling program. As soon as Bretta was able, I made sure she received their services.

So now, with day-by-day medical improvement, the heavy cloud of a worst-case scenario hung over our family as we waited for Bretta's menstrual period.

"Shouldn't you do a pregnancy test? Jenny asked.

"Yes, but . . ." I hesitated.

"But what?"

"But, what if we do the test and find that Bretta is pregnant?"

"Then you could do something."

"What would you have me do?"

My good Catholic, pro-life spouse didn't want to say the "A" word. Instead, she said, "You know—treat her."

"End the pregnancy?" I asked.

"Of course," she whispered.

I paused. Looked away. And tried to think how to phrase my response.

Jenny reached over and took my hand.

"You know it's against the law," I said.

"But she's our daughter," Jenny said. Her answer came with a sob and a tear.

Neither of us said anything for the next full minute.

"Maybe her period will start and we'll have the answer," I said.

8

At home, 1109 Westbrook Terrace

Bretta brought a beautiful voice into our family dynamics. We first recognized this fact at the North Hills Elementary Christmas program when, at age six, she sang a solo that brought down the house. This tiny little girl, one of the smallest children in the first grade, belted out "O Holy Night" in big, pure tones that filled the school auditorium. I don't know much about music, but even a dummy like me could tell our daughter had a special, God-given talent. Fortunately, her mother knew what to do and made sure Bretta got the best musical training available. For the next eleven years our daughter took voice and piano lessons, attended summer music camps, and made occasional trips to "the city," as we called New York, where she received coaching from the best teachers in Manhattan. This led to a voice major at CSU and her successful four years of study toward a Bachelor of Music Degree.

So when time for graduate school arrived, it seemed only natural that Bretta should go to Juilliard, and this brought another factor into the picture. Her maternal grandmother, Katherine Smithington Chase, lived in New York City. Over the years, my mother-in-law and I had been at odds—to say the least—over family matters. In the beginning, Katherine disapproved of her daughter's choice of a matrimonial partner *and* the move to Texas. Katherine openly voiced her opinion that the marriage probably wouldn't last and repeatedly offered Jenny the option of "moving back home" if things went awry. Jenny suggested I stay out of it and let her handle her mother. Most of the time I was only too happy to do so.

I knew that my mother-in-law had planned to come to Texas for Bretta's graduation. But the rape changed everything, and her trip had been cancelled. Jenny, however, called her mother frequently to share the news of Bretta's recovery. "Mother called. She wants to fly to Amarillo and help with Bretta's move home."

"Fine," I said.

"Be nice," Jenny replied. "Remember, Bretta is her only granddaughter."

I worried about the implications. With Bretta's recovery still problematic, the last thing we needed was family conflict.

"I said 'fine.'"

She gave me the infamous *Jenny glare*. "But I could hear the way you said it."

"Okay, let me try again," I continued. "Fiiiiiine, I'd love to have the old battleaxe here."

"Joe!"

"Seriously, we need to think about our options."

"What does that mean?"

"Together," I said "while there's still time, we need to look at all the various possibilities . . . at how we're going to handle this if things go south."

She backed up, her face settling into an *oh no* mask. "Not more bad news?"

"We've got to face the possibility that Bretta may be pregnant," I said.

Jenny stared at me. Then she nodded. I had the feeling she couldn't put her answer into words, and that by using nonverbal communication, she could avoid participation in a taboo subject.

"And we both know your mother's views on abortion."

The "a" word brought an even more dynamic emotion into our conversation. Again, Jenny did not speak. She nodded.

"We must prepare to do what we think is best for Bretta, not what your mother's religion dictates."

"Joe, we're all Catholic."

"Of course," I said. "But if there is conflict, Bretta comes first."

Jenny shook her head, this time vigorously. "Mother can see that. You're not being fair."

A little red light came on. Jenny had always taken my side in the ongoing battle between her mother and me. But pro-life rhetoric brought a new mix into the relationship. I could see that I needed to proceed with caution.

"Your mother is a very devout Catholic," I said.

"Yes," Jenny replied. "But so am I."

"However, she tends to see issues in black and white."

"What's that supposed to mean?"

"Sometimes, there's a little gray in the middle."

"Joe, quit beating around the bush. Say what you have to say."

I wanted to. Jenny, obviously, wanted me to. Even Katherine, if she were here with us, would want me to speak out, rather than offer my opinion in cautious, carefully guarded words. But that's the trouble with issues like abortion. They are so sweeping—so all encompassing—so powerful they tend to obliterate discussion.

"I heard a joke on the radio this morning. It reminded me of your mother," I said.

"Joe, this is serious," Jenny replied.

"This guy was told by his doctor he only had six months to live. So, he decided to invite his mother-in-law to come live with them, because, living with her for six months would seem like forever."

Jenny tried to react with anger. She couldn't do it. And I could see a bit of a smile as she called my name. "Joe, *please.*" she said, exasperated.

"Do you think you could get your mother to postpone her trip?" I asked.

Part II

JUNE

9

Northwest Texas Hospital, Amarillo

The day the hospital released Bretta, we took two cars—one for our patient and one for the flowers, plants, cards, wheelchair and crutches. Her broken leg was in a cast; however, her physical prognosis looked good. The cuts on her face were healing nicely, and the black-and-blue contusions had mostly disappeared. As we wheeled Bretta outside into the morning sunshine of a gorgeous springtime day, she smiled. The slow drive home was wonderful, and when we carried her into the house, her homecoming felt like a gift from heaven.

But there was an elephant in the room, and each of us knew it was there. What if she's pregnant?

One day passed and then another, but Bretta's menstrual period didn't come.

Then on the following Monday, June 9, four weeks after the rape, an evening when I had been on call at the hospital, I returned home late to find Jenny waiting up for me. She confronted me as I came in from the garage and said, "We've got to talk."

I followed her upstairs to our bedroom, and she closed the door, her face contorted with emotion.

"I went to Wal-Mart this evening, got an over-the-counter pregnancy test called First Response, and gave it to Bretta. The strip showed two lines."

"Pregnant," I said, not fully believing the word coming out of my mouth.

"Joe, what are we going to do?" Jenny asked, her voice quaking with a mix of fear and anger.

"I don't know." Immediately my mind began spinning with implications.

"I can't tell you how hard this was for Bretta. She cried for hours."

I pulled off my tie and threw it on the dresser, wishing I had a stiff drink.

"It was as though her spirit snapped—after all she's been through, the news was just too much. When I found her searching for my bottle of sleeping pills, I gave her two and hid the rest."

Jenny's crying increased into soul-wrenching sobs. She pulled a Kleenex from the box on the nightstand and slumped on the edge of the bed.

I flipped on the nearest lamp and sank down beside her.

"We've . . . got to do something . . . pregnancy," Jenny struggled to get the words out. "Bretta can't take it. And, God help me, I don't believe I can either."

"I've been thinking about what to do if this happened," I said, taking Jenny's hand.

"The new law—" she sniffled.

"What about it?" I said, my thumb stroking her palm.

"From what I've read in the newspapers, HB27 says it's okay to have an abortion if it's to save the life of the mother."

This was my Catholic, *pro-life* spouse talking. I could have given her a hard time about changing sides when religion and/or politics clashed with the reality of our daughter's health. But I didn't. Instead, I said, "Yes, to save the life of the mother would be the only way to perform the abortion legally."

"But this is exactly the case for Bretta," Jenny said, tears streaming. "She was ready to take her life this afternoon."

I gathered my wife into my arms. "Suicide doesn't count," I told her gently.

Jenny reacted with more sobs. "Damned politicians."

With my free hand I pulled more tissues from the box and gave them to her.

"I wish all *their* wives and daughters would get raped," she said, wiping the tears from her cheeks.

I placed the box on my lap and continued to hold her. "No, you don't. You wouldn't wish that on your worst enemies."

"My hairdresser had an abortion last month," Jenny said, her voice falling to a whisper. "She went to the Women's Clinic in Albuquerque."

"Obviously, Bretta's not in any shape to travel right now," I answered. "Maybe next month."

Jenny broke completely, worse than before. "Bretta needs help now! Can't you give her a pill or something?" She pulled more tissues from the box.

My frustration turned to anger, and I felt it nettle at the back of my head. But I bit my tongue and, in as calm and restrained a voice as I could muster, gave a simple response. "The morning-after pill has to be taken within seventy-two hours."

"Why didn't you or someone give her the damn pill?" Jenny wailed. "Doesn't anyone care about my daughter?"

Her stinging rebuke hurt, and I wanted to lash out, to tell her that other doctors had been in charge that night, and that, since HB27, it was now illegal for hospital personnel to give RU-284 or any of the morning-after pills. But I didn't. Instead, I pulled her in close and kissed her lightly.

Suddenly, we heard a crash from the downstairs bathroom—the one Bretta had been using. I ran down the stairs, Jenny right behind me. We found our daughter on the floor, semi-conscious, clutching the shower curtain, the curtain rod bent and lying beside her, half in and half out of the bathtub.

Apparently Bretta had slipped or fainted and grabbed the plastic curtain—the weight of her body pulling the rod as she fell. The clatter of the rod was what we had heard.

I knelt beside her, my physician instincts taking over. "Bretta, can you speak? What happened?"

"I botched it," she whispered. "Should've asked you."

Jenny screamed. Not a loud shriek, but a soft, high-pitched sound of horror. I turned and looked up at her face to see that she stared into the bathtub. Intuitively, I turned my head to follow her gaze, and I, too, recoiled at the sight.

A puddle of blood and a coat hanger.

10

Our home at 1109 Westbrook Terrace, 1:00 a.m.

Together, Jenny and I maneuvered Bretta so that she lay flat on the floor—a position where I could examine her. In a matter of seconds I determined that she was hemorrhaging from the vagina and that something needed to be done, immediately.

"We'll have to take her to the emergency room," I said.

Jenny nodded, as if in a trance.

Hurriedly, we loaded Bretta into the car.

Just as I had on that fearful night four weeks before, I drove the empty streets to the hospital's emergency room. But this evening our arrival was far different—no ambulance, no police, no flashing lights. A lone security guard sat at his desk just inside the back door. I recognized Dennis Smith, a normally friendly guy who usually smelled of stale coffee, often wore a "McCormack for President" button, and liked to pass out pro-life campaign literature. Tonight, I didn't care about his politics. All that mattered was caring for my daughter.

Dennis grabbed a gurney and helped me roll Bretta inside to the lobby of the ER. Except for two nurses who sat at the reception desk sipping coffee, the place appeared deserted. Elsa Jennings—the R.N. whom I'd known for almost a quarter century and who had helped deliver Bretta at this very facility twenty-three years ago—greeted me.

The two nurses took over and rolled Bretta into an examination room. On the way, Elsa introduced me to nurse Kathy Thompson.

"Kathy, Dr. Young's stretched out in ER2," Elsa said. "Would you get him?"

"Wait," I interrupted. "Who else is here tonight?"

"Just the two of us and Dennis," Elsa replied. "It's been quiet since we started the eleven o'clock shift. You're the first patient."

"Before you wake Young, let's examine Bretta," I cautioned. "We may not need him."

Together the two nurses helped me slide our patient from the gurney onto an examination table. In quivering voice, I told them about finding Bretta, the pool of blood, and the coat hanger.

"Vital signs," I ordered. "Get ready for a transfusion." The two nurses went to work immediately. Experienced and well trained, they knew what to do and were starting before I could get the words out.

"Kathy, we need a light sedative. Would you prepare an injection of Versed? Two and one-half milligrams."

She left to carry out my order.

"Elsa, I need to examine Bretta's cervix and see if it's perforated."

She nodded and went to get the necessary surgical equipment.

When both nurses returned, I administered the sedative and paused a minute for it to take effect.

While we waited, I lifted Bretta's hair and looked for her birthmark—the tiny pink spot behind her left ear. I almost smiled when I thought about how we'd promised each other to keep "our" secret of her pink freckle. And it reminded me of another incident, one that left a small scar behind her right ear. I turned her head and searched.

When I found it—an almost invisible line with faint marks where the stitches had been—I thought back to memories of an accident when she was only eighteen months old. While playing near a playground swing-set, an empty swing had caught her and sliced open her neck and head with a nasty cut. I had treated my daughter for that unusual injury with only one thought: *Do what's best for Bretta.* Tonight, looking at her as she gradually succumbed to the injection, I made a silent decision. Whatever the repercussions, I would do the same . . . now.

Elsa returned and arranged the surgery tray.

I started the procedure—the dilatation part of a D&C—which enabled me to widen the cervix so that I could examine the womb. We were in luck. Bretta's lining had not been punctured. The bleeding was either mostly or entirely from tears in the vulva, the external female genitals.

I breathed a sigh of relief. I knew what to do to help my daughter.

"We're almost done," I said. "No need to admit Bretta into the hospital. Kathy, would you start the paperwork?"

Kathy looked at me with uncertain eyes.

"List this as a gynecological examination—a treatment for vaginal hemorrhaging," I said, using my most authoritative voice.

She stood there for a long moment, staring at me, clearly questioning my request for her to leave.

I stared back, making the awkward situation a test of wills.

She blinked, then turned toward the door.

"Thanks, Kathy," I said to her back. "And would you ask my wife to bring our car to the driveway door? We're about ready to take Bretta home."

Kathy left, the door closed, and I turned my gaze to Elsa.

"I'm going to scrape the womb—a curettage," I said. "You'd better leave so you won't get into trouble."

"I'm staying," she said.

For a brief moment, we stood with our eyes locked, sizing each other up. Lately, it seemed like everything in my life was a test of wills. This time I caved and turned my focus to Bretta.

Elsa handed me the curette, a spoon-like surgical instrument used for abortions.

As I started to insert the instrument, my hands were shaking, and I almost dropped it. I backed off and took a deep breath.

"Want me to wipe your forehead?" Elsa asked.

Suddenly, I realized I was perspiring heavily. "Yes, please."

Elsa took a towel and mopped the sweat from my brow.

I turned back to Bretta and silently gave myself a pep talk. This was my daughter, the only one I would ever have. We had a special bond between us, something I had never been able to put into words. But she was my beautiful, special, little girl—the person for whom, more than any other, it was my duty to provide and protect. The full realization of this responsibility surged through my veins like fire. A dull anger gathered at the back of my mind as I tried to sort through the task at hand. Bretta was counting on me.

I took another deep breath, held it for a second, and then slowly exhaled. As the last bit of air left my lungs, I willed my heart to stop pounding. A calmness came over me, and I felt a steel-like resolve. My hands stopped shaking.

I took the curette and completed the D&C.

11

The ER, Northwest Texas Hospital

A few minutes and it was all over. We lifted Bretta into a wheelchair and rolled her out to the loading ramp where Jenny had brought the car around.

Dennis Smith was back at his desk. At that moment, I saw him as a nosy Bible thumper—a zealot too curious about other people's business. But he helped me ease a groggy Bretta into the rear seat. Jenny drove—I sat in the back with my daughter's head on my shoulder.

There are moments in a person's life we remember forever because of the intensity of our personal feelings associated with them. That slow drive home from the hospital, the feeling of Bretta's warmth as she slept with my arm around her, the peaceful contrast to a roller-coaster day filled with terror—a time that would remain in my memory always.

Fifteen minutes later, Jenny and I had our daughter tucked into bed. Jenny fussed with the covers, making sure that they aligned perfectly straight. Then she came to me and we embraced for a long moment.

Together we stood at the foot of the bed watching Bretta sleep.

"She's such a beautiful girl," Jenny said.

"Exactly what I was thinking," I replied.

"Why did this have to happen to her?"

"There is no answer to that, but—"

"But?"

"But the why of it is not important. What matters is how we help her recover."

Jenny tightened her embrace.

The next morning, after checking on Bretta, I drove to the hospital for rounds and then went to the office for a normal day of seeing patients. I felt tired—drained. Even Virginia, my head nurse, noticed.

"You look like the last rose of summer," she said. "You get any sleep last night?"

"Not enough," I said. "Would you get me a cup of coffee?"

"Coming right up." A moment later she was back with both coffee and orange juice. "Lots of sugar in the juice and you look like you need some sweetening."

"That bad?" I downed the juice in a single gulp. "My apologies for dragging you down."

"None needed," Virginia replied.

I sipped the coffee. It burned my throat but I didn't complain.

"Things okay at home?" Virginia asked.

"Yes, I think Bretta's turned a corner."

Virginia smiled. "I'm happy for you both." She handed me a patient folder.

I returned the smile, took the folder, and tried to liven our conversation. "And this morning's first supplicant for our medical attention is—"

Virginia's face widened to an ear-to-ear grin as she watched me read the name of an overweight hypochondriac. This fat woman was one of, if not *the,* least favorite of my patients. Normally I dreaded time spent listening to her long list of complaints. But that morning, I chuckled at Virginia's grin and charged forth to see what I could do.

Virginia shook her head and followed.

The ordeal took an hour, but I got through it—responding to every symptom, real or imagined.

When we finished, I went to my office for another cup of coffee and thought about calling my friend Isaac Levy to see if he was open for lunch. I had my hand on the phone when the receptionist handed me a note to call Elsa Jennings. The message said it was urgent. I dialed the number.

Elsa answered on the first ring. "Hello."

"Elsa, I want to thank you again for your help last night," I said. "As always, you were great."

She ignored my compliment. "We've got problems, Joe."

Her use of my given name jolted me and left me momentarily speechless. In our twenty-five years of working together, it had always been "Doctor Wright," "Doctor," or "Sir." I paused to think how to respond.

The brief silence heightened her next few words.

"Dennis and Kathy reported us to the hospital administration."

12

My office, the Medical Arts Building

Elsa's words hit me like a mule's kick. I pulled up my desk chair and sat, flustered, trying to think of what to say in response. Before I could form my thoughts into speech, Elsa lifted our conversation to a new level of bitterness.

"Dennis Smith is a self-righteous sonofabitch," she spat. "An asshole."

I'd known Elsa Jennings for more than a quarter century. That was the first time I had ever heard her raise her voice, let alone swear. "So what else is new?"

"He threatened Kathy."

"You know Kathy had no part in what happened last night," I said. "She has nothing to worry about."

"I know it. You know it. But Kathy's afraid of her own shadow. And Dennis can be very intimidating."

"Dennis doesn't have technical knowledge about medical procedures. He has no idea what to look for."

"No, but Kathy does. And right after you left last night, when I was busy with the laundry, he marched her into the examining room to gather samples of Bretta's DNA."

Her words gave me pause. "What did they get?"

"I'm not sure. It could be that they have blood and tissue scrapings from the curette."

I took a deep breath, thinking—damning myself for not having taken the time to flush all evidence of the procedure. If Dennis and Kathy had collected the tissue scrapings from Bretta's womb, they might prove that a D&C had taken place.

"Elsa, get some rest and quit worrying about this. If anyone asks, just tell them my daughter was suffering from vaginal bleeding. Say that I brought her into the ER last night for an examination."

"I'm sorry, Joe. If only I'd—"

"Nothing to be sorry about. You did a great job helping me."

"I should have cleaned the surgical pieces first—then gathered the laundry."

"No. You did everything perfectly."

"Stupid, stupid . . . ."

"Elsa, quit beating yourself up. I'll be forever grateful for what you did to help me and my family."

"I hope . . . I hope this turns out okay."

"Quit worrying about Dennis. He's nothing but a big blowhard," I said, hoping I sounded confident and reassuring. Inside, I was quaking.

"And a troublemaker," she added with conviction.

"Elsa, get some rest."

"I can only try," she said.

I went back to work, trying my best to concentrate on my patients and keep on schedule.

But my heart wasn't in it.

The morning dragged on. It became harder and harder to think clearly. By noon I was almost an hour behind, so I skipped lunch and took a minute to call home and check on Bretta.

"Honey, she's a changed person," Jenny reported. "A little sore, but she slept late and ate a good breakfast."

I felt like a load had been lifted.

"Any problems?" I asked.

"Nothing. Bretta even wants to help with dinner."

"Really?"

"She's going to make your favorite—strawberry shortcake."

We rang off, and I went back to seeing patients with renewed vigor. First we had a woman in her fifties with migraine headaches, then an overweight gentleman in his sixties with high blood pressure, followed by a dozen more with an endless variety of everyday ailments. The afternoon passed quickly—until I had a phone call from Ed Garfield, the hospital administrator.

"Joe, could you stop by my office this afternoon?"

"I guess so," I answered, a red light going off in my brain. "What's happening?"

"How about six o'clock?"

"Sure." My voice quivered. "Can't you tell me why?"

Garfield paused, as if weighing his response. "Sheriff Jack Richards wants to meet with us," he said.

The line went silent for a long minuet, then he cleared his throat and added. "Richards has had a complaint that you're involved in illegal medical practice."

13

Northwest Hospital, Amarillo

Edward G. Garfield and I go way back. Thirty years ago, we roomed together as fraternity brothers at Texas Tech. After college, he went into hospital administration, and I continued on to medical school. By the time I finished my internship in family medical practice, Ed had taken the job at this hospital. He lobbied hard to get me to move to Amarillo and hang out my shingle. Until now, a quarter century later, it was a decision I'd never regretted.

Shortly after six o'clock, I arrived at Ed's office to find Sheriff Jack Richards already there. Both looked grim. And when they stood to shake my hand, neither smiled.

"What's up?" I asked.

"You know Dennis Smith?" Richards asked without preamble.

I nodded. "Of course. Hospital security guard."

"He's made accusations against you." Richards handed me a two-page police form.

I scanned the report. Written in law enforcement jargon, I found it repetitive and laborious to read. "Whereas the alleged physician did illegally perform a dilatation and curettage procedure on Bretta Jean Wright," etc. It gave the location, the time and date. I thought it interesting that the report *alleged* me to be a doctor.

"So?" I looked at Richards, then Ed.

The Sheriff's gaze dropped to the floor.

"So, help us out," Ed replied. "We don't believe there's anything to this, but Dennis is giving a copy to the newspaper, and we have to do something."

"Have you talked with Winston Shoemaker?" I asked. We all knew the name of the managing editor of the *Amarillo Globe-News*.

"No," Ed replied. "We have no reason to."

Richards shook his head.

"May I use your phone?" I asked. "I think I'd better call him."

Ed scooted it toward me. "The number is 555-1200."

I dialed and looked at my watch as the phone rang. It was 6:20 p.m. The woman who answered told me Winston had left for the day. Because we often played golf together, I knew the home number—I dialed it and recognized his voice when he answered.

"Winston, this is Joe Wright."

"Joe, what an unexpected pleasure."

"I'm here at the hospital with Ed Garfield."

"You've found some news in the local medical world?" he chuckled.

I ignored his attempt at humor, but appreciated the fact that it sounded like he didn't know anything yet about my circumstances. "We're talking with Sheriff Jack Richards about a charge that's been filed against me."

There was a pause, and I could imagine the smile fading from

Winston's face. "Really. What's the charge?"

"Abortion."

Winston paused again. I could hear his breathing. "Let me talk with Ed."

I passed the phone and, with a sense of apprehension, listened to one side of the conversation.

"No. No corroboration. Just an accusation."

Ed held the receiver to his ear for a long time without saying a word. Finally, he said, "I agree. And yes, when we learn something, I'll call."

Ed handed the phone to the sheriff. "Winston wants to talk with you."

Again we listened to a one-sided conversation—mostly a long string of negative answers. At the end, Richards said, "All right, we'll call you if something develops." Then he hung up.

"What'd he say?" I asked, the slight tremor in my voice betraying my anxiety.

"The *Globe-News* is going to sit on it for a while. However, Winston wants us to call him before we talk with any radio or television reporters. He's afraid the broadcast media will try to scoop him."

"What's the hospital's position?" I asked, my temper rising.

"Waiting. So far, all we have is an unsubstantiated complaint," Ed said.

"Damned right, so what else are you thinking?" I addressed the question to Sheriff Richards.

"Off the record?"

I nodded. So did Ed.

"Randall County Deputies brought your daughter to this hospital. And we've been working double shifts trying to find the thugs who raped her. Whatever your daughter needs, I say you should do it. You'll get no flak from me."

I relaxed a little, but tried not to outwardly show my relief. "Thanks, Jack," I said.

"But, you understand," he added quickly, "I've sworn to uphold the law. And if you've broken it, I'm the one who'll have to arrest you."

14

At home, 1109 Westbrook Terrace

The next week brought good news, semi-good news, and bad news. The good news was that Bretta continued to improve. She smiled a lot. And she got a walking cast on her leg so she could move around without crutches. Seeing her return to "a more-normal" day-to-day living routine caused the family's spirits to soar.

The semi-good news was the void—the absence of anything in the newspaper about me and my troubles with the law.

The bad news was that presidential candidate McCormack announced his plan to come to the Texas Panhandle and make a political "sweep" of the area. The broad range and comprehensive quality of his campaign schedule defied logic. As I read the details in the morning newspaper, I found that—after he opened with a rally in Canyon—he planned a two-day visit to Amarillo.

Why would a national candidate bother to visit a sparsely populated area like the Texas Panhandle, let alone spend two days here?

That afternoon, Winston Shoemaker called, and I found out.

"Joe, KAMA-TV is going to break the story about you tomorrow morning."

I felt my gut tighten, a sinking feeling as I waited for his next statement.

"We're going to have to run it."

"What exactly are you publishing?"

He gave me a blow-by-blow account—specific, graphic details of how I had taken Bretta to the ER and performed the D&C. Their article would name Dennis Smith and Kathy Thompson as their sources, report the medical evidence submitted, and chastise local police and hospital officials for "trying to hide the story."

My stomach dropped to my toes. "Winston, you won't name Bretta, will you?"

"My sources tell me that Channel Four will give both her name and yours," he said. "I'm sorry, Joe. Wouldn't do any good for me to withhold them."

I paused, trying to frame my words about the normal custom of withholding the name of a rape victim. But I never got the chance to speak them.

"It's out of our hands, Joe," Winston said with finality.

I could see it wouldn't matter what I said.

"Thanks, Winston. You sat on this for a week, and I appreciate what you tried to do to protect me and my family."

He rang off without a word of sympathy.

With a heavy heart, I finished my appointments, went by the hospital to make rounds, and then headed home to tell my family.

After dinner, I gave the news to Jenny, Bretta, and Brent.

"Oh, *no*, that's just great," Jenny said, her face a mask of anger. "The women at church will think we've turned pro-choice."

My daughter clenched her teeth, stuck out her jaw, and said, "Well, I'm glad, Mom."

"Bretta!" Jenny shrieked. "How could you? This is not something to be proud of."

"I'm not proud, but I'm not embarrassed, either."

Jenny turned her wrath on me. "This is your fault. I thought if you did the abortion, you would do it discreetly—that no one would know."

Before I could answer, Brent jumped in. "Why don't the newspapers write about the three bastards who did this?" he asked. "That's the story. Or doesn't anyone care about that?"

Good point, I thought. Sometimes it's only the youth who, because of their naiveté, can cut through all the bullshit and speak to the gut issues.

"Brent—" I started to lecture my son about political thinking. About how a story of three thugs who raped a girl on her way home from the library didn't have the "sizzle" to arouse voters like an abortion controversy. Before I could get the words out, he stood and paced the floor, ready to lecture me.

"Dad, this whole mess has gotten out of hand," Brent said.

"Hey, I'm the victim," Bretta cut in. "I have nothing to hide."

"This is all because of your misjudgment," Jenny said, piercing me with her glare. "We could have avoided the embarrassment, the loss of face among our friends, and the threat against your medical practice if only you'd have exercised a bit of caution."

For the next hour we wrangled—a down-and-dirty family free-for-all. The more we talked, the more I realized that Bretta and Brent—even Jenny—didn't want words of caution from me.

With heartbreaking slowness, I climbed the stairs and dressed for bed. As I brushed my teeth I thought about how the local media might soften their publicity about me. Perhaps a candidate like McCormack, a minister with Christian ideals, wouldn't name me or my daughter for political gain. The more I turned it over in my thoughts, the more I hoped for the best. I climbed into bed and pulled up the covers, thinking we had at least a fifty-fifty chance this might blow over, and if it did, the story would die a natural death.

I was wrong.

15

At the breakfast table the next morning

The *Globe-News* used my name in their headline. Channel 5 referred to me as "Local Doctor," but as their television presentation continued, they gave extensive biographical specifics about me, my family, and my medical practice.

Both broadcast and print media went into great detail about the dilatation and curettage—the who, what, where, and when. Comparatively little coverage was devoted to the rape and the fact that law enforcement had yet to file charges against any suspects.

The rape was old news.

The news of the day was me—the doctor who had allegedly broken the law.

The result was that I had set the stage for Reginald Q. McCormack and his campaign activities in Texas. Overnight, McCormack had jumped from a third-place, little-known candidate to a spotlight grabber. The *Globe-News* carried five different stories that featured something about him. The headlines screamed:

MCCORMACK COMES TO TEXAS

TV SPEECH TO ORIGINATE FROM AMARILLO

ROPER PREDICTS MCCORMACK TO SKYROCKET

MCCORMACK BREATHES NEW ENERGY
INTO PRO-LIFE MOVEMENT

MCCORMACK'S CAMPAIGN FINANCES SURGE

As I read story after story, my stomach churned. I had never thought of myself as pro-choice, or for that matter, pro-anything in politics. For most of the past twenty-five years, I had been too busy to vote.

Now my name and my family—and most of all, my personal reputation—were inextricably linked to the pro-choice movement.

I didn't look forward to going to work.

At the hospital, I hadn't been there fifteen minutes before Ed Garfield called me into his office.

"Joe, I'd like you to consider letting other doctors look after your patients at the hospital."

I flinched. "You're barring me from practicing here?"

"Not if we can avoid it."

"Suppose I said 'no' to your request?"

"Then we'd have to have a hearing, a media event."

I stood speechless for a moment, thinking.

Ed brought up the name of another local doctor. "You remember a couple of years ago when Nicholas Zahrenski was thought to have a drug problem?"

"Yeah. Mel Campbell and I helped to cover some of his patients."

"No formal action was ever taken against Nick. We just made the arrangements."

I nodded. And for the first time I realized how Ed had saved that doctor's professional reputation. Zahrenski was again bringing his medical practice to the hospital.

"That won't work for me," I said. "The way they've plastered my name in the newspapers, every person who can read will always think of me as the abortion doctor."

"But that's old news," Ed replied. "What you're trying to do is avoid creating *new* news."

I could see his point. I pondered what to do about it. "What do you suggest?" I asked.

"Go to your patients one at a time. Explain that you're cutting back, temporarily, and that you're asking 'doctor so-and-so' to make your rounds. Hell, Joe, it's what you do when you leave town for a couple of weeks to go fishing."

I reluctantly agreed, but only because I didn't know what else to do. And so, without fanfare, I relinquished my hospital privileges.

16

Amarillo, the Medical Arts Building

Busy doctors hate meetings. Which is why Melvin Campbell, Harvey Adams, and I rarely met to discuss our partnership. By mutual consent, the Adams-Campbell-Wright Clinic meandered along with our staff scheduling the patients, taking care of the finances, and making most of the day-to-day decisions.

But this was different. I knew I needed to confer with Mel and Harv, so I ordered sandwiches, chips, and Cokes from Hoagie's Delicatessen and scheduled a lunch meeting in my office.

Harv came on time, chose turkey and swiss on rye, and pulled a chair up to my desk. "What's up?" he asked, claiming a corner of the desktop to set his Coke and chips on.

I suggested we wait until all three of us were present. We spent the time munching our sandwiches and exchanging banal chitchat.

Mel arrived ten minutes late with an attitude. "Let's do this quick," he blustered, not bothering to take either a seat or a sandwich.

"I guess you've heard, the hospital jerked my privileges," I said.

Mel shrugged his shoulders. "It was just a matter of time," he replied. "Why didn't you take your daughter to Albuquerque?"

I looked at Harv, waiting for him to add his condemnation. Instead, he took another big bite of his turkey and swiss.

"Northwest Hospital is the hotbed of community gossip," Mel continued. "Thirteen seconds after you finished your supposedly secret D&C, half the population in the Texas Panhandle probably knew about it."

"I didn't expect to keep it a secret," I replied, remaining calm with an effort

Harv laughed and reached for a his bag of chips.

"Oh?" Mel said. "I guess that's why you picked two a.m. for the procedure?"

"Look," I said, setting my sandwich aside. "Will you guys cover for me at the hospital until I work through this?"

"Of course," Harv replied at once.

Mel shook his head. "This is only the beginning. What're we gonna do when they strip your license?"

His words halted the conversation.

Harv took the last bite of his sandwich.

After a pause that weighed heavily, I gave a truthful answer. "I don't know," I said.

"We'll cross that bridge when we come to it," Harv added.

"Or maybe I'll sell out to you two, go to some other state, and open a practice where the politics are less combative."

Mel turned abruptly, a scowl on his face. "Might be good to leave now, before they send you to prison." He stomped out of the room, slamming the door.

Harv and I looked at each other. He took a long swig of his Coke—an obvious effort to avoid saying anything.

I waited.

"He'll cool off," Harv finally said. "Meanwhile, don't worry about your hospital patients. We'll cover for you."

"Thanks. I was pretty sure you would."

"Anything else?"

"Yeah. I'd like you and Mel to talk this over without me. Any time you want me to leave the partnership, just say the word. I don't want to drag you down."

Harv smiled—a big, toothy, making-fun-of-me look. "You're not going anywhere, Joe. Hell, all three of us know you're the best damn G.P. in Texas."

17

At home, 1109 Westbrook Terrace

That night we watched television. I had to admit, Reggie McCormack was a spellbinding speaker. He knew just how to tell a story, to shape it with detail and suspense, to make it so compelling that his audience hung on every word with bated breath until he delivered his punch line. One of his stories was about a doctor in the Texas Panhandle who was killing babies.

His punch line was yours truly.

He didn't use my name. I was simply "the good doctor" in Amarillo. Then he moved on to indict doctors all across America—misguided doctors who were killing babies. "Something must be done," he insisted.

Applause—loud and lengthy—poured out of the television.

"Are you with me?" he shouted, eyes ablaze with passion.

The crowd roared their assent.

Jenny left the room and went upstairs.

Brent and Bretta stayed with me until the program ended.

"That guy could sell refrigerators to polar bears in Alaska," Brent grumbled, rose from the sofa, and headed for his room.

I stretched, trying to ease the tension in my limbs.

"Dad, am I supposed to feel guilty about having an abortion?" Bretta asked, her features taut, her back stiff. She shifted uncomfortably in her chair, waiting for my answer.

"Some people do," I answered as calmly as I could.

"Well I don't."

"And that's okay."

"It's like my leg," she said. "Those guys—they did this to me, and I had to go to the hospital to get it fixed."

"And you'll recover," I assured her.

"But I feel the same about the rape."

"And from that, too, you'll recover," I repeated with conviction, "if you let yourself."

She hobbled over, sat on my lap, put her arms around me, and kissed me on the forehead.

"Why can't this guy McCormack understand that, like my broken leg, I needed you to fix the result of the rape for me?"

"Give him time," I answered. "Maybe he will."

Bretta sighed. "Yeah, when pigs fly."

"Can I tell you something that may surprise you."

"What?"

"Basically, I'm against abortions."

"Oh, really?" She frowned, shook her head. "You trying to make me feel guilty?"

"No, of course not."

"But, you just said . . ."

"Yes, I'm against them, but you needed one."

"So, you did it."

"Yep."

She relaxed her embrace, drew back, and looked at me.

"And I'd do it again," I said through a smile. "You trying to compare me with people who are against abortions like McCormack?"

She hugged me, tighter than before. "Dad, you're the last person in the world I'd compare with Reginald Q. McCormack."

"Well, that's reassuring."

"Dad, I . . ."

"What?"

"I love you," she said, and there were tears in her voice.

18

Driving to Rick Husband International Airport, Amarillo

Jenny had convinced her mother to postpone the visit. But I knew it was inevitable. So, when Katherine Smithington Chase came to Texas on Thursday, June 19, I vowed to put my best face on it. And on the day of my mother-in-law's arrival, I drove Jenny to the airport with an upbeat, positive attitude.

In the car, Jenny led the conversation. "Joe, be nice."

I glanced at her, then turned my eyes back to the road. "Hey, the last thing Bretta needs is a family feud," I said.

"Remember, Mother's only going to stay one night."

"Oh, couldn't she stay longer?"

Jenny looked out the window for a long minute. I could partially see the reflection of her face on the glass. She appeared to be smiling, trying to regain her composure. When she turned back to me, however, the stern look was at full glare.

"This is not funny," she said. "For Bretta's sake, you've got to bury the hatchet—at least for the next twenty-four hours."

I returned her glare with my own exaggerated look of innocence. "Don't worry. I'll be good as gold. Scout's Honor."

Jenny groaned and looked out the window again. So we arrived at the airport, parked the car, and went in to pick up our guest.

I checked the monitor and found Katherine's flight—twenty minutes late.

"How about we go for some coffee?" Jenny suggested.

"Sure," I replied. And we made our way to the nearby airport coffee shop.

Jenny found a table. I picked up two cups of coffee and a newspaper.

We sipped our coffee, an unspoken truce between us. And it seemed likely we'd get through these next two days without open hostility.

I turned my attention to the news of the day. Unfortunately, it was all about McCormack. Once again, the *Amarillo Globe-News* had plastered a huge photo of the presidential candidate on the front page to accompany their story about his forthcoming visit.

"Joe, maybe it would be better not to read the paper for the next few days," Jenny said.

"Yeah," I folded the paper and laid it on the table so that the McCormack photo was face down.

"Let's just concentrate on Bretta, try to help her recover," Jenny said.

"And make your mother's visit as pleasant as possible," I replied.

That stopped the conversation. Jenny looked at me, confused. She didn't know whether or not I was being sincere.

"Seriously," I said, "I'm going to do my best to make your mother feel welcome."

Jenny reached over, took my hand, and started to say something. I expected it would be a repeat of the speech I had heard many times about how much she would appreciate any effort on my part to show kindness to her mother.

I never heard her words.

Because at that moment, the airport PA system announced the arrival of Katherine's plane. We both knew not to be late. So, we quickly gathered up our stuff and headed to the authorized passenger exit area.

Katherine came down the corridor dressed to the nines. She immediately hugged her daughter. Then she offered to shake my hand. The three of us proceeded to the luggage carousel. For an overnight visit, she brought three bags, which I carried to the car along with my newspaper. The bags went into the trunk, and I thoughtlessly tossed the newspaper into the back seat with Katherine.

A mistake.

A big mistake.

We left the airport and started west on I-40. Jenny engaged in chitchat with her mother. How was the flight? How crowded was the plane? They kept it up, mostly leaving me out of the conversation until we arrived home. I gathered the luggage. Katherine picked up the newspaper and carried it into the house.

I lugged the suitcases back to the guest bedroom. When I returned to the kitchen I found Katherine reading the newspaper.

Usually, the Wright family ignored McCormack's election activities. He had his world; we had ours. I worried about my medical practice, my wife, and my children, while he labored over the election, his campaign, and the national political scene. So, even though we each became involved in the abortion issue, I thought it really didn't matter.

Until Katherine came to visit.

My mother-in-law started reading the article to my wife. Then she set the paper aside and enlightened us with her opinion of the candidate.

"I just love McCormack," she said.

This comment got Jenny's full attention. Mine, too.

"Have you been watching his television speeches?" Katherine gushed. "He's such an engaging speaker."

Jenny glared at me. I knew the look. It warned me not to say anything.

"I sent him a hundred dollars," Katherine continued.

I almost gaged. Katherine seemed oblivious to her granddaughter's recent ordeal and my involvement in its resolution. Shakespeare must have had it right when he wrote *discretion is the better part of valor.* I decided to leave the room, quietly, and let Jenny discuss politics with her mother.

Somehow, we survived.

And Katherine went back to New York the next day.

That evening I found a mother-in-law joke in the *Readers Digest* that I thought especially appropriate.

"What's the punishment for Bigamy? Two mothers-in-law."

19

Amarillo, Texas

On the following Monday, the McCormack campaign brought its bus to Amarillo. They also brought a half dozen cars—with PA systems mounted on top—that drove around town playing loud, patriotic music interspersed with announcements about two political rallies.

Hundreds of volunteers blanketed the city with handbills urging attendance. Virginia Cotton, my office nurse, found one under the windshield wiper on her car and brought it into the clinic.

"Thought you'd want to see this," she said as she handed it to me and then walked on.

I scanned it quickly, then went back to my desk and reread it slowly. I especially noted the location of the noon rally.

TODAY

REGINALD McCORMACK

Independent Candidate for President

Two Rallies in Amarillo

12 Noon at the Corner of 4th Avenue and South Polk Street

7:00 p.m. at Dick Bivins Stadium

Hear McComack's message in person;
Learn how he plans to stop the murder of Babies;
Join the national movement to overturn *Row v. Wade;*
Help in the fight to return pro-life values to our country;
Learn the facts about abortions taking place in your home town.

TODAY

The Medical Arts Building was located at the corner of 4th Avenue and Polk Street. McCormack was staging his noon rally on my doorstep.

I went to the south side of the clinic, to the suite of rooms used by Mel Campbell. He was examining a patient, so I spoke with one of his nurses.

"Let Mel know I need to speak with him briefly. I'll wait in his office."

A few minutes later she came back. "Dr. Campbell said to tell you he's tied up with this patient and won't be able to talk with you. He suggests you write him a note, and he'll call you, probably this afternoon." She handed me a notepad and pen, then turned and left the room.

I could read the implications. Mel was trying to distance himself from me and my problems.

I left without writing a note and moved on to the other side of the clinic where I found Harvey Adams. "Need to speak with you," I said. "Can you give me a sec?"

"Sure." He pointed to his office and led the way.

Once inside the office, he closed the door and offered me a seat. "What's up?"

I handed him the McCormack flyer. "Have you seen this?"

"No." He scanned it for a second. I could tell the moment he read the line about the location of the rally outside our clinic.

Harv grinned as he handed it back. "Are you surprised that McCormack's got you in his crosshairs?"

I shrugged. "I suppose not. What do you think we should do?"

"Nothing."

Harv's carefree attitude gave me pause—as it always did. "I'm trying to keep you and Mel from being dragged into this," I told him, my voice and expression serious.

He chuckled. "I think it's a little late for that."

"Maybe I could get a restraining order?"

Harv looked at his watch. "First, it's probably too late. And second, I think that's a bad idea."

"Damn it. I want to do something."

"Well, I have a suggestion," Harv said with another grin. "At noon, when McCormack has his rally, go out there and stand in the front row where everyone can see you."

I thought about it for a second, and then I looked him in the eye. As our gaze met, I could feel the electricity pass between us.

"Okay," I replied. "You're on."

20

4th Avenue and Polk Street, near the Medical Arts Building

As the morning dragged on, everyone at the clinic worried about the rally—me most of all. Between patients, I went to the window in my office and watched the preparations. At eleven o'clock, a flatbed truck pulled up and parked at the corner.

When I came back thirty minutes later, a van with political signs—and loudspeakers mounted on the roof—had parked next to the flatbed and was now blaring *The Stars and Stripes Forever.* A few people gathered around the speaker's platform. Most wore political buttons, signs, or hats.

And a little voice in my subconscious began to raise some doubts. Maybe my attendance at this rally wasn't such a good idea. I left the window to meet with my last patient of the morning.

At ten minutes to twelve, I returned to join Harvey Adams and several other members of the clinic staff who were peering out the window. We could see a hundred or so people gathered around the speakers platform, the music louder than ever, and McCormack's campaign bus parked a half block away.

Decision time.

I dreaded going out into the crowd and wondered how I'd handle the personal confrontations. Suppose one of my neighbors approached me? I could see this might get embarrassing, ugly, or both. But at noon, I swallowed my pride and my reservations, tried my best to put on a brave face, and walked across the street to join the political rally.

A lady handed me a McCormack button.

I took it and, when she turned away, stuck it in my pocket.

Reggie McCormack worked the crowd, shaking hands, thanking people for coming. I elbowed my way into the front row, near the speakers platform, fearful of what he'd say to me, wondering what to offer in response. I watched with apprehension as the candidate—accompanied by several others—made his way toward me.

Then it happened.

He smiled, shook my hand with a firm clasp, thanked me for coming, and moved on to the next person. In less than ten seconds, it was over.

Suddenly it dawned—McCormack hadn't recognized me.

I'd assumed he would know me from newspaper photos. And as he climbed the steps to the platform microphone, I searched the crowd. It surprised me how few faces I could identify. Having lived in this city for over a quarter century, I prided myself in knowing many of its citizens. Then my eyes caught the license plate on the van with the PA system—South Carolina—and a realization came over me. A great many, maybe even most, of these people were outsiders, supporters McCormack had brought to Amarillo with him.

I relaxed.

A woman wearing a McCormack red-white-and-blue vest and carrying a small American flag came to the mike. The music stopped and the crowd quieted.

"I'm Diane Evans from Austin," she said, "chairwoman of Texas's Right-to-Life Committee."

People clapped. Some cheered.

"We've had a great victory in our state this year. We passed HB27."

The crowd applauded, whistled, and cheered, much louder and longer.

"Last night the nation's political spotlight focused on Amarillo." She paused. "Texas is leading the nation in anti-abortion legislation."

The people responded. A young woman standing next to me whistled, a shrill, ear-piercing sound that hurt. I was witnessing, up close and personal, a truly emotional response.

Ms. Evans held up her hand to quiet the crowd. "We're here this morning to honor our candidate, the next president of the United States." The applause started. "I ask that you join me in welcoming Reggie McCormack!" She yelled the last few words, doing her best to project over the roar.

I had thought the previous applause loud, but I was wrong. This time the crowd went berserk, and the volume was deafening. They whistled, yelled, cheered, clapped, and created an ovation that I was sure could be heard in New Mexico. The loudspeakers joined in with a replay of *Stars and Stripes*. I stood there, the only person not cheering and clapping. The woman with the loud whistle gave me a dirty look, so I moved my hands a little and tried to fake being an active McCormack supporter. The ovation lasted a long time—several minutes.

McCormack stood at the microphone and basked in the response. When the prolonged applause finally died, he spoke eight words. "Ain't it great to be in Texas?" Again the crowd roared. And I marveled at this guy's political instincts. *Charismatic* was the only word I could think of.

"All life is valuable and a gift from God," he said. "Are we pro-life?"

As expected, the crowd exploded with enthusiastic, affirmative responses.

"When pregnancy occurs, that is God's hand at work in our lives. Do we believe in God?"

Another overpowering, positive response.

"Fetus, from the Latin, meaning little one. Should a fetus have the right to life?"

Over the swell of applause I began to wonder how long the crowd could keep this up. Apparently, McCormack read their response the same as I. He changed his approach.

"Choice. We hear a lot about pro-choice and the freedom to choose. But can anyone claim they have the *right* to kill an innocent baby?"

This time he wanted a negative response from the crowd. He got it, but it was noticeably less vociferous.

"Choice? Yes, but there are right choices and wrong choices. Some choices have led to terrible slavery, death to Jews, dead babies." Then he segued to the topic of the day. "Just recently, here in this very city, a doctor chose to take the life of his daughter's baby."

21

The McCormack Rally

McCormack never mentioned my name. It wasn't necessary. Everyone in the crowd knew the person he was chastising. I wondered if I should identify myself. I looked across the crowd, searching for someone who might recognize me. I tried to do it surreptitiously—brief glances timed with crowd response—so that the movement of my head faded into a sea of audience reaction. Three times I scanned the audience to my right. While it was difficult to look closely at people's faces without alerting them, there didn't seem to be anyone I knew.

Then, while McCormack rambled on, I switched to those on my left. Again, with quick, furtive sweeps, I searched the sea of humanity. On the second attempt I found a familiar face.

Dennis Smith.

Immediately I turned away, facing the front, looking slightly to the right so as to give as little profile as possible. It didn't seem that he had spotted me—at least he didn't give any sign of recognition. For the next few minutes I stared at McCormack, totally absorbed in my thoughts, trying to think what to do.

People clapped.

The rousing music began to blare again.

I had no idea what was happening.

The woman next to me mumbled something and looked at me expectantly.

I leaned over and tried to speak into her ear. "Sorry, I couldn't understand you."

She responded by standing so close I could smell her subtle perfume. She said, "Wasn't that wonderful, what he said about the Texas Panhandle leading the way?"

I nodded, smiled, and clapped my hands in time with the music.

Gradually the crowd scattered.

Out of the corner of my eye, I saw Dennis approaching the steps to the platform.

Looking down, trying to hide my face, I moved in the opposite direction, toward a group of people at the intersection waiting for the light to change before crossing the street. Hoping I was still safe in my anonymity, I elbowed my way into the crowd.

We waited.

Finally, the light changed.

As we surged forward, I felt a hand on my shoulder and heard a deep masculine voice speak my name.

"Dr. Wright."

I turned to find Dennis Smith. Most of the crowd continued ahead, crossing the street. A few stopped, apparently interested in who was calling my name.

"Good morning, Dennis," I said.

"Did you find our candidate's remarks interesting and helpful?"

"Not particularly."

"Too bad. It's people like you who need enlightenment."

"Dennis, that's your opinion."

"No, Dr. Wright. It's the law."

I turned to walk away, only to find that the light had changed again. I was trapped.

"This morning a group of us called on the Potter County District Attorney," he said, staring hard at me. I assumed he was gauging my reaction.

I looked away, ignoring his lecture. To my dismay, more people gathered around.

"We insisted that he file charges against you."

The light changed. I moved first, trying to get away from Dennis.

"We want to make sure you aren't killing any more babies here in Amarillo," he shouted, dogging my heels.

I moved faster, almost running to the door of the Medical Arts Building. When I glanced back, Dennis had suddenly given up his pursuit.

"You should be ashamed, taking the life of your own grandchild," he yelled after me.

It was the last thing I heard as the door closed behind me.

22

At home, 1109 Westbrook Terrace

The kitchen smelled of garlic and pasta as Jenny put the finishing touches on the Italian cheesecake we were having for dessert. One of the qualities I admired most about my wife—she was a great cook. My mouth watered in anticipation of a sumptuous meal.

"Bretta got her cast off today," Jenny said. "Dr. Olsen says Bretta can start driving next week."

"Where is she?" I asked.

"Upstairs in her room."

"Everything okay?"

Jenny hesitated a moment before answering. "I'm not sure," she said. "Bretta's been in her room all afternoon—ever since we got back from the doctor."

"I'll go check on her," I said, eager to look at her leg without the cast. I grabbed my *doctor's bag,* went upstairs, and knocked on her door.

"Who's there?"

"Norma Lee."

Bretta opened the door. She looked a little pale, a little worn out. "Hi," she said.

I paused for a moment, thinking how small and childlike she looked standing there in her faded jeans and oversized wooly slippers. "You're supposed to say 'Norma Lee who?' And then I say, 'Normalee, I don't go around knocking on doors, but do you want to buy a set of encyclopedias?' And then we have a big laugh."

She didn't laugh, but she cocked her blonde head to one side and smiled. "Dad, knock-knock jokes went out with the horse and buggy."

"Really?"

She rolled her eyes. "Try 'em with your patients in the nursing home. Maybe they'll think they're funny."

"Speaking of patients, how's the leg?" Time to change the subject, obviously.

"Dr. Olsen says it's fine, and that if I'm careful for the next month or so, it'll be good as new."

"Want a second opinion?"

"Sure."

"Pull up your pant leg, and stretch out on the bed. Dr. Knock-knock will give you his expert opinion."

While she removed her slippers and eased down on the bed, I glanced around the room. A pile of used tissues lay heaped on the nightstand by her cell phone. I studied her face. Her eyes looked red, as though she'd been crying. I pulled a chair next to her bed, sat, and gently lifted her leg.

"How's it feel?" I asked.

"Good," she said. "Almost like old times."

"I'm going to flex it. Tell me if it hurts." I shifted it slowly until it was almost vertical, then eased it back down. I did it three times. "Feel anything?"

"Just normal."

"Now let's bend the knee." While flat on her back, I manipulated her leg to a chair-like position—thigh vertical, calf horizontal. Then I lifted it three more times, moving faster and rougher with each repetition. "How's the knee?"

"Okay."

"Just *okay,* not great? Or good as new?"

"Dr. Olsen is not as rough as you."

Very gently, I returned her leg to the bed. "Want to tell me about the pile of tissues and the red eyes?"

She hesitated. "It has nothing to do with my leg. Something personal." She looked away.

"Dr. Dad, personal physician, at your service." I gave her my best 'daddy' smile, striving to sound reassuring.

Bretta reached for the Kleenex box and pulled out two tissues. She used one to dab her eyes, the other to blow her nose.

"Not trying to be nosy," I said. "Just offering. Sometimes it helps to talk with a person you know is on your side."

She rolled off the bed and adjusted her pant leg, then sat in her desk chair to tug on her slippers. I could see tears shimmering at the edge of her eyelashes. When she finished, she grabbed two more tissues.

"I hate it when I can't stop crying and feeling sorry for myself," she said, blotting her eyes.

"Something happen today?" I asked softly, hoping she would open up.

"I talked to Nathan. You know, he never came to visit me while I was in the hospital. And he hasn't called. Finally I couldn't stand it any longer so I called him."

"And what happened?"

"He's dating someone else."

"You and he have been an item for most of this year?"

She nodded. "When I had the lead in *Annie Get Your Gun*, he wanted to show me off as his main babe."

"I remember, at the reception, after the closing performance. Your mother and I wondered if things were getting serious."

"I thought they were—"

Then Bretta lost it. And she broke down completely.

I held out my arms, she fell into my embrace, and I held her a long time. When her sobbing eased, we both sat, she back in her desk chair, me on the side of the bed. I handed her the box of Kleenex, and she blew her nose again.

"When I was the leading lady, he loved me," she lamented. "Now that I'm damaged goods, he doesn't want to have anything to do with me."

"Bretta, you don't know that," I said, but my heart was breaking for her. Anger toward Nathan rose up in me, because Bretta had probably called it right.

"What other reason is there?" she cried, tears threatening to spill once more.

I stood, held out my arms again, and stayed with Bretta until she regained her composure. Then I gave her a light sedative and suggested she lie down—try to rest. As soon as she was asleep, I went downstairs and talked with Jenny.

When Brent came home a few hours later, the three of us conferred about a support plan for Bretta. We decided to act as normal as possible, to try to be upbeat and cheerful, and to offer family support when the opportunity presented itself.

Jenny had prepared a beautiful dinner of Bretta's favorites—manicotti, Caesar salad, and Italian cheesecake. Brent went upstairs to call her, and when she came down I was surprised—and relieved—to see her looking fresh and relatively upbeat. The evening went well and closed on a happy note.

23

At home, 1109 Westbrook Terrace

I knew it was only a matter of time until another mother-in-law visit. Jenny gave me the news at Saturday morning breakfast. "Mother called last night," she said.

"How nice," I said as I read the recap of McCormack's visit to Amarillo. I couldn't decide which news was worse.

"She wants to spend some time with Bretta."

"And what does Bretta want?"

"I haven't checked. But Mother offered to take us out to dinner, to celebrate Bretta's cast removal."

"That's not time with Bretta. That includes others." I wanted to add "such as me," but I didn't.

"Joe, Mother's coming." She expelled a long sigh.

"When?"

"Tomorrow. American Airlines, flight 487, 7:35 p.m. I was hoping you'd go with me to meet the plane."

Trapped.

A number of thoughts roiled through the gray matter, the frontal lobe of my brain. Would the repercussions be worse if I didn't go? Probably. Why couldn't Katherine arrive at a time when I was at work? Several other scenarios flashed by—all of them bad.

I caved.

"Of course, I'd love to greet your mother."

So, on a beautiful summer evening, Jenny and I picked up Katherine and all of her designer luggage. In the car, on the drive home, we talked about the special dinner Katherine had planned for Bretta. Jenny led the conversation.

"Mom, we like your idea of taking the family out to dinner tomorrow night. It'll be Bretta's first outing."

"I'm delighted to hear it," her mother replied. "Have you selected a restaurant?"

"We have reservations at your favorite," I chimed in. "The Amarillo Golf and Country Club."

Katherine shook her head and gave me a narrow look. "I've never said that was my favorite," she stated flatly.

Immediately, I could see my mistake. Katherine doesn't like to have her preferences—her values—characterized by her son-in-law. I looked at Jenny with a plea for help.

Jenny, too, could see my mistake. "Mom, what Joe meant was that the Country Club is Bretta's favorite. We thought, since this is her first time out, we should let her pick."

"Of course," Katherine replied. "We should do everything we can to lift her spirits."

"The whole idea is doing something that will distance us from the doom and gloom of these past few weeks," Jenny continued.

"And I love the Amarillo Country Club," Katherine replied.

Looking at my wife, I rolled my eyes.

Jenny gave me the warning look.

I studied the road and concentrated on my driving.

Jenny and her mother filled the rest of the twenty-minute trip with chit-chat.

And I breathed a sigh of relief. That was Sunday evening. Monday I would be at work all day. This wouldn't be so bad.

So, Monday evening I sat in the living room dressed in my Sunday suit, white shirt, and best red tie. My shoes were spit-polished to a mirror shine. The clock read 6:30 p.m., plenty of time for a fifteen-minute drive to the Amarillo Country Club and our seven o'clock dinner reservation. I waited for three women—Jenny, Bretta, and my mother-in-law. While waiting, I reread the bad news in the morning paper.

MCCORMACK'S AMARILLO VISIT restated the details of his successful appearances in the Texas Panhandle. On the positive side, it appeared I was no longer in first place for the area's "hot news." The paper didn't state it in so many words, but it left no doubt that McCormack had taken my place and risen to the top of everyone's "new news" list.

Jenny appeared, dressed in her finest, a stunning black sheath and pearls. "How do I look?" she asked.

I put down my newspaper, stood, and made a facetious inspection. I circled her with a frown on my face. "People will look at you and say, that must be the daughter of a prominent New York City society dame."

"I shouldn't have asked." Jenny laughed and gave me a playful tap in the stomach.

I looked at my watch to see that we had less than twenty minutes for the drive.

"You have Bretta's corsage?" she asked.

I held up a white carnation. "Right here."

"Don't forget to mention her hair. She spent the afternoon at her hair stylist. First time since all this happened."

I nodded.

Bretta came into the room with a bright, upbeat glow. She looked stunning. I don't know anything about the coiffure of hair, but hers appeared magnificent. "Wow. Very elegant. And I love the hair." I held up the carnation and smiled.

"Oh, Daddy. You shouldn't have." She giggled like a little girl and moved closer so I could pin it on.

"How's your grandmother doing?" I asked as I finished the job.

"She's in the bathroom," Bretta replied.

I checked my watch again. Six forty-five. Unless we left now, we'd be late for our reservation. I looked at Jenny and rolled my eyes.

Jenny gave me *her look*. In our twenty-seven years of marriage I had learned its meaning—well. In no uncertain terms, it said, "Don't say it."

I didn't. But I thought it. And as I sneaked another look at my watch, Katherine appeared—complaining.

"Joe, your house needs a guest bathroom."

I helped her with her coat, thinking we needed a nearby motel more than a guest bath.

She rattled on. "How can you expect me to get ready for a social event like this when I have to share a bathroom with Bretta?"

I helped Jenny and Bretta with their coats.

"I can't believe you've lived out here in cow country all these years in a house with only two bathrooms."

The four of us piled into the BMW. Thankfully, that brought an end to my mother-in-law's harangue. She and Bretta took the back seat.

Jenny sat in front with me.

As we backed out of the driveway and headed south on Westbrooke Terrace, another problem arose—my cellphone rang. From the back seat, I received more advice. "Good lord, do we have to talk on the phone tonight?"

"Please." Jenny whispered. Her eye contact said it all. Nothing could possibly be more important than Bretta's dinner. I pulled the phone from my pocket, turned it off, and in so doing noticed that the call was from my lawyer, Isaac Levy. I didn't give it a second thought.

"Thank you," Jenny said as she leaned over and lightly kissed me on the cheek.

The Country Club had decorated our table with balloons and a little homemade banner that read, "Bretta Wright, Amarillo's Sweetheart." Their festive touch thrilled our daughter and set the tone for the evening. We needed a happy time for Bretta and, even though one member of our group continued to whine and complain, Monday night provided it.

Later that night in bed, I read the jokes in *Readers Digest.* Apparently, the editors have a proclivity for mother-in-law humor. Maybe that's why I like the Digest so much? Anyway, my favorite was about a new policeman who takes the department's entrance exam.

The examiner asks, "What would you do if you had to arrest your own mother-in-law?"

The student replies, "I'd call for back-up."

I read the joke to Jenny.

She didn't think it was funny.

24

At home, 1109 Westbrook Terrace

The next day, we all had our assignments. I went to work. Brent went to school. Bretta had doctor appointments. And Jenny took her mother to the airport.

All went well until dinner. Brent was late. We went ahead without him. Then, after dinner, while we were cleaning up and loading the dishwasher, the doorbell rang. I went to the door to find Sheriff Jack Richards, two university policemen, and our son.

Brent didn't look so hot.

Sheriff Richards took the lead. "We need to talk," he said.

"Come in," I said and held the door open. I led the way and gestured to the chairs in our living room.

Jenny and Bretta joined us. Jenny took one look at Brent and left the room for washcloths and first-aid supplies. Bretta and I went to Brent to examine his wounds.

Brent's shirt was torn, his lip cut and bleeding, and for sure, a black eye was on the way. "What happened?" I asked, as I tried to examine him.

"Fist fight, over behind Jones Hall, one of the men's dormitories at CSU," Jack Richards said. "But I'd like you to hear Brent's side of the story."

"Yes, let's hear it," I said.

Brent stood silently, using the sleeve of his torn shirt to dab his lip.

"Son, I want to know what happened."

Brent shook his head, looked down at the floor, and mumbled, "You wouldn't understand."

I turned to Richards. "Tell me what you know."

He held up a clipboard and read from notes. "At 5:14 p.m., we received a complaint from University PD that a fist fight was in progress behind Jones Hall. UPD called us because one of the participants was not a university student. Turned out, the non-university fighter was Brent."

He flipped a page and continued.

"The other participant was a CSU student named Nathan Martin."

"Ah," I said. "I see. Bretta's Nathan."

"Witnesses said it began as a verbal argument inside the dorm and that Brent started it. Then it escalated to fisticuffs with Nathan Martin as instigator."

"And when did police get involved?"

"About ten minutes after the fight started. It was a mismatch. Some of the other students called University Police to come stop it."

I nodded. "As I remember, Martin is four or five years older, six inches taller, and forty or fifty pounds heavier."

Both policemen smiled. Richards chuckled. "You're right, but the reason we called it a mismatch is because Brent was beating Nathan—

badly. Blood all over the place," he chuckled again. "Nathan's."

Jenny returned. She and Bretta started working on Brent's wounds.

"I think we're almost finished here," I said to Jenny. "If you'll hold off just a minute, I'll help you."

I turned, and led the three officers to the door for a more private word.

"So, have charges been filed against Brent?"

"No, and probably won't be," Jack said.

"What does Brent need to do? What's our responsibility?"

"Honestly, Joe, I think a good father-to-son talk is all that's needed," Jack turned and gestured back at Brent. "He needs to stay away from Martin. No more fights."

"I'll take care of it," I said. The officers left, and I closed the door after them.

Jenny cleaned the wounds.

I put three stitches in a cut lip.

When we were finished, Bretta walked Brent up to his room. It seemed to me that our son and daughter were closer than I had ever seen them.

25

The Office of Levy and Cox, Attorneys at Law

I knew I needed a good lawyer. Isaac Levy held the reputation as the best attorney in the Texas Panhandle. It helped that he had a personal interest in me. Fifteen years ago, his daughter Sarah had been injured in a terrible automobile accident on I-27 just east of Canyon. At that time Sarah was a high school cheerleader, returning from a Friday-night football game in Lubbock. She'd been riding in the "death seat," the right, front passenger seat of a car driven by her boyfriend, a freshman at CSU. A drunk driver, headed in the wrong direction, came up the off-ramp and met them head on. Police estimated the speed of each car at highway levels—a closure of approximately 140 MPH. Even with seatbelts and airbags, the horrific crash should have caused certain death for everyone, especially a passenger in the right front seat.

However, fate sometimes creates a series of lucky circumstances. In this case, the location of the accident was close, the ambulance came quickly, and I arrived at the ER at almost the same time as Sarah. The bottom line was, we saved her life—something Isaac had never forgotten.

Now, at our first "professional" meeting, Isaac gave me a robust greeting, and then I watched as he poured two cups of coffee. When he handed a cup to me, I could see the look of a determined legal expert. He wanted to help me in my hour of need, just as I had worked for his daughter in hers.

"I've filed a restraining order," Isaac said. "This gives you back your license to practice medicine."

"Until?" I asked.

"Until they prove their case."

"Isaac, that won't take long. I did the D&C."

He shook his head, and his face changed to the "lawyer look." I knew that look. It reminded me of the expression a kindergarten teacher would use with an errant child. Isaac didn't say, "Tisk, tisk." He didn't have to. His condescending manner implied it, and his pause in the conversation let it expand into the focal point of our meeting.

"I did it," I repeated.

"You don't get it, do you?"

Now it was my turn to give him the silent treatment. I could have said *get what*, or *please explain.* But I didn't. Instead, I took a sip of coffee—waiting him out.

"The question is not 'Did Joseph Wright do the D&C,'" he said. "The question is 'Are we going to allow Texas Law to contradict US Law?'"

"And . . . ."

"And I don't think any Potter County jury is going to rule against you."

"Isaac, I think you're forgetting something. There's a reason we've been called 'The most politically conservative county in Texas.' Why do you think McCormack chose Amarillo as the site for his national broadcast?"

He smiled, silently.

"I don't see how we can win. Hey, it was our representative who coauthored House Bill 27.

"Joe," he said, "it's a win/win situation. We can't lose."

I took another sip of coffee. "I guess you'll have to explain."

"First, I think we'll win. You're a respected physician. This D&C was needed because it was the result of a gang rape." He paused, a lawyer's pause, a pause that signaled he was about to deliver his major point. "And she was your daughter."

I nodded. "And the procedure was against the law."

He shook his head in disagreement. "There's not a jury in Texas that would rule against a father's effort to protect his daughter."

"Depends on how you define *protect*."

"Okay, substitute the word *help*."

"Semantics," I said. "The law is the same no matter which word you use to describe what I did."

"Joe, I don't think we'll lose, but suppose we do?"

"Okay, suppose we do?"

He smiled. "We'll appeal."

We talked some more. Isaac's verbal description of our strategy reminded me of a merry-go-round. If we didn't win we'd go around to the next legal hurdle, and if that didn't give us the result we wanted, we'd keep going round and round until we found a legal venue where we did win.

Isaac projected that even if the local trial ruled against me, that we'd appeal, that I would continue to practice while we waited, and that the wrangling could go on for a long, long time. I left, thankful I had a good lawyer.

But deep down, I couldn't escape an ominous feeling of futility—it seemed likely that the wheels of justice would eventually ruin my life.

Part III

JULY

26

July 5, The Potter County Courthouse, Amarillo

We put the trial off as long as we could. Isaac filed legal documents asking that it not be held until next fall. But District Attorney William Robert Tredwell—everyone called him Billy Bob—knew that he had a "hot potato," and that the political consequences of any delay would return as bad news at the next election. So, on the day after the Fourth of July, amid massive media coverage, we gathered at the infamous Potter County Courthouse.

The term, infamous, could have been created to describe the old building. In the 1970s, it had been the site of the longest and most expensive murder trial in Texas history when a Fort Worth oil billionaire named Davis won acquittal for the murder of his wife. Davis, reportedly the wealthiest person ever to be tried for murder, hired Racehorse Haynes as his attorney and paid millions for a spectacular defense. Even today, more than a third of a century later, critics referred to the verdict as, *not guilty by reason of wealth.*

My first impression of the large room was its smell. A musty odor harkened to past battles where lives hung in the balance, fortunes were distributed, and hordes of people came to watch. A wooden railing divided the room into distinct areas—one part for the participants, the other for the audience. The spectator section with its wooded benches was at least twice as large, and I estimated it would seat over a hundred people. On that memorable July morning, every space was occupied.

An elevated desk dominated the front of the courtroom. A massive, high-backed, mahogany chair flanked by two flags, a U.S. flag on one side, a Texas flag on the other, left no doubt where the judge would be seated. Directly in front of the judge's bench, centered in the room, stood a raised platform and chair with a placard that read "witness stand." I assumed that the small table and chair nearby were for the court reporter. A uniformed bailiff, wearing a gun and a badge, sat at a small table by the window. Another wooden railing separated the jury box with its twelve chairs along the far wall.

Two large tables, furnished with two chairs each, sat in the center of everything. Billy Bob and his assistant sat at the first. Isaac and I headed toward the second. En route to our seats, we paused to shake hands with the opposition. Formal introductions and stiff body language left no doubt about an adversarial relationship. I looked at my watch to see that it was almost nine o'clock.

A few minutes later, the bailiff stood and in a loud, commanding voice, said, "All rise." A door on the east wall opened, and a large, heavyset man in a black robe entered. The bailiff continued. "The forty-seventh district court of Texas is now in session, the Honorable David Gleeson presiding. You may be seated."

Judge Gleeson used his microphone. He called the two lawyers to approach for instructions about jury selection.

I could write a book about the next three days, about the endless haggling, about the flimsy reasons that both sides used to dismiss a potential juror. About the words "pro-life" and "pro-choice," which were forbidden and avoided like the black plague. Judge Gleeson had ruled them as pejorative. As such, the mere utterance of either term by a prospective juror was grounds for dismissal.

"We want as many women as possible," Isaac said.

"And who do we *not* want?" I asked.

"Catholics and rednecks" came the blunt reply.

"Really?" Catholics, I could understand. But rednecks? I hadn't thought about any prejudicial views they might bring to the jury box. "Why the latter?" I asked.

"Rednecks tend to see issues in black and white. They don't want to haggle about the minutia, about the exceptions, about the fine points of an issue."

As usual, Isaac was right. And as the jury selection progressed I could see his insight at work in the questions he presented to a well-known rancher.

"How do you feel about mad cow disease?" Isaac asked.

"It's deadly," the rancher replied. "You get it, you die."

"How many cattle do you presently own?" Isaac asked.

"That varies from day to day," he replied. "We're constantly buying and selling."

"On average. During the month of June, how many cattle on an average day?"

"About 500,000. We're one of the largest cattle operations in the Texas Panhandle."

"And how many cases did you have of mad cow disease?"

"None."

"None?" Isaac paused, his face reflecting an obvious, perplexed expression. "You're sure that out of a half-million cattle, you didn't have a single case?"

"Yup."

"How many cases of mad cow in the entire state of Texas?"

"None."

"None last year?"

"None, ever. Texas has never had a case of mad cow."

Isaac picked up his clipboard and studied it for about fifteen seconds. I could feel the tension building. He was getting ready to deliver the *coupe de grace*, a question that would disqualify the juror.

"Would it surprise you to know that the NIH, the National Institutes of Health, has discontinued all research in Bovine Spongiform Encephalopathy—what is commonly known as mad cow disease?"

"No. Nothing surprises me about the government."

"The reason given by the NIH, and I quote, is that 'mad cow disease is not dangerous.' They say that your chances of getting the disease are less than a combination of being struck by lightening and winning the lottery, all in the same day."

"The government lies. I see it every day."

Isaac handed the rancher a newspaper. "I'm merely quoting the *New York Times.* They report statistics for worldwide deaths last year from mad cow disease and compare the number with a total of lottery winners and deaths by lightening. I suppose the *New York Times* is also lying?"

The rancher looked defiant. "I don't care what you say, mad cow disease is deadly, and I'm afraid of it."

"And you also believe Dr. Joseph Wright should be sent to prison?"

"Objection," yelled Billy Bob. "That's asking a prospective juror how he's going to rule on the case."

Isaac raised his hand before Judge Gleeson could respond.

"Your Honor," Isaac said. "We ask that this juror be dismissed."

"So ordered," the judge replied.

Jury selection inched on—hour by hour, day by day—until at the end of the third day, twelve jurors and two alternates had been selected. The judge rapped his gavel and said that opening statements would begin the next morning at nine o'clock.

Isaac told me he thought we had done well. Of the twelve jurors, seven were women, and he was especially pleased that no Catholics had been chosen. The two alternates were both men—one a farmer, the other a rancher—but he hoped that we might get through the trial without the need to call on either.

That night I drove home more nervous than ever. My fate was now in the hands of these twelve local citizens. Isaac called it a win/win situation. But when it's your future on the line, you can't help but think of all the bad things that could happen to you. I tried to put it aside, to focus on the positive—an effort that failed miserably.

27

The Potter County Courthouse

Billy Bob made his opening statement. Isaac responded with his. It was interesting to hear two such different versions of the same story. Billy Bob stated that he would prove, "beyond any reasonable doubt," that I had performed an abortion, that I had broken the law, and that I must suffer the consequences—a prison sentence and loss of my medical license. Nothing new. Like a parrot, he just repeated the same old rhetoric that had filled both the print and broadcast media for weeks.

Isaac started with one word, *caution*. He spelled it, C-A-U-T-I-O-N. Then he gave a spellbinding speech about this being the first trial under the new law, about precedence, about how the decisions made by this jury would affect history. I thought his presentation more memorable for what it didn't say than for any specifics about whether or not I was guilty.

The "opening statements" took almost two hours.

Judge Gleeson declared a fifteen-minute break. When we returned, he looked at the prosecution and said, "Call your first witness."

"I call Dennis Smith," Billy Bob announced.

I almost didn't recognize Dennis. Wearing a dark suit with a red-and-gold striped tie, he looked like an ad for Brooks Brothers. The bailiff administered the oath, and Dennis took the stand.

Billy Bob began slowly, asking Dennis to give his name, where he lived, where he worked, how long he had lived and worked in Amarillo—a series of questions to portray the witness as a model citizen. This took a long time, probably a half hour or more, and, I thought, it siphoned all the excitement out of the trial. It seemed obvious to me that everyone in the room wanted to hear testimony rather than a long, pedantic recitation about the witness's background. And I could hear a rustle of impatience as people shifted in their seats. Finally, Billy Bob got to the point.

"Do you recall the events that occurred at Northwest Hospital in the wee hours of the morning of June10," Billy Bob asked.

"Yes, sir," Dennis replied.

"Tell us what happened. Be as specific as possible."

"I worked the graveyard shift, midnight to eight a.m. I was the security guard at the emergency entrance to the hospital. It was a slow night; for the first couple of hours we had no patients."

"Nothing happened?"

"Until 1:47 a.m. I keep a log, and that's the time I wrote down."

"And what happened at 1:47?" Billy Bob asked.

"Dr. Wright drove up with his daughter and his wife," Dennis replied.

"Go on."

"Dr. Wright started to carry his daughter into the ER, but I fetched a gurney and helped him roll her in."

"Who else witnessed this?"

"The two nurses on duty: Kathy Thompson and Elsa Jennings."

"Go on. What happened next?"

"We wheeled the patient into examination room ER2. Kathy started to call Dr. Young, the MD who was on duty that night, but Dr. Wright stopped her."

"The defendant, Dr. Joseph Wright, ordered nurse Kathy Thompson not to call the physician on duty?"

"Yes, sir."

"Was that unusual?" Billy Bob asked.

"I've worked the ER for going on ten years. In all that time, this was the only instance I've ever known that to happen," Dennis said.

"Why do you think Dr. Wright did not want another doctor present for the treatment of his daughter?"

"Objection," Isaac said. "Calls for speculation."

"Sustained," Judge Gleeson replied.

"Okay, just tell us, what happened next?" Billy Bob asked.

"I went back to my security desk. Dr. Wright closed the door."

"But you were suspicious?"

"Yes, sir," Dennis said. "When a doctor brings a female patient into the ER at two o'clock in the morning, doesn't summon the physician on duty, and sends the nurses out of the examination room, it's clear something shady is about to happen."

"Objection," Isaac said. "That's opinion not supported by facts in evidence."

"Your Honor," Billy Bob pleaded. "I'm leading to the facts."

"I'll allow you to continue, subject to presentation of those facts. Get on with it."

"Yes, Your Honor." Billy Bob turned to the witness stand. "You say Dr. Wright sent the nurses out of the room?"

"Just one nurse, Kathy Thompson." Dennis replied.

"And nurse Elsa Jennings," Billy Bob continued, "who is a long-time friend of Dr. Wright, stayed to assist with the abortion."

"Objection," Isaac yelled.

"Sustained," replied the judge, his face showing a mean scowl. "Mr. Tredwell, you know you can't imply something like that. Next time you use a blatantly pejorative term without first showing a factual basis, it'll be a $1,000 fine."

"Sorry, your Honor," Billy Bob replied. "I was just getting ahead of myself."

"Get on with it, but stick to the facts."

I loved it when the judge reprimanded Tredwell. And for a moment, I sensed a wave of empathy from the jury. Unfortunately, it didn't last long as he cautiously returned to his witness.

"Mr. Smith, did you question Nurse Thompson?"

"Well, we talked. She was a little miffed about being kicked out of the room."

"And you remember the conversation?"

"Absolutely. I'll never forget it."

Billy Bob moved to the side, to give everyone a full view of the witness. It was a subtle gesture, but it had the effect of turning a spotlight on Dennis. The courtroom became deathly quiet.

"Tell us what Nurse Kathy Thompson said."

"She said Dr. Wright's daughter, Bretta, had taken a coat hanger, that she'd tried to do a self-abortion, that she blotched it, and that she was bleeding heavily. Dr. Wright did a pelvic exam, a dilatation, and determined that her uterus was not perforated."

"So, Bretta Wright's attempted abortion had failed."

"Kathy was there. She saw it. She couldn't stop talking about it."

"What happened next?"

"Kathy was asked to leave."

"So, Kathy left, and after that we don't know what took place in the room?"

Dennis smiled. He puffed up like a detective with an *ah-ha* moment. "Fifteen minutes later, Dr. Wright and his daughter left. Immediately, Kathy and I went into the room to clean up."

"And . . . ?"

"And we found the curette."

Billy Bob stepped to the evidence table and picked up a clear, plastic bag that contained a stainless steel medical tool. Shaped somewhat like a large spoon, it looked discolored with what could have been blood and human tissue. "Is this *the* curette?"

"Yes, sir. It has my tag attached to the handle."

"And you took this to the hospital administration?"

"Yes, sir."

William Robert Tredwell turned to Isaac Levy and said, "Your witness."

"I have no questions for this witness," Isaac replied.

28

The Potter County Courthouse

The trial continued for two days. Billy Bob presented Kathy Thompson to confirm Dennis Smith's testimony. Kathy stated that a curette was an instrument used to scrape the womb in a dilatation and curettage—a D&C, an abortion.

"And, on the night of June 9, or the early morning hours of Tuesday, June 10, you found this curette in the ER examination room number two?"

"Yes, it has the tag attached, signed by Dennis Smith and me."

"It's discolored—it looks like what could be dried blood."

"It *is* dried blood. When Dennis and I found it, it was bloody and had fragments of human tissue on it.

"What did you do with the curette?"

"Hey, this is not rocket science," Kathy said. "When you leave the room in the middle of a pelvic exam, and fifteen minutes later you find a bloody curette, you know that it's evidence."

"Evidence of what?"

"Evidence of a D&C. Obviously, Dr. Wright had just performed an abortion on his daughter."

"There's no other possible explanation?"

"That's what a curette was designed for—scraping the uterus. It had fresh blood on it, showing it had just been used. The only patient in the room was Bretta Wright. What other explanation could there be?"

"So, you saved the curette?"

"Yes, we carefully put it in a plastic bag—attached the tag with date, time, and our signatures—and turned it over to the hospital administrator, Edward Garfield."

"Thank you," Billy Bob said. Then he turned to Isaac. "Your witness."

Isaac stood and walked over to the witness stand. "You don't like Joseph Wright, do you?"

"That's not true, I like all the doctors," she replied.

"But he asked you to leave the examination room?"

"Well, yes."

"And Dennis Smith has testified that you were *miffed* about being asked to leave."

"Dennis exaggerates."

"So you have nothing against Dr. Wright?"

For a few seconds, Kathy looked down at her shoes as though trying to decide what to say. When she looked up, she stared at me for a moment and then looked away. I had the feeling of a Judas Iscariot betrayal.

"He plays fast and loose with the rules," Kathy said. "Doctors think they are better than the rest of us—that the rules are for little people, but not for them."

"Really. All doctors?"

"To a degree, yes. But some act more high-and-mighty than others.

Dr. Wright, in my opinion, is the worst of the bunch."

"So, you want to see him sent to prison?"

"No, but—"

"But, what?"

"I don't think he should be allowed to get away with this."

"Can you prove Dr. Wright broke the law?

"I think *we* just did."

"You actually saw him do an abortion?"

"No, but—"

"But you want him punished and you'll do everything you can to make that happen?

"You're putting words—"

"Your Honor," Isaac said. "I have no more questions for this witness."

The hospital's ethics committee, two MDs and the hospital administrator, Ed Garfield, all testified that the curette had been turned over to the police and that Dr. Joseph Wright's hospital privileges had been suspended.

Billy Bob said, "The prosecution rests."

Isaac called Dr. Harvey Adams, one of my two medical partners.

"Dr. Adams, how long have you known Joe Wright?"

"Fifteen years," Harvey replied. "We're partners in the Adams-Campbell-Wright Medical Clinic."

"As a fellow doctor for fifteen years, you've had an opportunity to form an opinion about Joseph Wright's medical ethics?"

"Yes, we work together. I know everything there is to know about his medical practice."

"And . . ."

"I think he's the best family doctor in Texas. He has a mind like a medical encyclopedia. Very knowledgeable. Highly skilled. When I need consultation on a difficult medical problem, I always go to Joe."

"Have you ever known him to play 'fast and loose' with the rules? To violate normal medical ethics?"

"No. Joe Wright is the most ethical physician I know."

"Fifteen years, and he has never committed an illegal act—something that you, as a doctor, would consider an unethical medical practice?"

"Never."

"Thank you, Dr. Adams," Isaac said. "Your witness."

Isaac's questioning had taken less than five minutes. In contrast, Billy Bob hammered Harvey Adams for almost an hour. Over and over, he asked variations of one basic question: *Had Dr. Wright ever done something, anything, unethical?*

To his credit, Harvey backed me to the hilt. According to Harv, I was not just clean, I was *squeaky* clean.

Finally, the judge had heard enough. "Mr. Treadwell, we need to move on."

"One last question, your Honor," Billy Bob answered. Then he turned to Harvey and asked, "Do partners in the Adams-Campbell-Wright Clinic have an informal CYA agreement?"

"CYA?"

Billy Bob smiled, a sardonic facial gesture that mocked Harvey's questioning response. "Come on Dr. Adams. Everyone knows CYA."

"I'm sorry, I guess you'll have to enlighten me."

"Cover your ass."

"Objection," Isaac said.

"Overruled," the judge said. "Answer the question."

Harvey's face turned red, and the courtroom turned eerily quiet. So quiet we could hear the sound of air moving through the air conditioning system. The sudden quietness brought a heightened focus on the wintness and his answer to a loaded, confrontational question. I could see it coming. Normally, Harvey Adams was a soft-spoken, easy-going, even-tempered individual. But if you cross him, he can explode—I'd seen it a couple of times in our fifteen-year partnership.

"No," Harv said, his voice soft, almost a whisper. Then a little louder, "And I resent the implications of your question." He moved forward in the witness chair, finger pointed at the district attorney, each word louder, "You have no basis to imply that Dr. Wright, Dr. Campbell, or I would engage in nefarious acts for the financial benefit of our clinic." His voice filled with rage as the volume grew. "For fifteen years, we three doctors have given our sweat, our blood, our lives to caring for Amarillo citizens and their medical problems. We've built our reputations, day by day, year after year, through consistent, high-quality, always ethical medical practice."

The judge cut him off with a loud rap of his gavel. "Mr. Tredwell, you said that was your last question."

Like a dog with his tail between his legs, Billy Bob gave up without another word and returned to his seat.

"Mr. Levy?" the judge asked.

"No, Your Honor. I think the witness has answered the question.

Then Isaac paused. For about fifteen seconds, he stood perfectly still, looking down at his notes. The courtroom came to a screeching halt. Isaac's intention was to focus all attention on him, on what he would say next. It was the most dramatic moment of the four-day trial. I'll never forget those next three words:

"The defense rests."

29

The Potter County Courthouse

Closing arguments. Isaac went first. "Remember the word *caution*, "he said. "We all know this is the first trial to come under the aegis of Texas House Bill 27. You've seen the attention given to us by the media. Presidential candidates have come to Amarillo because of this trial. Like it or not, we're going to be scrutinized in a way that can only be called historic. Legal scholars will look at you and your decision with a microscope. Every aspect of these past four days will be debated in America's judicial system. You need to get this right."

Isaac paused, took a drink of water. He had everyone's undivided attention.

"Let's reexamine the facts. The prosecution has failed to prove that Joseph Wright broke the law. Yes, we've heard some people say, 'They think he performed a D&C on his daughter.' But that doesn't meet the standard of *proof beyond any reasonable doubt.* We've seen a bloody medical instrument called a curette. But again, there's no proof that Joe

Wright used it to commit an illegal act. No one can say, 'He did it,' with absolute certainty."

Isaac paused and looked at the jury. I could see him meeting each juror, eye to eye, making sure they would evaluate his next few words with special concentration.

"The stakes could not be higher. These past few days we've learned that Joe Wright is not just a good doctor, he's a good man with an untarnished reputation. And more than that, he's a devoted father. The prosecution is trying to use that *good father* image to imply that he committed an illegal act to help his daughter. But that's not proof."

Then Isaac came over and put his hands on my shoulders.

"I'll close with the same word I used three days ago in my opening statement. It's spelled C-A-U-T-I-O-N. Don't allow the media's histrionics to stampede you into lynch-mob mentality. The prosecution has not proved Dr. Joseph Wright guilty. Do the right thing. Vote to acquit. Return this good doctor to his family, to his community, to his outstanding medical work."

I wanted to lead a standing ovation. There was electricity in the room. I could sense it, and I thought, if we asked the jury to vote at that instant, it would be a unanimous win for the defense.

Unfortunately, William Robert Tredwell had his final turn in taking pot shots at me. As Isaac took his seat, Treadwell rose and cleared his throat. Positioning himself directly in front of the jury, he began.

"Ladies and gentlemen of the jury, I agree with the defense on an important point—Joseph Wright is a good doctor."

Years ago, my high school debate coach told me to *watch out when your opponent agrees with you.* I still remember the words, *he's about to turn them around and use them against you.*

"But you can't allow a good doctor to use his medical skill to break the law. Yes, his daughter had recently gone through a terrible ordeal. Yes, Joe Wright wanted to help his daughter. No, you must not allow him to sneak off into the night and commit an illegal act, an abortion."

Then Billy Bob switched to a lesson in American history. He started in the 1700s with the country's founding fathers, the constitution, the concepts of democracy that had now become the bedrock of American jurisprudence.

He spoke with elegance.

Then he challenged Isaac's closing argument and his statement about absolute certainty.

"We all know about circumstantial evidence. Every day, we see convictions that are based on it. Why? Because, like this case, crimes are often committed behind closed doors, in the middle of the night, without someone present to witness the event. Mr. Levy made a big point about having someone say 'He did it.' Well, you heard the testimony. We presented six different people who said 'He did it.' The circumstances were so compelling, there could be no other explanation."

And then he came to his point.

"The 'Rule of Law,' that has made our country great, is very fragile. If we allow one person to *break the law,* what is to keep us from allowing a second, a third, a hundred? A basic premise of the American justice system is fairness—we treat everyone equally."

I thought, at this point, William Robert Tredwell would quit. But he didn't, and he proceeded to lay a guilt trip on the members of the jury.

"I like Dr. Wright. And I'll bet you do, too. He's a good doctor, a good man, a good father, and we all feel sorry for his daughter. But I've taken an oath to enforce the rule of law, and so did you. When you were sworn in as members of this jury, you held up your right hand and said, 'So help me, God,' that you would uphold the law. It has now come time to do that. He's guilty. He broke the law. You must vote to convict him."

The judge then gave a lengthy charge to the jury.

One by one they filed out.

I thought we had a chance.

An hour later they came back and gave their verdict. Guilty.

We lost the case, and two bailiffs promptly arrested me.

30

The Offices of Cox and Levy, Attorneys at Law

We lost the trial. I went to jail. But, without telling me, Isaac had filed an appeal to the Texas Supreme Court. Within hours, I was released and had my medical license reinstated. The next day I met with Isaac in his office.

"Isaac, you son-of-a-gun. You knew we wouldn't win. You were stringing me along, making me think we had a chance."

He handed me a cup of coffee, the standard ritual at the beginning of every Isaac Levy office conference. "You remember, I told you the trial was a win/win situation for us?"

"Yeah, but I guess you neglected to explain."

"There was always a chance we might win our case at the district court."

"But, we didn't."

"A possibility—that was the first half of win/win.

"And the second half?" I asked.

"An appeal to a higher court," he said. "The appeal has now been sent to the Texas Supreme Court. Again, we have a chance."

"How long will this take?" I groused.

"Who knows?" he answered with a shrug. Isaac picked up the carafe, gestured to refill my cup.

"I'm fine," I said. "Tell me about the timeline for an appeal to the state Supreme Court."

"Normally—"

"Isaac, you and I both know this *ain't* a normal situation." I took a long draw of coffee. "Hell, everyone in Texas knows it."

He took a sip of his coffee and then turned to the computer on his credenza. I watched silently as he went from screen to screen, searching a database of records from the Texas Supreme Court. A couple of minutes went by before he turned, halfway facing me.

"I have three possible timelines," he answered. "First, 30 percent of all appeals never get heard. They're still there, waiting, and probably will die without ever being reviewed by the court."

I frowned. He and I both knew this possibility had nothing to do with my case.

"Normally—and I know you see your appeal as anything but normal—the average case takes eighteen months from the date it is filed until the court renders a decision." He turned back to his computer screen.

I sipped my coffee, knowing that eventually he'd answer my question. Finally, reading from his electronic data, he gave the response I'd been waiting for. "The all-time, fastest response from the court was a case called 'The Sons and Daughters of Davy Crockett versus The San Antonio Alamo Foundation,' which occurred last winter."

"And?"

"And it took two weeks."

We talked some more. Isaac projected that I would continue to practice while we waited, and that the wrangling could go on for a long, long time. I left, thankful I had a good lawyer, and wondering how fast the wheels of justice would take to ruin my life.

31

At home, 1109 Westbrook Terrace

Ignorant, oblivious, uninformed—words that describe my knowledge of legal matters—so what does a person do to learn about the appeal process? Go to the Internet. I did and I was surprised.

I found that Texas had two judicial possibilities. The Supreme Court of Texas is the court of last resort for noncriminal matters. A different court, the Texas Court of Criminal appeals, is the court of last resort for criminal cases.

My first impression—since I had been arrested and sentenced to five years in prison—was that I had a criminal case. Isaac said, "No, that the essence of my appeal was a matter of law confrontation—a problem that challenged existing federal law." My case would be heard by the Texas Supreme Court.

So I went back to the Internet to a website titled *Texas Supreme Court* and found the following material:

> The Supreme Court of Texas is composed of a chief justice and eight associate justices. Each member of the court must b at least thirty-five years of age, a citizen of Texas, licensed to practice law in Texas, and must have practiced law (or have been a lawyer "and/or" a judge of a court of record for a total of) at least ten years. The chief justice and the associate justices are elected to staggered six-year terms in state-wide partisan elections. When a vacancy arises, the governor of Texas may appoint justices, subject tot senate confirmation, to serve out the remainder of an unexpired term until the next general election. At the current time, six of the current justices, a majority, were originally appointed by Governor Rick Perry. The current justices, like all the judges of the Texas Court of Criminal Appeals, are all Republican. The court meets in Austin in a building located on the state capitol grounds, behind the Texas State Capitol.

As I read the above, the "facts and figures" about the Supreme Court of Texas, I marveled at how little I knew about it. I was born in Texas, raised in Texas, educated in Texas, and—except for a couple of years to complete my medical training, a residency in New York—lived all my life in Texas.

Over the years, I occasionally noticed elections where an unfamiliar name was listed on the ballot as running for a seat on the Texas Supreme Court. And I remember some passing thoughts about "being bothered" by the process—of voting for candidates that I knew little or nothing about, and of being involved in the election of candidates for an office that seemed remote, unimportant, or both. Until I had a case on their docket, I hardly knew that the Texas Supreme Court existed.

Out of sight, out of mind.

Suddenly, this had changed.

So, I read and reread the data carefully. I studied it, trying to wring out every drop of information, overt or covert. If these nine people were going to decide my future, I wanted to know as much as possible about them, about their background, and especially about any possible bias they might bring to a contentious subject like abortion.

The more I read, the more I didn't like what I found—a very conservative court with probable bias toward a "pro-life" position on abortion issues.

Texas is a Republican state.

And in other branches of government, we seem to have—at least the appearance of—a two-party system that was, I thought, alive and flourishing in Texas. In every gubernatorial election, we have had Democratic candidates who made a creditable race. And I had even heard talk about the possibility that, as our Hispanic population continued to increase, a return to a Democratic majority in the legislature.

It was a fact—the Texas Senate and the Texas House of Representatives both had a sizable minority of Democrats.

But a citizen, any citizen, hopes for a bipartisan quality in all three aspects of government—executive, legislative, *and* judicial.

So much for hope.

In the judicial branch of Texas state government, any possibility for bipartisan thinking appeared nonexistent. The Texas Supreme Court was solidly Republican—nine justices, nine Republicans. And the political system, that of holding statewide elections for six-year, staggered terms, virtually guaranteed that the state's majority party would shut out any Supreme Court justices from the minority party.

As I analyzed my chances with these nine jurists, the old cliché about "slim and none" came to mind. And the part about slim "having left town" didn't seem humorous anymore.

I was stuck. So I didn't bother to attend the court proceedings in Austin. Isaac represented me. And he missed the timeline. Isaac's projection of "a long, long time turned out to be dead wrong.

Texas v. Wright set a new record for speedy process, and the Texas Supreme Court ruled against me two days later.

32

At home, 1109 Westbrook Terrace

Isaac Levy was good. Damn good. The Texas Supreme Court gave its ruling against my appeal at nine o'clock, and I lost my right to practice medicine. But Isaac had anticipated their decision and, without telling me, had prepared the next step in our legal battle.

By noon, I had my license back.

That morning, in less than three hours, Isaac processed three legal actions. First, he filed a brief with the US Supreme Court challenging our state's ruling—on the basis that House Bill 27 was unconstitutional. Isaac alleged HB27, which directly contradicted existing law, denied a woman her right to reproductive freedom. Therefore, as long as *Row v. Wade* continued as the law of the land, no state had the right to prohibit abortions.

Second, he processed an injunction with the Texas Supreme Court, blocking all their legal actions against me, pending a ruling by the higher court.

Third, he filed a restraining order against the Texas Medical Licensing Board, which had the effect of maintaining my right to practice medicine until our appeal at the national level was decided.

I was back in business. The date was Monday, July 13, just three days after Bretta got her cast off.

Life goes on.

And my medical practice, except for treating patients at the hospital, felt surprisingly normal. In some ways I liked it better. Without the demands of checking on patients in the mornings and evenings, I worked shorter days.

A more leisurely morning schedule gave me time to read the newspapers. Unfortunately, the news was mostly bad. The *Amarillo Globe-News* now had a reporter traveling with the McCormack campaign, and the paper gave daily reports of Reggie's political fortunes. Day after day I read how the Democrats and the Republicans were losing ground, and about how McCormack's pro-life issues were making *Roe v. Wade* the central issue of this year's election. Worst of all, my name, and the appeal over my medical license, appeared in almost every article.

I thought it blatantly unfair that the name of a local doctor would become national news. And, as a family, we made a new rule—we wouldn't talk about it. So, like the old saw about an elephant in the room, we conversed about Brent's school, Jenny's museum, my patients, the plans for our family's future—anything but the issue that dominated our lives.

All of us except Bretta. Once in awhile, she felt she had to talk about it.

Bretta had a direct stake in the publicity. The more the national press raised my notoriety, the more it reminded the outside world of her status as the infamous victim. On that July evening, she came to me for advice and sat beside me on the sofa in the den.

I muted the sound on the television.

"Dad, I'm having second thoughts about going to Juilliard this fall," she confided.

My heart sank. This had been Bretta's dream for years. "Why's that?" I asked, deliberately keeping my voice even to mask the alarm I felt.

"People no longer react to me as a singer. They see me as that girl who had an illegal abortion."

I didn't respond for a moment, waiting to choose my words carefully. "The quality of your voice becomes an afterthought?"

"Exactly, and I don't know what to do about it."

"Nothing you can do . . . for now. But, I think you'll probably find that not *everyone* is going to feel that way."

Bretta didn't like my answer. Her reaction was—as it had been for all her twenty-three years when she didn't agree with parental statements—silence.

I reached over and held her hand.

"I'd like to drop out of school and get a job," she said, a quiver in her voice.

All of a sudden she seemed so fragile. Though I hated what she was telling me, I didn't want to object too strongly. "What kind of job?" I asked.

"One with a low profile. McDonald's had an ad in this morning's paper."

I tried not to let my disappointment show. "Whatever you want, we'll support your decision." Though my heart was not in my reply, I managed to keep my voice even.

She squeezed my hand. "Thanks, Dad. I knew I could count on you."

"You don't have to decide tonight."

She sat up, giving me a stern look. "You waffling on me already?"

I grinned. "Of course."

"One thing I've decided, for sure. I'm not going to graduate school this fall."

I nodded, and I could see a flash of the old independence that had characterized her personality through the years. "But you might think about other low-profile jobs, some that require a college degree and pay more."

"Jobs where they let rape victims fade into the shadows?"

"You bet." I let go of her hand and playfully punched her on the shoulder. "Seriously—a job where you can keep your options open."

Our eyes locked and she flashed a big, toothy grin. "Weasel," she said as she stood.

"You asked for my advice."

"I know." She leaned over and kissed me on the forehead. "And I have a little gift for you. Wait here." She left to go upstairs to her room.

A gift? The thought stirred memories of Bretta as a little girl—when she gave me tokens of her affection. Once, when she was three years old, she gave me a dandelion . . . I still remember it.

Bretta came back down the stairs and handed me a small box wrapped in white tissue with a red bow. It had a heart-shaped tag with an inscription:

"To Dad, the guy I love more than anyone else in the world."

"Wow." I choked.

In Texas, real men are not supposed to cry, but in spite of my efforts to hold back, I felt moisture gather in my eyes. At first I just blinked and squeezed my eyelids, trying to stop the reaction. Finally, I gave up and wiped my eyes with my sleeve.

"Well," Bretta said. "Aren't you gonna open it?"

I ripped off the tissue paper to find a little box stamped, Top of Texas Catholic Bookstore. The box measured only two inches by four inches by ½-inch thick. "Must be a very small book?" I asked.

Bretta shook her head, impatiently. "Open it."

I had to work at it, but when I finally got the little box open I found a bronze medallion. It was about an inch in diameter and had a tiny chain attached so that it could be worn around the neck. I thought I recognized the image. "St. Jude?"

Bretta smiled. "The patron saint of impossible causes."

I laughed. "So I'm an impossible cause?"

Bretta's smile vanished and she took my hand. "No, Dad, but I was . . . until you came to my rescue." She squeezed my hand. "You're my very own St. Jude."

Then she gently took the medallion and hung it around my neck.

33

Amarillo, the Medical Arts Building

Bretta's decision to decline her graduate assistantship at Julliard hit me like a dagger through the heart. The rape was an awful, terrible thing. But to give up her future? The morning dragged and, as patient after patient came to my treatment rooms, I found it hard to concentrate, to give my complete, undivided attention to their medical needs.

Virginia, my chief nurse, noticed. Between patients, she closed the door and confronted me. "You okay?" she asked.

"Sure," I replied. "I'm fine."

"You don't look it or act it."

"Hey, I'm all right. Where's the folder for the next patient?"

Virginia proffered the file and a cup of coffee. "Something's not right," she said. "If you'll tell me what it is, maybe I can help?"

I took the folder in one hand, the cup in the other. "Thanks, this helps." I sipped the coffee and found it scalding hot.

"And?" Virginia gave me a look of expectation.

Virginia and I had worked together for almost a decade. Over that time we developed a professional relationship that extended beyond normal office rapport. And our patients benefitted from this joint approach. Because we cared for one another, trusted one another, depended on one another, we used two brains, two sets of eyes, ears . . . two individual, medical perceptions to reinforce each diagnosis and treatment. We were more than a doctor and a nurse—the typical boss and assistant—we were a team.

So when she gave me that look, I felt compelled to tell her about Brenda.

"The office." I nodded down the hall and led the way.

She closed the door.

I sipped my coffee, a momentary pause, thinking about where to start.

"And?" she asked.

I unbuttoned my shirt and pulled out the little bronze medallion. "Ever heard of St. Jude, the patron saint of impossible causes?"

Virginia looked at the icon. "You know I'm Methodist, but, yes, I've heard of St. Jude, and I know that Catholics hold the saint in high regard."

"Bretta gave this to me last night."

"Oh?"

"She considered herself an impossible case, and that I came to her rescue. I was her St. Jude."

"How sweet." Virginia smiled. "I'll bet not many fathers receive a medallion from their daughters."

"Yes, I teared up."

Virginia's smile faded. She shook her head and said, "I don't understand. Most dads would be busting their buttons if their daughters had given them a St. Jude award. There's something you're not telling me?"

I nodded. "Yeah, there's more." Then I told her about Bretta's decision to cancel Juilliard.

"What's she going to do?"

"She's reading the classified ads, looking for a job. She mentioned McDonalds."

"Oh, no," Virginia looked horrified.

I shook my head, a double negative, a gesture of agreement.

"She's throwing away her future," Virginia said. "You can't let her do it."

"Obviously, I can't make her go to graduate school," I replied as I looked at my watch.

"Surely, there must be something you can do," Virginia insisted.

I looked down and shook my head again. "Last night, my brain turned to mush. All I could think about was the need to support her."

"I understand," Virginia said, her voice only a whisper. "She needs her father's support."

"And we have patients waiting." I set my coffee down and opened the folder.

"Heavy." Virginia shook her head. "Thanks for sharing this with me. But I know you. You'll find a way to help her."

Together we headed to treatment room number one where we found our next patient—a seventy-year-old obese woman with type-2 diabetes. Normally, I would take the lead and offer counsel about exercise, nutrition, and weight loss, about how vital it is to maintain low blood sugar, and the disastrous consequences of not doing so. On this day, however, I just didn't have the push.

I looked at my nurse, rolled my eyes, and she took over. This patient was facing the possible loss of her feet, her vision, or both. I watched and listened while Virginia read her the riot act—stern, harsh medical advice, which thc patient needed.

While Virginia was doing this, my mind drifted. Over and over the same thought kept repeating—dominating my thinking to the point of blocking rational thinking. ? What does a person do to help a rape victim?

Specifically, what could I do to help Bretta?

Or most importantly, as a father, what could I do to help my daughter?

34

The next morning, at home, 1109 Westbrook Terrace

We have a small television in the kitchen which I sometimes watch during breakfast. The next morning I turned it on to find a special news bulletin; "US Supreme Court Justice John Paul Stevenson has died," the newscaster stated. "At age eighty-seven, his passing was not unexpected—"

I went outside to fetch the morning paper. When I opened it, the headline surprised me.

I'd never seen such extensive coverage devoted to the death of a Supreme Court justice.

Back at the breakfast table, as I read the news, I realized the stories were not so much about Justice Stevenson as they were about his replacement. Speculation ran wild with names of possible candidates. Even more conjecture went into an accompanying article about how this new justice might affect the balance of judicial opinion on abortion. Just from reading one day's news, I sensed that political pressure ran rampant for a pro-life appointment.

As soon as I got to the office, I called my lawyer. He suggested we go for lunch at the Burger Barn, a gourmet hamburger place near his office. I arrived first and found a table in the corner, away from the crowd. Isaac arrived shortly, and we each ordered the "All-American," the restaurant's signature sandwich.

"You've heard the news about Justice Stevenson?" I asked.

He chuckled. "Even an Eskimo native living at the North Pole now has every minute detail about the death of John Paul Stevenson."

I smiled in response, acknowledging the obvious stupidity of my question. "How's it going to affect us?"

"I think it's both good news and bad news. Which do you want first?"

"Good. I need some good news."

"Okay. The good news is this probably puts our appeal on hold. We're controversial. In fact, I think we're probably the most controversial case on their docket. Current political wisdom tells us the court will not take up any major, controversial cases until the new justice is appointed."

I nodded. And I remembered a story in this morning's *Globe-News* that expressed the exact, same opinion. "And the bad news?"

"The bad news is we're gonna get a new justice who is pro-life."

"You seem awfully sure about that," I said, hoping he might be wrong.

"Hey, the president's a Republican. And in case you haven't noticed, the Republicans are losing ground to an Independent named McCormack."

The waitress brought our hamburgers. I looked at the huge sandwich with a sinking feeling. Our discussion of Reginald McCormack's right-to-life campaign—especially its effect on the president's choice of a new Supreme Court appointment—destroyed my appetite.

Isaac picked up his burger and took a big bite.

I stared at mine.

"Joe, you can't let this affect you," Isaac said. "It's not unexpected."

"I can't help it," I replied. "It's like someone is tightening a noose around my neck."

Isaac took another big bite. Silence reigned as he chewed his food and I continued to stare at mine.

"Look at it this way," he continued. "First, the president has to pick a candidate. That'll take some time."

I picked up my burger and took a bite—a small one.

"Next, the appointee has to be interviewed and then confirmed by the Senate," Isaac said.

I chewed, then managed to swallow.

"My guess is the Senate will adjourn for their August vacation," he carried on, "and postpone any action on the confirmation until they return in September."

"But we don't know that," I argued.

Isaac shrugged. "We don't know the sun will rise tomorrow morning, either, but I'm expecting that it will." He took another big bite of his burger.

I felt compelled to work on mine, so I forced myself to take another small nibble.

"And even if the Senate confirms a hard-hitting, extreme right, super-conservative new justice, the court is not likely to take up their most controversial case until things have a chance to settle," Isaac said. "I predict it may be a year until they rule on something as contentious as your appeal."

"Meanwhile, I continue to practice medicine in the Texas Panhandle?"

"*Roe v, Wade* is settled law," he replied. "And we have a presidential election coming up. A vote of the people may have a strong effect, maybe even a mandate, on the abortion question. All of this could have powerful implications for the court."

I pushed my plate away. The half-eaten burger looked more unappetizing than ever. "You're saying that if McCormack wins the election, the court will rule against me?"

Isaac laughed, a big, Texas guffaw.

People turned and looked at us. I searched for the check.

"We have some uncertainties to worry about," he said. "However, a McCormack win is not one of them."

I assumed he was implying that McCormack had no chance of winning the election. I nodded, mulling everything over. Isaac finished his burger, I left money for the check, and we said our goodbyes.

Driving back to the Medical Arts Building, my thoughts about the future weighed heavily. It appeared my appeal might form the basis for new law.

Roe v. Wade had become infamous, the most recognized case title in the history of the United States Supreme Court.

I dreaded that *Texas v. Wright* might become even more notorious.

36

At home, 1109 Westbrook Terrace

The process of naming a candidate for the Supreme Court did not go as expected. In the days immediately following the death of Justice Stevenson, I carefully followed the political analysts. The vast majority of print and broadcast commentators predicted the president would study his list of possible candidates and—since the Senate was not going to do anything until after the August recess—hold off the announcement of his nominee until late August or early September. Many envisioned that, most likely, the president would announce this major decision over the Labor Day weekend.

Everyone failed to consider McCormack's competitive instincts.

Reggie saw a political opportunity of historic proportions. Which it was. And as the summer doldrums sucked all the political energy from Washington, the McCormack campaign revved up its efforts. Already well organized and operating at peak efficiency, Reggie mobilized a massive national effort to support the appointment of Evelyn Jones, one of the country's foremost, anti-abortion jurists. McCormack's carefully planned media blitz surpassed anything yet seen in national politics. It included full-page ads in all of America's leading newspapers, primetime TV commercials on every major network, and hourly radio announcements throughout the entire country.

Every advertisement extolled the name of Evelyn Jones.

That morning, Isaac and I met for coffee at Starbucks. "So, who's Evelyn Jones?" I asked.

"Only the most famous judge in America," replied Isaac. "You already knew that, right?"

"Yeah, I do now, but I'd never heard of her until McCormack began running his ads."

Isaac ripped open a pink packet of saccharine, dumped the contents into his cup, and stirred it with a spoon. "Neither had 95 percent of the country."

"Damn. I can't believe this guy. Where's he getting the money to run such expensive ads?"

"He's raising it as he goes. I checked with a friend who works for a national advertising agency—a big-time executive on Madison Avenue. He told me McCormack places the ad, then hopes the money comes in to pay for it."

"God, that's risky," I said, shaking my head in disbelief.

"He learned it by studying the operating practices of TV evangelism," Isaac replied. "And you have to admit, it's working."

I didn't like it. And it made me sick to talk about it, so I paused and tried to come up with something to change the subject.

Isaac jumped in before I could think of anything remotely interesting. "Did you see the editorial in this morning's *USA Today*?"

I shook my head. "What did it say?"

The waitress came with a carafe of fresh coffee. Conversation ebbed while she topped off our cups. I took a sip and waited.

"The editorial writer believes the president now has only two basic choices," Isaac said.

"And they are?" I blew into my cup to cool it. The hot vapor fogged my glasses.

"One, he can defer to McCormack's pro-lifers and appoint Ms. Jones."

"Or?"

"Or he can wait—probably until Labor Day—to appoint his own nominee, who will also be a strong pro-life jurist, only not as well known as Evelyn Jones."

I didn't know how to respond to that.

"You interested in a little bet on the side?" Isaac asked when I didn't say anything.

"Sure," I replied. "I'll make you a bet the president takes his own sweet time and waits until after Labor Day to make an announcement. So when it's over, when a candidate is nominated, loser buys the coffee."

"You're on," he said, and we shook on it.

As we parted, the smirk on Isaac's face infuriated me. He thought he had a sure thing.

That evening, the president nominated Evelyn Jones.

37

At home, 1109 Westbrook Terrace

Luckily, I'd saved copies of recent newspapers—those with ads about Evelyn Jones. I dug them out and reread McCormack's sales pitches. Jones lived in Dallas. She served on the 14th Circuit Federal Appeals Court and had earned a strong reputation as a right-wing, all-out, super conservative. Her nomination gave the media a field day.

The two aspects of her nomination that received the most coverage were its *speed* and its *impact.*

The swiftness of the president's action startled everyone. More importantly, it served as political motivation for the Senate to fast track the confirmation process. The *speed* question received an immediate answer when, the day after Justice Stevenson's funeral, the confirmation committee opened hearings.

The question of *impact* provided even more grist for journalists, and they had a feeding frenzy on the possibilities. As I read article after article—and editorials ad nauseam—the details of her political biography produced a wide variety of conservative possibilities.

Age fifty-seven, a graduate of Rice and The University of Texas Law School, Evelyn Jones had devoted her life to the practice of law. Never married, she had worked for one of the largest and most prestigious law firms in Houston, where she specialized in oil and gas litigation. After making partner at an early age, she left a lucrative seven-figure income to become the Dallas City Attorney. For the next ten years she compiled an outstanding record as a hardworking, incorruptible, highly skilled lawyer. This—and the fact that she made no bones about her pro-life stand on abortion—caught the attention of Ronald Reagan, who appointed her to the federal bench.

One other important presidential consideration was that Ms. Jones didn't look the part of an anti-abortion hardliner. Now in her second decade as a federal judge, she projected a grandmotherly appearance that belied her firebrand politics. Her soft-spoken, feminine mannerisms were thought to make her bulletproof in the contentious Senate hearings.

When I met Isaac at Starbucks on the last Tuesday in July, I paid for the coffee.

"How about another bet?" he asked, grinning.

"I don't think so," I replied.

Isaac laughed.

I grinned back, but I wasn't laughing. This was serious.

"Editorial writers are taking bets on when the Senate vote will take place."

"Hell, don't ask me," I replied. "I've missed every prediction."

"You're not the only one."

I nodded. "The editorial in this morning's *Amarillo Globe-News* says the Democrats have conceded."

Isaac picked up two pink packages of sweetener. He offered one to me. I tore it open, dumped it into my cup, and stirred.

"I can see why," Isaac agreed as he sweetened his coffee. " I watched her last night with Hardball journalist Chris Matthews. After it was over, he described her as an unassailable, mild-mannered, matronly candidate."

"So much for hardball." I moved the spoon around in my cup. "How long before the vote?"

"Not long, I should think."

"What happened to your Labor Day prediction?"

"Look, I was lucky to win this cup of coffee." He turned away, stirring as he spoke and looking off in the distance behind me. I could almost see the wheels turning inside his head.

"You've got an idea?" I asked.

He smiled.

"Go ahead. Lay it on me."

"What if I could arrange for you to testify at the hearings?"

I chuckled. "At the Evelyn Jones confirmation hearings in the Senate?" The notion seemed ridiculous.

Isaac nodded, looking more serious than ever.

I quit laughing.

"If I can set it up, would you do it?"

"Sure," I replied with carefree glibness.

At the time of my one-word answer, the likelihood appeared not just remote, but impossible. I was just a small-town doctor in the most sparsely populated area of Texas—a nobody. The only people invited to testify at Senate hearings for Supreme Court justices were big names—powerful political figures or nationally recognized leaders.

Isaac gave me the eye, his smug, lawyer-like grin. It was an expression that normally exasperated me.

This time, I just laughed at him.

38

At home, 1207 Westbrook Terrace

That evening, Isaac called. "You're on," he said, barely giving me a chance to say hello. "We fly to Washington tomorrow. You testify before the Senate Judiciary Committee at ten o'clock on Thursday morning."

"You're kid . . . kidding?" I stammered, dumbfounded.

"I called the ranking member of the committee, Senator Williams of Massachusetts. He's a Democrat, pro-choice, and short on people to speak against the Jones appointment. When I gave him your name, he jumped at it."

"Isaac, I can't." I stiffened and tightened my grip on the receiver. Everything in me rejected the idea.

"Too late. You told me this afternoon you'd do it. You're already committed."

"But, I don't know what to say. I'm not prepared. I—"

"We'll work on it on the plane. I'll help you."

"Isaac, this is crazy."

"No, it's an opportunity. And I've booked our flight—American Airlines #107, leaving Amarillo at 10:05 tomorrow morning. We change planes in Dallas, arrive Washington Reagan, 4:26 p.m."

"Isaac—"

"I'll pick you up at eight-thirty tomorrow morning."

For a moment I stood there gripping the receiver, my mind whirling.

He hung up.

"Bad news?" Jenny asked, rinsing off a salad plate and placing it into the dishwasher.

"The worst." I re-cradled the phone. Then I told her what had happened.

Jenny kissed me lightly on the lips. "Honey, you can't have it both ways," she said, and went back to loading the dishwasher.

That was the last thing I wanted to hear from my wife. I stomped off—went upstairs to watch TV.

C-Span was airing an interview of Evelyn Jones with Senator Williams. I watched as she parried questions so effectively that even a skeptical, pro-choice liberal like Williams couldn't find a way to criticize her conservative politics. He closed with a comment about testimony the Judiciary Committee expected to hear on Thursday.

"I understand that Reginald McCormack is scheduled to appear before your committee?" Jones asked.

"Yes, he's one of the witnesses," Williams replied.

"I guess you know, I'm a great admirer of Rev. McCormack," Jones continued.

"No, I didn't." The senator looked away from the camera, a subtle gesture of disapproval.

"I probably wouldn't have agreed to this nomination had it not been for his entreaty," Jones said, oblivious to Williams and his body language. "He's a hard man to turn down."

"The committee hears testimony from various viewpoints," Williams commented.

"I'm sure you do," Jones replied. "However, I'm mighty pleased to have the support of such an elegant spokesman."

Williams signed off, wishing Evelyn Jones "good luck" with the committee hearings.

I thought about competing against her *elegant* spokesman.

My stomach twisted. It felt like I'd swallowed a rock and the lump had just hit bottom.

39

American Airlines, flying to Washington

We had to take a small propjet from Amarillo to DFW—one of the disadvantages of living in the sparsely populated Texas Panhandle. Then, from DFW to Washington Reagan, we relaxed in first class on a big jet, sipping vodka tonics while Isaac tried to coach me on my testimony.

"Speak slowly, look confident, try to make eye contact," he said.

"Is McCormack going to testify?" I asked.

"You can count on it," Isaac replied. "And he'll come reeking with self-confidence."

"What do you think he's going to say?"

"That Jones is a terrific lawyer and an outstanding jurist."

I nodded. I supposed that was pretty much a given. "So you want me to say she's a lousy attorney and a poor judge?"

"No," Isaac said, shaking his head. "Because she's not."

I frowned, confused. "Then how can I counter McCormack's

testimony?"

"Emphasize her bias."

"Okay," I said. I settled back into my seat, working my head into the headrest. "So what's her bias?"

"Good God, Joe, haven't you been paying attention? McCormack calls her the most ardent pro-life jurist in the country."

"I read his ads," I said. "I've never seen that statement in writing."

"Of course not. He keeps it verbal, and only by innuendo. If it's documented, people like you could use it against the nomination."

Whizzing along at 35,000 feet, sipping cocktails in the comfort of roomy, leather seats, I thought about what Isaac had gotten me into. Testimony for a high-profile US Supreme Court nomination was sure to be nationally televised. My words would be scrutinized by both sides of the abortion issue. Senators and media specialists—even the country at large—could and would pounce on any perceived slip. I felt an uncomfortable tightening in the pit of my stomach.

Isaac continued with a litany about Evelyn Jones, and he handed me a fact sheet of her judicial record. I scanned it, using only half of my concentration. With the other half I tried to listen to his suggestions as to how I could deflect questions about my testimony. The more we talked, the more it seemed to me that I was taking the job of hatchet man—a role repugnant to me.

The captain announced that passengers should make preparations for landing. A female flight attendant followed immediately with the standard message about putting away all electronic devices and returning our flight tables to their upright and locked position. I looked out the window to see the Washington Monument off in the distance.

That evening we had dinner in the hotel coffee shop and went to bed early. Isaac wanted us to get a good night's rest in order to be at our best for tomorrow's big day. We agreed to meet for breakfast when the restaurant opened at six o'clock.

The next morning, after a quick bite, we hailed a cab and by seven o'clock were headed for the Caucus Room of the old Senate Office Building. Located just a short way northeast of the capitol, the Russell Building—as it was now called—was famous as the site for many historical events.

At 7:30 a.m., an hour and a half before the Jones hearing was scheduled to begin, it surprised me to find dozens of people in the room, busy with preparations. Uniformed capitol police met us at the door and guided us through security. Technicians hustled around checking the mikes and PA equipment. Television crews hauled in their cameras and electronic paraphernalia.

Isaac left me to go check on details of the hearing. I stood at the back of the room and tried to stay out of the way. On a small table near the doorway, a stack of brochures titled *The Caucus Room, An Historic Site in American Government*, caught my eye. I picked up one to study it.

The history started shortly after the completion of the building in 1912 with an investigation of the sinking of the Titanic. The infamous inquisition was held there on April 22, only a week after the ship went down. Skipping over a number of famous events of the 20s, 30s, and 40s to a paragraph titled "The Early Days of Television," I read about the 1954 clash between Senator Joseph McCarthy and the US Army's counsel, Joseph Welch. It was broadcast nationwide from the Caucus Room and turned the tide of public opinion—eventually leading to the Senate's censure of McCarthy. In 1960 John F. Kennedy used the room to declare his presidential candidacy. The Ervin Committee conducted the Watergate hearings in the room in 1973.

As I read about the building and its historic events, a chill rippled down my spine. The famous site exuded an aura of both history and melodrama, and I couldn't help but be moved by its sense of political power.

Isaac returned. "Follow me," he said. "We have reserved seats in the front row."

Together, we walked down an aisle from the back of the room to the front. I estimated 500 chairs for the audience. Along the front wall on a raised, circular platform, we could see microphones and seats for the Senate Judiciary Committee. Directly facing the dais—at the focal point of the room—was a small table, a single chair, and a mike. Isaac and I stood there for a moment and looked around.

In a very short time I would be seated in that chair at the small table—the so-called "hot seat"—under bright lights with video cameras rolling. One word came to mind:

Intimidating.

40

The Russell Senate Office Building, Washington, DC

We still had some time before the hearing, so instead of standing around with me getting more and more nervous, Isaac and I left to go for coffee. When we returned, the Caucus Room had filled, and a line stretched down the hallway. I checked my watch—9:30 a.m. Fortunately, we had our reserved seats in the front row among those who were to testify. Without asking, I took my lawyer with me and headed toward the front.

A few minutes later, we watched the media gather around the doorway. Television lights and flash cameras created a stir as Reginald Q. McCormack made his entrance into the room. Several people clapped. He and his group took seats in the front row, across the aisle from me. I noticed that one of his aides immediately scanned the room, checking for recognizable faces. His gaze came to a screeching halt when he found me, and our eyes met for a moment. Then the aide turned back to confer with McCormack.

A minute later, McCormack stood and made his way over to me. "Dr. Wright," he stated without preamble.

I stood.

He offered his hand. "Good to meet you," he said.

I shook it and tried to think of something to say. "Yes," was the only word that came to mind.

"This place is really a zoo, isn't it?" His smile was huge—it struck me that I'd never seen so many teeth in one mouth. Somehow, when displayed on TV, it had never seemed so radiant, so full of energy.

"Yes," again, the only word I could think of.

He moved closer, so close that the smell of mint mouthwash overwhelmed my rational thinking. I tried to back away, but my chair was too close. I felt trapped.

"We're in this together," he said. "We're both looking for a way to help families with their everyday problems."

My thoughts, running at lightning velocity, went back to a quote used by the D.A. at my Amarillo trial. I remember his directive—*when your adversary says he agrees, watch out, his next statement will be to take your position and transform it slightly to use against you.* I started to say the same word, yes, again. Instead, I said, "No."

McCormack blinked.

"No, we're on opposite sides," I reaffirmed.

At that moment, the person on my right moved, creating a slender opening. I sidestepped away from McCormack's in-your-face dominance.

"You're not trying to help families?" he asked, his face now almost three feet from mine. "Maybe I could quote you on that."

"I'm trying to help women with their health problems," I answered. "You can quote me word for word."

He smiled his big, toothy smile, looked at his watch, and then said,

"Any quotes about what you're doing to babies?"

The chairman, Senator Dawkins, a Republican from Pennsylvania, rapped his gavel. "The hearing will now come to order."

I never had a chance to respond.

But as the senator rapped his gavel again, and the room began to quiet, I thought about McCormack's question. It was one of his favorites, and he used it repeatedly. I made a mental note to prepare a good response—to have it ready for the next time.

41

The Caucus Room of the Russell Senate Office Building

Senator Dawkins took charge. As he spoke, the TV cameras rolled, and it was immediately clear to every person in the room that he was not addressing us—his remarks were directed at the television audience. He gave a long-winded commentary about the American tradition of appointing Supreme Court justices, about the openness of the process, and about the committee's efforts to assure fairness. I thought his statement was more meaningful for what he didn't say—that this was August, that Congress was anxious to get out of town, and that this nomination was going to be processed in record time.

Finally, near the end of his remarks, the information we were waiting for trickled through. The committee had agreed to hear testimony from five individuals: the president of the American Bar Association, a noted Republican conservative; the attorney for Planned Parenthood, a woman whose views were obvious; the Rev. Reginald McCormack; me; and finally, the nominee, Evelyn Jones. That morning they would hear the first four, with a limit of twenty minutes for each, and after lunch they would devote an unlimited amount of time to Jones. Dawkins didn't say it, but he certainly implied that the committee's vote would be taken late that afternoon, after Ms. Jones's testimony.

Senator Dawkins called for the ABA president.

The guy really looked like a lawyer. He wore a dark, pinstriped suit straight out of an Armani ad. His red-and-gold-striped tie, with matching handkerchief peeking out of his upper left coat pocket, looked expensive and very suave, almost over the top. He gave strong, elegant support for the Jones nomination.

Next came the lawyer for Planned Parenthood. She, too, wore a dark suit and gave a visual impression of formal, legal testimony. But she made a mistake—at least in my opinion. She framed her presentation, and her answers to the committee's questions, in feminist rhetoric. It hit me as belligerent and, therefore, offensive. I was pulling for her, but in the end, I thought she lost votes for our side.

Then McCormack took the seat.

The television evangelist came across like a pro—which he was. And compared to the previous two persons, he raised the hearing to a new level of audience interest. His deep bass voice came over the PA with stentorian authority. I could easily imagine that "the voice of God" was addressing us, and as a result, found myself sitting forward in my chair. I noticed that those nearby were also moved to a new, more attentive posture.

As Isaac had predicted, McCormack extolled Jones's qualities as a terrific lawyer and an outstanding jurist. But while Isaac had envisioned what McCormack would say, he failed to predict the manner in which it would be said. McCormack's Southern drawl, his down-home choice of words, and his light sense of humor, all combined to captivate the listener.

Midway through McCormack's testimony, I quit listening and scanned the row of senators facing me. All were staring intently at McCormack, hanging onto every word, reacting to his subtle humor. Even the Democrats were smiling.

Then I turned in my seat to peer around the room. Every face that I could see was obviously engaged by McCormack's winsome charm. The audience reminded me of a time many years ago, when on vacation in Los Angeles, Jenny and I attended a live broadcast of *The Johnny Carson Show*. Each person in the audience had been caught up in the celebrity of the moment. Today the same thing happened. In the questioning, McCormack turned the senators' questions into a series of humorist's straight lines, and he quipped answers back that played to the audience.

The hearing turned into a barrel of laughs.

The twenty minutes flew by until Senator Dawkins called time and rapped his gavel.

He thanked Reggie McCormack for his testimony. Then:

"Dr. Joseph Wright of Amarillo, Texas . . . would you take the chair, please?"

42

The Caucus Room of the Russell Senate Office Building

Isaac gave me a pat on the back and whispered, "Break a leg." I knew what he meant. The old rhetorical admonition, what one actor would say to another as he or she went on stage, was intended to encourage, to bring out a sterling performance, one that could even suffer broken bones in its effort to win favorable audience reaction. But in my case, I almost took it literally. After sitting for over an hour, my foot had gone to sleep, and I limped toward the chair. Not an auspicious way to enter the national spotlight.

I took the oath.

"Do you have a prepared statement?" Senator Dawkins asked.

I nodded.

"Proceed." He looked at his watch. "You have twenty minutes."

I started to read, but my voice wouldn't work. When I tried, what came out was a croak, a whisper, an unintelligible, raspy facsimile of the words. Thank goodness they had placed a glass of water on the table. I stopped, took a drink, and then tried to clear my throat.

"Sorry," I said, my voice better, but far from normal.

"That's okay," Senator Dawkins replied. "Take your time. You have eighteen minutes left."

A wave of laughter rippled through the audience.

Their laughing at me was the last thing I had expected, and it unnerved me. My hands began to shake. Fear surged through my brain. It paralyzed my ability to think rationally, and I found myself in a moment of panic. I felt lightheaded, unable to move. I'm not sure how long I sat there seized with immovable muscles, but eventually, through the fog, I heard someone calling my name.

"Dr. Wright?" Senator Dawkins asked over the PA. "Are you all right?"

I tried to clear my voice. In so doing, I took a big breath. It helped.

Isaac, who had been seated in the front row about ten feet away, came over and put his hand on my shoulder. "You okay?"

The touch and voice of a friend brought reassurance. I took another sip of water.

"I'm fine," I said. And for the first time, my voice sounded normal.

Isaac went back to his seat.

"Dr. Wright, are you able to go ahead with your statement?"

I didn't answer his question. Instead, I started reading.

"The nominee before this committee has a notable background in the law. She holds degrees from prestigious universities, and her work as a lawyer and a jurist gives impressive evidence of her intelligence and command of legal issues. And her gender gives this committee an opportunity to correct an imbalance to the court that has been long neglected. We need more women justices. It would seem that Evelyn Jones would be an ideal candidate. Except for one important qualification—bias."

Some words evoke an emotional response. Like waving a red flag in front of a bull, they ignite passions that shut out the intellect. When I said the word "bias," I sensed a change in the room. All of a sudden, no one moved. The audience grew deathly quiet. No one breathed.

"I'm Catholic," I said. "My wife's Catholic. We've raised a Catholic family." I paused to let the words sink in. "We're pro-life. We oppose abortion."

If I thought "bias" was the inflammatory word, I was wrong. It paled in comparison to the "A" word. And once I had said it, the room exploded.

A female senator from California, noted for her pro-choice, feminist rhetoric, pounced on me like a pit bull. "Dr. Wright, we're talking about an inviolable personal choice, one that involves a woman's body, her personal health, her future."

I tried to answer, "Yes, I understand your point, but I was going to say that my statements refer only to extremist views."

"How do you define an extreme position on abortion?" asked a senator from South Carolina.

"That's difficult to . . ." After only three words, another question cut me off.

"Does any candidate who openly states a personal position, as either pro-choice or pro-life, qualify as an extremist?" asked another.

Again, I tried to respond. But it soon became obvious that there was no answer to questions about abortion. No middle ground. People like me were on one side or the other, and nominees like Evelyn Jones were, too.

My appearance in the Caucus Room had turned into a political fight, a down-and-dirty verbal row. When it was obvious that the exchange had become hopeless, Senator Dawkins rapped his gavel. The hearing broke for lunch and would resume at two o'clock to question Ms. Jones.

Isaac and I walked over to the Food Court at Union Station for a sandwich. He tried to put the best face on my pathetic performance. "You did good," he said.

"You've always been a lousy liar," I replied.

We bantered back and forth a couple of times, but deep down, we both knew my testimony and this trip had been wasted. At lunch I changed the subject.

"What time is our flight back to Amarillo?" I asked.

He pulled his ticket out of his coat pocket. "Six fifteen," he answered. "We'll need to catch a taxi no later than four o'clock."

I nodded. And I thought to myself that the issue was already decided. We wouldn't miss anything if we left now.

But we didn't leave.

Instead, we went back and listened to Evelyn Jones parry questions for two hours.

Obviously, the procedure didn't matter. Only one aspect of her nomination was under consideration—her stand on abortion. And no senator on the committee was going to change his or her position. The vote was a foregone decision.

We landed at the Amarillo airport on time at 9:45 p.m.

In the car on the drive home, Isaac turned on the radio for the ten o'clock news. The lead story gave us the result. The committee narrowly approved Evelyn Jones, and she would face a confirmation vote by the full Senate the next morning.

Part IV
AUGUST

43

The Medical Arts Building, Amarillo

It felt good to be back in the office, seeing patients. I found that I had a new celebrity status. Apparently, everyone had watched me on TV, choked voice and all.

"I thought you did well, in spite of your illness," my head nurse, Virginia, said.

"They showed a close-up of your forehead. You were perspiring so heavily I thought you might faint," another said.

"Nice recovery," Virginia added. "And I thought your point about bias would be considered."

"Me, too," the other nurse replied. "But I'm pro-choice."

"And in the end, that's all they cared about," I added. Then, deliberately changing the subject, I asked, "Who're we seeing first this morning?"

She gave me the name, a longtime patient with chronic arthritis. I prescribed the strongest medication I could, and then, in rapid succession, we saw a dozen cases that ranged in age from six to sixty, with medical problems that ran the gamut from constipation to diabetes.

Midway through the morning, Isaac called, and I agreed to meet him for lunch at the Burger Barn. I arrived, ten minutes late, and found him in the corner with two hamburgers—one he'd ordered for me.

A waitress came with coffee. "Are you the guy who was on television yesterday?" she asked.

"Well—"

"I thought you were sick or something."

"Yes, I—"

"You look okay today. You take cream?"

I shook my head. "No, thanks." She shrugged her shoulders and moved on to the next table.

Isaac picked up the conversation as I took a bite of my hamburger. "You heard about the Senate's confirmation?" he asked.

I shook my head. "No," I mumbled with my mouth full.

"Evelyn Jones passed—easily. Even some of the Democrats voted for her. She'll be sworn in when the Court reconvenes in October."

Conversation lapsed while we finished our sandwiches. I thought about the last couple of days, about McCormack's impressive TV appearance, and especially how it contrasted with mine. Lost in thought and wrapped in self-pity, I voiced my misgivings. I didn't mean to say it out loud, it just slipped through my lips as an aside. "My nurse thought I looked sick," I mumbled.

Isaac looked up. "Nurse, what?" he asked.

I felt my face flush.

"You okay?"

I nodded.

"Talking to yourself these days, are you?" Isaac grinned.

"Let's change the subject," I suggested. "Bretta has fallen off my radar. Politics has taken over my life to the point that I haven't done anything for her."

"Okay, let's talk about Bretta." Isaac picked up his cup and held it to his lips with both hands, elbows on the table, a look of benevolent concentration as he sipped his coffee.

"She's lost her sparkle," I said.

"In what way?"

"When she comes home, she goes to her room. Her daily routine is becoming more and more reclusive."

"I don't know your daughter well, but I've heard she's an outstanding singer—you told me she had a scholarship to go to Juilliard?"

"All that is on hold. She turned down the graduate assistantship."

"How much is she singing?"

"Zero."

One of the most impressive aspects of Isaac's personality is his ability to quickly focus on important details. And he does it with incredible placidness, like a prophet, delivering the message with equanimity.

"Maybe that's the answer."

His words hit me like a bullet between the eyes. And I resolved, silently, to do something about it. Conversation changed to pleasantries. We said our goodbyes and agreed to meet next week.

That night, after dinner, Brent took his trombone and went to a rehearsal. Bretta went to her room. I helped Jenny clear the table and load the dishwasher.

"Isaac Levy and I had lunch today," I said.

"The Burger Barn?" she asked.

"Yeah, and we talked about Bretta's singing."

"What's there to talk about?" Jenny asked, sadness in her voice.

"That was Isaac's point. He thinks it could be a key factor in her recovery."

Jenny stopped, turned and faced me. "I've been thinking the same thing. Singing was the central activity in her life."

"Was," I said.

"I haven't heard her sing since . . . ." Jenny couldn't get the words out.

"So, how can we change that?" I asked, gently.

Jenny stood perfectly still, looking down at the floor, obviously in deep thought.

I finished loading the dishwasher, added the soap, closed the door, and pushed the buttons to start the wash cycle. Then I went over to stand by my wife. I put my arm around her and asked, "What can we do to help our daughter?"

Jenny kissed me, a light brushing of our lips.

"I think you should be the one to talk to her. Tell her you haven't heard her sing lately, and you'd like to hear something."

"How about we talk to her together?" I asked.

Jenny shook her head. "She'll feel like we're ganging up on her. I think it better if you speak to her alone. You initiate the idea. Later, when the opportunity presents itself, I'll back you up."

So, that night, I went to have a father-daughter talk about singing.

44

At home, 1109 Westbrook Terrace

I went to Bretta's room and knocked on her door.

"Who's there?" she asked.

"Radio," I said, my voice as big and officious as I could make it.

"Okay, I'll bite. Radio who?"

"Radio not, here I come."

Bretta opened the door. "Dad, we've had this conversation. Knock-knock jokes went out fifty years ago."

I smiled. "I heard that one last week on Garrison Keillor's radio show."

"And I'll bet he stole it from some hundred-year-old joke book."

"Okay, here's a new one," I smiled. "How many musicians does it take to change a lightbulb?"

"Oh, no."

"Five. One to change the bulb, and four to get in free because they know the guy who owns the socket."

"Dad—"

"I also heard that one on Keillor's show."

"You came to tell jokes?"

"Well, I have something I want to ask of you."

"Okay, ask."

"This is a sit-down-to-ask favor," I gestured toward her desk and chairs.

"Sure." She led the way and we each took a chair. "What's up?"

"Your mother and I are thinking of having a little dinner for some friends. And, as a part of the social evening, we'd like you to sing. Something short. Maybe just two or three numbers."

Bretta started shaking her head. Slow, short movements. A nonverbal response. It was as though she was expecting our conversation to go North, and I had just caused it to go South.

"D . . . D . . . Dad, I don't know."

"Would you think about it?" I asked. "We don't need an immediate answer."

"Dad, I really don't—"

"Would you think about it?" I reached over and held her hand. "Please?"

She smiled. "Okay, I'll think about it."

We stood.

I kissed her on the forehead. "Thanks." I turned and started out the door.

"When is this event?" she asked.

"We don't have a date." I stopped in the hallway, looked back, and gave her my best smile. "We'll set one when we have a singer."

The next evening when I came home, I found Bretta at the piano, vocalizing. As Jenny prepared dinner, beautiful, crystal-clear, high notes bounced through the house. Our soprano sounded good. Really good. And the music, even though it was only arpeggios and exercises, gave me, and I think our entire family, a feeling of returning to normalcy.

That weekend, the doorbell rang, something unusual in recent days. I went to the door to find Bretta's accompanist, Michael Railton. Before I could say anything, Bretta joined us.

"What's happening?" I asked.

"Practicing," Bretta said.

"Oh . . . well . . . welcome, Michael," I said, and backed away.

So she and Michael went through some familiar arias, things I had heard on her senior recital and her audition for Juilliard. I'm pretty ignorant when it comes to music, but I remembered a Mozart piece that had lots of high notes and a Puccini song from *Madam Butterfly.*

Especially, I remembered a spiritual called "Go A'way from My Window." Of all of Bretta's repertoire, it was my favorite. That afternoon, Bretta's beautiful clear voice gave special meaning to the words, "Go a'way from my window . . . ." An emotion filled our house, and I could feel a special communication as the music and the words reached out to our family. The words—about all who hoped for love, for caring, for others, for the best in human relationships—seemed so appropriate. The last line, "my love for you," ended with a beautiful, crystal clear note that started soft and tapered down to nothing. The word "you" ended so softly, I couldn't tell when Bretta stopped singing.

Their rehearsal lasted about an hour. I checked the buttons on my shirt to make sure they hadn't popped.

During the last song the phone rang. Jenny answered, and a lengthy conversation ensued. She was still talking after the accompanist left.

I listened and figured out the identity of the caller when I overheard Jenny use the word "Mother."

The rehearsal had helped my spirits.

After the phone call, Jenny's news didn't.

"Mother overheard Bretta's singing," she said.

"So?"

"She wants to come to our dinner and hear Bretta."

"Fine."

"She's only going to stay with us one or two nights."

"Fiiiiiiiiiiiiiiiiine."

"Jim Bob, please."

"Hey, this is just what I need—she probably has some advice about my next senate hearing."

45

At home, Amarillo

We scheduled our dinner for the next Friday evening. Jenny invited Harvey Adams and his wife Cindy. I invited Isaac Levy and his wife Sarah. Counting Brent, Bretta, and her accompanist, Michael, along with Jenny and me, that would be nine people—a nice, small number for a quiet dinner at home.

And we added another place for our special guest—Katherine Smithington Chase. Life goes on.

Thursday evening, the day of my mother-in-law's arrival, we had a little family skirmish about going to the airport to pick her up. I thought Jenny would do the honors. After all, Katherine was *her* mother. But Jenny nagged me to go with her. Finally, I said, "Okay, but only if Bretta goes, too." Jenny passed the buck, something I've noticed she does frequently when circumstances involve her mother.

Jenny said, "I just want someone to go with me. You can go, or you can bring Bretta—your choice."

So, I found myself in Bretta's room . . . negotiating. "I'd like you to go with us to the airport," I said. "Your grandmother will expect you to be a part of the welcoming committee."

"Sure." When she said the word, Bretta gave me her *I know what you're up to* smile. "You want me to deflect the sparks that fly when you two get together."

"Not true," I protested.

"Mom says that twenty-eight years ago Grandma tried to block your marriage and that you've been fighting ever since."

"I can't believe your mother would say such a thing."

"Dad, I've got eyes."

"Then you can see that I've won her over and that she now has a special place in her heart for Texas and for her son-in-law."

Bretta laughed. "Yeah, I know that special place. It's a four-letter word, starts with H."

Jenny called from the back porch, interrupting our banter. "Time to go."

I looked at my watch. "Her plane isn't scheduled to arrive for two hours."

Bretta interrupted, "Mom wants to take the BMW to the carwash before we go to the airport."

I shook my head. "The inspector general—"

"Come on, Dad, it's no big thing, and if it makes Grandma happy—"

So, the three of us piled into the BMW, drove to Sooper Carwash, and paid for "The Works," their most expensive and thorough cleaning. Thirty minutes later, with a heavy "new car" aroma wafting around us, we drove to the airport.

My mother-in-law looked spectacular when she came through security. Dressed to the nines in Fifth Avenue's finest, she hugged and kissed Jenny and Bretta. Then she turned to me and held out her hand.

I shook it.

On the ride home, Katherine conversed with her daughter and granddaughter. This relegated me to the status of a nonperson being held incommunicado. So I let my thoughts roil, and they went back to Bretta's room. I realized how beautifully clean and neat it was—ready for inspection. And I thought about the thousand or more times I'd complained about my daughter's messy room. Grudgingly, I had to admit, my mother-in-law was a genius at intimidation.

The next morning, I was glad to have a place to go—my office. I could leave Jenny to prepare for the dinner *and* host her mother. And I made a conscious effort to make it a good day for my patients, my staff, and me. If there was conflict with my mother-in-law, I did not want anyone at the office to be aware of it.

Apparently, I couldn't quite bring it off.

Midway through the morning, Virginia, my head nurse, asked for a conference.

"How about a cup of coffee in your office?" she asked. This happened just after we had dismissed an elderly patient with a severe sinus infection.

"What's wrong?" she asked. "You seem distracted. You weren't listening very closely to her symptoms." She shook her head, an obvious gesture to emphasize my lack of judgment.

"Virginia, did I ever tell you your headshaking reminds me of someone?" I asked.

"Who's that?"

"My mother-in-law."

"Good." She smiled, an ear-to-ear show of teeth. "I understand she's a top-notch motivator."

"Nag."

"But a good one?"

"World class." I smiled back as I thought about Katherine's nagging prowess. And I honestly couldn't imagine anyone better.

"So, you're blaming your mother-in-law for today's distraction?" When it comes to our medical evaluation of a particular case, Virginia has a gentle, but effective, way of way of keeping the conversation on track.

I retreated to the coffee pot, poured myself a second cup. "Could we change the subject?"

"Hey, I'm only trying to help." She smiled. "In case you've forgotten, I'm on your side."

I thought about Virginia, about her loyalty, about the twenty-plus years we'd been working together. "Yeah, I know."

"Tell me what's troubling you," she said. "Sometimes it helps to verbalize, to tell a friend."

I took another swig of coffee, looked at my watch, and caved. I told her about the trip to the airport, the car wash—everything.

Virginia held out her coffee cup. I picked up the carafe and refilled our cups.

"A memorable trip to the airport with your mother-in-law?" She chuckled, making light of my woes.

"Virginia, do you know what it's like to listen to her whining and complaining for two, solid hours?"

We paused, and I could see the wheels churning in my nurse's head.

We sipped our coffee in silence.

"I have a suggestion," she said, after a while.

"Let's hear it," I responded. "I'm desperate."

"Kill the old battleax with kindness. Give her a nice gift."

"Tried that," I said.

"What happened?"

"When she came for her visit last month, I gave her a waterproof, shockproof, anti-magnetic, unbreakable watch. Expensive, too, I might add."

"And—"

"She lost it. Couldn't find it anywhere."

46

Friday evening at home

The dinner went well. Jenny is at her best in planning, preparing, and presenting a small, formal—one might even say gourmet—dinner party. And of all the dinners we've shared over the years, I could not remember one any finer.

The entrée—roasted duck—was to die for. And I'd picked up a bottle of Dom Pérignon to celebrate Bretta's special occasion.

It was a memorable, happy, upbeat evening. So much so that even the inspector general—my mother-in-law—couldn't find anything to criticize.

And I didn't say a word when she drank half the champagne.

But the highlight of the evening was Bretta.

She looked beautiful, even stunning, in a white, floor-length dress. And so poised it reminded me of her performance at that elementary school Christmas program almost twenty years ago when she was too young to know about being nervous. When she was six years old, she just sang from the heart. And it wowed everyone.

Friday night, there in our living room, as we gathered around our baby grand piano, she did the same.

She and her accompanist had prepared two arias by Mozart and Puccini, and the spiritual by Niles. A short program, only fifteen minutes.

As Michael played the introduction to the Mozart, I found myself perspiring. But Bretta sang with poise and confidence, and when she came to the high notes, she popped them out like there was nothing to it. I started to relax.

I put my arm around my wife and squeezed as Bretta sang the opening notes of "Un bel di,"—"One Fine Day"—the most familiar melody from Puccini's *Madam Butterfly*, and one of the most beloved in all of operatic literature. To my untrained ear, Bretta sounded better than ever.

Note after note floated out into our home with a beautiful, effortless intensity. And because it carried an emotional, human message that words could never express, I felt the adrenaline surging through me like electricity.

Jenny put her lips to my ear and whispered. "Not so tight."

Only then did I realize that I was holding onto her with all my might. I eased my grasp, tried to relax.

Jenny pulled a Kleenex from her purse and dabbed her eyes.

I withdrew my arm and gestured for her to hand one to me. As I wiped the tears, I looked down the row at our guests to see that they, too, were also wiping their eyes.

Bretta finished with the spiritual, "Go a'way from my window . . .". It was the hit of the evening, as I knew it would be. We clapped until our hands hurt. Then, as guests are supposed to do after a fine dinner and an extraordinary evening's entertainment, we stood around, making small talk with another glass of champagne.

When I had the chance, I spoke with Isaac.

"How about lunch at the Burger Barn tomorrow?" I asked.

"Sure," he replied. "What's up?"

"I have something I want to talk with you about."

He shrugged. A silent acknowledgement that he understood. This was something more than chitchat at a dinner party.

Gradually, the guests departed.

I helped Jenny with the cleanup.

And we went to bed feeling good, really good, about Bretta.

At noon on Saturday, I went to meet Issac—lunch at the Burger Barn. I arrived, ten minutes late, and found him in the corner with two hamburgers—one he'd ordered for me.

Isaac picked up the conversation as I took a bite of my hamburger. "What's up?" he asked.

I shook my head. "A minute," I mumbled with my mouth full.

"If you're worried about Evelyn Jones, she'll be sworn in when the court reconvenes in October."

I shouldn't have taken such a big bite. All I could do was shake my head and continue to chew.

Conversation lapsed while we finished our sandwiches. I thought about our trip to Washington, about McCormack's impressive TV appearance. Especially how it contrasted with mine. Lost in thought and wrapped in self-pity, I voiced my misgivings. I didn't mean to say it out loud, it just slipped through my lips as an aside. "McCormack made me look like a hick," I mumbled.

Isaac looked up. "McCormack what?" he asked.

I felt my face flush.

"You okay?"

I nodded.

"Reminiscing the senate hearing, are you?" Isaac grinned.

"Let's change the subject," I suggested. "The reason I asked you to meet with me today is to find out if you've heard anything new about the hunt for the rapists?"

Isaac looked at me like I was speaking a foreign language. "Whoa. Where'd that come from?"

His reaction made my already dour mood sink to even lower depths. I wanted to lash out at his words, at his insensitivity to my question—about the need to find the bastards who had done this to my daughter. Instead, I bit my tongue.

The silence between us said it all.

"Sorry," he said, after a few moments. "We haven't talked about the rapists for a month. You caught me off guard with that question."

"That's the problem," I said, feeling my face flush again. "Nobody's talking about it anymore."

"The old saying, 'out of sight, out of mind,' is a time-worn statement, but true."

"So, we talk about Evelyn Jones, Reggie McCormack, the Supreme Court, politics, ourselves—everything except justice for Bretta. Do you understand how angry that makes me?"

Sometimes Isaac pontificates. He backs off, looks at the world, and places our problem, or problems, into a perspective that sounds like it comes from an Old Testament prophet. This was one of those occasions. He set down his hamburger, looked squarely into my eyes, and in his most officious voice, gave me his admonition.

"Maybe it's time for you to call on the police again."

47

Randall County Sheriff's Office

I asked to see Jack Richards. The receptionist told me to take a seat. Five minutes later Richards came through the security door in full uniform, sidearm strapped to his belt.

"Joe. Good to see you." He held out his hand and smiled.

I stood and shook it—without returning the smile. "Can we talk?"

"Sure." His smile disappeared as quickly as it had come. "Let's go back to my office."

I followed him down a narrow hallway, past a number of tiny rooms, to the corner office, a large room with desk, credenza, bookcase, and three chairs—two of which were guest chairs positioned in front of the desk. He offered one to me and took the other. A coffee pot on the credenza filled the room with gurgling sounds and the aroma of fresh brew.

"How's Bretta?" he asked.

"Physically, good," I said. "Emotionally, not so good."

"It takes a while. Perhaps when school starts and she gets back to singing—"

I shook my head. "Bretta doesn't plan to go to Juilliard this fall. She contacted them and turned down her graduate assistantship."

Richards frowned. "I . . . I'm really sorry to hear that. What are her plans?"

"She wants to stay in the area, close to home. She's looking for a job."

The coffee pot hissed, and a mist of hot vapor wafted out into the small room. The gurgling ceased.

"I think coffee's ready," Jack said. "May I pour you a cup?"

"Yes, please."

He filled two Styrofoam cups and held up a small container of condiments.

I nodded. "Pink."

"Me, too." He set the two cups of coffee on the front of his desk, and then added two pink packets, two spoons, and two napkins.

"How're you coming with your hunt for Bretta's assailants?" I asked after sweetening my coffee and taking the first sip.

He shook his head. "Nothing new."

"Talk me through it. Suspects. Clues. How many are working the case?" A familiar mix of anger and frustration stirred in me, and I suppose it showed.

He slumped back into his chair, holding his cup with both hands—body language that signaled a long and difficult answer. "Last May, right after it happened, this was our number one priority. Every officer I could shake loose was working the case. Most of us volunteered for extra shifts and weekends, but—" He paused.

"But what?" I asked.

"But it was the end of the semester," he said. "Students scattered. The campus became deserted."

I felt a sense of cold fury seeping into my blood, and I struggled to control it, to keep from lashing out. Purposefully, I sipped my coffee to give myself thinking time.

Richards reached over and pulled a thick, three-ring notebook from the vertical file behind his desk. I guessed it to be at least 500 pages. "We sent teams east to Oklahoma City and west to Albuquerque."

"What about Amarillo?"

"Two teams worked it for more than a month. I personally committed 100% of my time to the case for all of May and most of June. After checking every suspect, every lead, we interviewed all the music majors to see if anyone had even a guess about who could have done this."

"And you came up empty," I said, stating the obvious. "So, what are you doing now?"

He didn't answer. Instead, he stood, walked over to get the coffee pot, turned, and gestured to me. "More?"

I shook my head.

Silently, he filled his cup.

I couldn't hold back any longer. I shouted, "You're telling me that law enforcement isn't doing a goddamned thing to find the bastards who raped my daughter."

His face turned red, and I could see he clenched his teeth. I thought he might hit me.

But he didn't. Without saying a word, he eased back into his chair and slid the big notebook over to me. "Here's the file. You tell me what to do that hasn't already been done—several times."

I *wanted* to be angry, to lash out at someone. Obviously, Jack Richards wasn't the one. I hadn't come here to pick a fight with him. I opened the file and leafed through the first twenty pages or so. Most were reports of interviews. Some were summaries. With each page my rage lessened, and I felt my breathing slow to a more normal rate.

Feeling chastised, I closed the notebook.

"Sorry, Jack, it's just—"

"No apology needed."

"I didn't come here to bite your head off."

"I know you didn't," he said. "But, Joe, these guys will slip up. And when they do, we'll nab 'em."

I set my coffee cup on the desk, looked down at the floor, and uttered a prayer. It came out as a whisper, an exchange among the three of us: God, Jack, and me.

"I so hope you're right."

48

Driving home on Westbrook Terrace

No doubt about it—I felt depressed. And as I made the fifteen-minute drive home, I tried to analyze my options—what could Joseph Wright, MD, do about it? I ruled out medication—my depression wasn't that serious. And for that and many other reasons, I discounted the need for services of a psychologist or psychiatrist.

My cellphone rang. The caller ID showed my home number.

"Hello."

"Supper's ready," Jenny said. "Where are you?"

"Five minutes away. What's on the menu?"

"Lasagna. I'm putting it on the table as we speak." She sounded a little distracted, but I chalked it up to her last-minute meal preparations.

"Yum. I'll drive faster."

We rang off, and I had another thought about depression. Quit thinking and worrying about the rapists, about national politics, or about me. Concentrate on home, family, and Jenny's lasagna.

Immediately I felt better. And wondered if we'd have garlic bread to go with the pasta.

When I opened the door from the garage, I could smell the garlic. I took a minute to clean up, then joined Brent and Jenny at the table. The lasagna looked and smelled wonderful. So did the garlic bread. I smiled.

"Where's Bretta?" I asked.

"She said she doesn't feel like eating," Brent replied.

Jenny passed the garlic bread. I took a slice. Brent took two.

"What's wrong?" I looked first at Brent, then Jenny.

No one answered.

"What are her symptoms? Upset stomach? Maybe I can help."

Brent stared at his mother. "Mom?"

Jenny slowly lowered her fork. "She got some disappointing news this afternoon," Jenny said. "She's upset."

I laid my fork accross my plate and sat back, away from the table. "What happened?"

"She thought she had the job as elementary music teacher at Texland," Jenny replied. "It's a small school northwest of Dalhart—a tiny rural community where she'd be far away from all the publicity."

"I know. She told me the contract was in the mail," I replied.

"The principal called," Jenny continued. "They're not going to hire her."

"Why not?"

"Bretta said they wanted to interview more applicants."

"School's starting in two weeks."

"I think it's the abortion thing," Brent said. "I heard her side of the conversation, and she asked, 'You're not hiring me because of my dad?' Then she slammed down the phone."

"When was this?" I asked, my appetite now waning.

"Late this afternoon, not more than thirty minutes ago."

The three of us stared at Bretta's empty chair. No one spoke.

I stood. "She in her room?"

Brent nodded.

I took the stairs slowly and tried to organize my thoughts. What could I say or do that would be supportive? How could I best help my daughter? I knocked on her door.

"Who is it?" came a small voice.

"Little ole lady," I answered.

"Little old lady, who?"

"Hey, you can yodel. Maybe we can get you a job in a country-western band."

She opened the door. "Dad, I heard that joke fifteen years ago in grade school."

"But you answered."

"That's because it's so old I'd forgotten it."

"Tell me about the Texland job." I entered the room and sat on her bed.

She teared up. "It was a lousy job. I really didn't want it." She went to her desk, grabbed several tissues.

I stood and gave her a hug.

Bretta seemed to relax a little. "Ah deed to blow mah nosth," she said, sniffing.

I let her go and returned to my seat on her bed.

She took more tissues, blew her nose, and wiped her eyes.

I patted the bed. "Come sit. Tell your old Dad what happened."

She sat beside me, her shoulders slumped.

"It was a little bitty school out in the middle of a wheat field. The nearest civilization is Dalhart, and it's twenty-nine miles away."

"Brent said they're not hiring you because of me. He said you slammed down the phone."

Bretta sat up, her back straight, anger in her face. "Old Big Mouth. How did I ever deserve him as a kid brother?"

I chuckled, put my arm around her. "But he loves you."

"And I love him—sometimes. But that doesn't excuse his blabbing about my private conversations."

"And he wants you to come have dinner with us," I added as I stood.

She remained seated.

"Come on," I said, pulling her up.

She sniffed, then smiled. "Do I have to promise not to whack him?"

49

My office, The Medical Arts Building

The next morning, I called Isaac Levy and asked if he could clear his schedule and go with me to Texland that afternoon. "It's a hundred and five miles," I said.

"Well, I guess so," he replied. "What's up?"

I told him about Bretta losing her job, and we made arrangements to meet.

Next, I called the principal at Texland Elementary and made an appointment for three o'clock. Then I asked my nurse to clear our schedule for the afternoon, which she did.

At noon I stopped at McDonald's for hamburgers, fries, and Cokes. Then I picked up Isaac at his office and headed north on Highway 287. We ate lunch in the car while we talked strategy.

"You didn't reveal much on the phone this morning," Isaac said. "What exactly is our goal?"

"I want to find out why these yokels promised my daughter a job and then reneged."

"You just want information? Nothing else?"

"For now."

"You don't care about the job?"

"No."

"Or damages?"

"What damages?" I asked.

"If they promised Bretta a job, and she passed up other employment opportunities because of their promise, she can sue for compensation," Isaac explained.

I thought about that for a moment. "I don't believe that's the case."

Isaac sat quietly for a while, obviously thinking about the possibilities. I slowed as we passed through Dumas and headed northwest on US-87, a two-lane blacktop to Dalhart.

"Okay, so tell me again why we're spending this whole afternoon driving to a small school out in the middle of nowhere?" he asked.

"Because I'm mad," I answered.

"Not a good reason."

"And I'm trying to stand up for my little girl."

"That I buy." He smiled. "Fathers are supposed to defend their daughters."

"I want to punch this guy in the nose."

"Surely we can do better than that."

"I'm all ears," I said. "What can we do to make him regret that he bullied her and reduced her to tears?"

"That's easy," Isaac said. "We can sue."

I thought about it as we drove on.

After a brief silence, Isaac changed the subject, and we talked about quail hunting and fly-fishing. Isaac knew some great streams in the Colorado Rockies, just a couple of hundred miles on past Texland, where he said rainbow trout would practically jump out of the water and into the creel.

We passed through Dalhart, the largest town in the northwestern corner of the Panhandle. I followed the signage pointing north on US-87, "Texland, 29 miles." A few minutes later we drove into a tiny farming community with a sign that read, "Texland, population 507." I started counting the buildings: a combination filling station/grocery store, a post office, only a handful of houses, and a cluster of three, red-brick structures with school buses out behind. We parked in front of the smallest, an older building with an ancient wooden sign above the door that read, "Texland Elementary."

Inside, the first door on the right stood ajar, and we found a secretary sitting at her desk, typing on her computer. For a welcome she gave us a big frown. "You here to see Mr. Burney, our principal?" The not-so-subtle message—*you're the trouble-makers?*

"Yes, please. I'm Joseph Wright. This is Isaac Levy."

"You're the abortion doctor?"

"Yes," I answered. "Would you like one?"

She turned beet red.

Isaac interrupted immediately. "Please forgive him. He's just trying to be funny." Isaac gave me a scowl that would wilt fresh lettuce.

The surly secretary rose, went to a door behind her desk, rapped, cracked the door, and said, "They're here."

"Show them in," a bass voice said.

50

The Texland Elementary Principal's Office

Maurice Burney was tall and looked like an over-the-hill basketball player. He stood behind his desk, stoic, with a worried look on his face. I held out my hand. "I'm Joe Wright," I said. He shook it, reluctantly, as though I had leprosy.

"This is my lawyer, Isaac Levy."

The color drained from Burney's face, and he backed away. "W . . . Wh . . . Why do we need a lawyer?"

"I'm hoping we don't," I replied. "But my daughter, Bretta, tells me that you called her yesterday afternoon to say that the contract you promised was not in the mail."

"That's our right," he said. "We're trying to hire the best teachers."

"Bretta was an honor student at CSU, is an outstanding musician, and came to you with glowing recommendations. We'd like to know who you've found with better qualifications."

"That's confidential information," he blustered.

Isaac intervened. “You’ve heard of the ‘Freedom of Information Act?’ It’s the federal law that requires all government agencies to release information to the public.”

Little drops of perspiration started breaking out on Burney’s forehead. “I . . . I’ll have to check with the superintendent and the school board,” he stammered.

The three of us stood there, waiting for the next word of confrontation. The pause gave me a moment to think, and I realized that Burney was scared. His bluster was a cover-up for something.

“I think you and I need to talk,” I said to Burney. I turned to my lawyer, and could see sparks as he returned my look. Then, in a softer voice, I asked, “ Isaac, could you let me have a few moments with Mr. Burney—alone?”

“I’m not sure that’s a good idea,” Isaac warned.

“Just a few moments,” I repeated.

“We’ve driven a long way to get this information,” Isaac said. “I think you need me to be a part of this discussion.”

I gave him a look that ended the argument.

He shook his head, picked up his briefcase and left, closing the door behind him.

Burney took out a handkerchief and wiped his brow.

“When you called Bretta yesterday, she cried,” I said, “Your rejection devastated her.”

He nodded. “I could tell she took it pretty hard. I *am* sorry for that.”

“It’s been tough this summer. She’s been through a lot.”

“Look, Dr. Wright, I like your daughter. I’m the one who wanted to hire her.”

“What happened?”

“A member of our school board objected. He didn’t want a teacher who'd had an abortion."

"Really?"

"This is a small, conservative community. *Very* conservative."

"And the school board hires the teachers?"

"Usually, they let the superintendent and me make those decisions. But if it's controversial, then the board calls the shots."

"And Bretta's controversial?"

"No." He shook his head. "Not exactly. At least not as far as I'm concerned." He looked straight at me. "But *you* are. There's no question about that."

Burney's comment stopped me. I looked out the window and could see a herd of Black Angus grazing. For the next few seconds, my thoughts roiled.

"I'd like to talk to this school board member," I said.

"You'd probably get me fired." Burney fidgeted, clearly fearful of the prospect.

"Small town politics?"

"I'm three years away from retirement," he said. "If I can hang on just a little longer, my wife and I can take my teacher's pension and move away from all this pettiness."

I stood and held out my hand. "They say the weather's nice in Florida."

He took it. And his handshake was completely different—firm and warm. "I wish the best for you and your daughter. She deserves better than a teaching job in Texland."

I met Isaac outside, and we drove back to Amarillo.

"There's no question," Isaac said. "If we sued, we could win."

"Forget it," I said.

51

The office, the Medical Arts Building

The following morning, Bretta's problems dominated my thoughts. I could see that Texland had too many issues, and someone should counsel my daughter about moving on.

That someone was me.

I thought about how to phrase my advice, what words to use.

Yes, we could sue. Yes, we would probably win. And yes, we'd get her appointment back and shove it down their throats. But at what cost? Even if she did a super job of teaching music, that school board member wouldn't acknowledge it. All he could see—the only thing he would ever care about—was Bretta's rape incident. And the fact that she had an infamous abortion doctor for a father.

I stewed about it all day. Between patients, I practiced different ways to convey my concerns to my daughter. But that evening, at home, I found that she didn't need counseling. Bretta had it figured out before I approached her. "Dad, I'll find another job," she told me, and the genuine optimism in her voice made me believe she meant it.

Coincidentally, the next day my office manager resigned for reasons having nothing to do with me, my family, or abortions.

I knew I should talk with my partners first, but that night at dinner I popped the question. "How about going to work for me?" I asked Bretta as I passed the potatoes.

She blinked. "Doing what?"

"Office manager. Booking appointments. Looking after the business side of a doctor's office. Linda Hinders resigned because her husband is being transferred to Iowa and she, obviously, wants to move her family and follow him there."

"When would I start?" Bretta asked, without much enthusiasm.

"Right away. The first day of classes is Tuesday after Labor Day, and Linda wants her kids to start the school year in Iowa."

Bretta took a big serving of potatoes and passed the bowl to Brent.

Dinner conversation lapsed as Bretta thoughtfully picked at her food.

"No rush," I said. "You could let me know next week."

"I'll take it," she answered.

Brent and Jenny stopped eating.

"Hey, I don't need an immediate answer," I said, wanting her to take her time. "You should think it over."

Bretta set her fork down. "Is this a serious offer, or are you just saying something to cheer me up?"

"It's serious. But I don't want to pressure you. Think about it. Talk it over with someone."

"I don't need to think about it. I want the job."

Both Brent and Jenny resumed eating. Clearly, they thought the issue was settled. Jenny and I exchanged a glance. I could tell she was pleased—and very relieved.

"Pass the bread," Bretta said, her decision *made*.

"You'll like working with the clinic staff," Jenny said. "They're really great people."

"It'll be nice to have you here this fall," Brent added. "I was worried about parental issues without your help. You know how unreasonable Mom and Dad can be."

Bretta bunched her fist and playfully hit him on the shoulder. "You're on your own, pal."

I handed the bread to Bretta, picked up my fork, and speared a big bite of green beans.

The next morning I called a doctors' meeting with Harvey Adams and Melvin Campbell. We gathered in my office, and I closed the door.

"Linda Hinders is leaving," I said, getting right down to business. "I'd like to hire Bretta as our new office manager."

"Bretta?" Mel asked, looking a little bewildered.

"My daughter," I replied.

"Your daughter?" he asked, his face conveying an unmistakable negative reaction. "How old is she?"

"Twenty-three."

Mel shook his head, his frown deepening into an angry scowl. "She's just a kid," he objected. "A kid with no management experience, I might add."

I started to respond, to defend my daughter, but Harv held up a finger signaling me to be quiet.

"I think we should give her a chance," Harv told Mel, asserting his own brand of authority. "What could it hurt? And it'll save us from having to do interviews."

Obviously, this wasn't the time for me to say anything. I eased back into my desk chair.

"Nepotism," Mel said, shaking his head.

"She's a sweet girl," Harv replied. "The others will like her. I say we give her a trial period of three months."

Mel heaved a loud sigh of exasperation and glared at me. "Go ahead, then. Hire her. Hell, in three months the Supreme Court will have ruled against you, and the whole Wright family will be moving to another state." His face changed to a half-smile, one that conveyed condescension. "I hear there's a medical shortage in Alaska."

A cold chill rippled down my spine, and I thought about the reality of his prediction.

"I'll speak with Bretta," I said. "She can start next Tuesday."

Mel stomped out.

Harv gave me a thumbs-up and closed the door as he left.

52

At home, 1109 Westbrook Terrace

Three months after I'd lost my hospital privileges, my new routine of skipping rounds at the hospital started to feel normal. I wasn't sure I wanted to go back to those twice-a-day trips across town. Especially the mornings.

I loved the extra hour at the start of the day—the luxury of sitting at the breakfast table, drinking a relaxed second cup of coffee with Jenny and reading the newspaper. It brought a sense of opulence and comfort to the beginning of my daily routine. Except for one thing:

McCormack.

I told myself I'd skip any headline that carried his name. I tried, but each day his campaign activities and his rise in the polls made for such compelling reading it became impossible not to look. Reginald Q. McCormack was news—the biggest news of the current presidential election.

The last Saturday in August—on a slow news day coming into the

Labor Day weekend— Gallup, Roper, and *USA Today* reported that the impossible had happened. A single-issue, independent candidate had become a serious contender. George Roper even predicted that, if the current trend continued into November, McCormack would become the frontrunner. When I read that, I literally felt sick at my stomach.

"You look awful," Jenny said, looking up from the sports section she'd been reading. "Are you ill?"

I arranged the front page of the *Amarillo Globe-News* and laid it flat on the table so she could read the headline:

McCORMACK ON BALLOT
IN ALL 50 STATES

"How would you like a TV evangelist for your next president?" I asked.

Jenny smiled. "I have to admit, he's a good-looking S.O.B."

I pulled the newspaper back and studied the huge photograph just below the headline. It showed the candidate in Washington, the awe-inspiring Lincoln Memorial in the background. Reggie's face carried innocence, along with a winsome smile that had become his public persona. The strategy of his campaign handlers was to sell him as "non-political." This made his naiveté, the fact that he'd never held an elective office, a plus. It was a fresh approach and obviously, it appealed to a lot of voters.

That scared me.

Another reason he scared me was his unrelenting attack on me as a person.

At noon, Isaac Levy and I talked about it over lunch at the Burger Barn.

"I suppose you watched McCormack's TV special last night?" Isaac said, obviously baiting me.

I grinned, took a small sip of coffee, and burned my tongue. "Hell, no."

"Joe, you need to disregard your personal feelings and study your opponent."

Isaac's admonition surprised me. "What do you mean, *my* opponent?"

"Don't you know he's using you?"

"I'm trying to stay out of this whole troublesome campaign." I took another sip of too-hot coffee. "I consider myself apolitical."

Isaac frowned. Clearly, he didn't agree with my stand. "And as your lawyer, I'm telling you, you don't have that luxury." He looked around, then held up his cup signaling the waitress for a refill.

I thought about his point of view. Maybe my stick-your-head-in-the-sand approach was foolish, but I couldn't see an alternative. I didn't have any desire to confront McCormack, nor did I have the platform with which to do it. McCormack was a famous, national figure. I was a nobody, a small-town, West Texas doctor. He was a spellbinding, charismatic speaker. I couldn't address the local Kiwanis Club without stuttering.

"Forget it," I said, shaking my head to reinforce my refusal.

"The least you could do is pay attention when he castigates you on national television," Isaac said.

"All right. You know I didn't watch the program, so what did he say?"

"That you're a murderer. That you've killed thousands of babies."

Though this really wasn't amusing, I chuckled. "What's the penalty for exaggeration?"

"Not funny."

"The truth of it is, I rarely do a D&C. And most of the time the patient isn't pregnant—so it's not an abortion. It's a common, routine, gynecological procedure to clean the uterus."

"You don't get it, do you?" Isaac countered, sounding exasperated.

"Get what?"

"One or a thousand, you're still an abortionist. That's all McCormack cares about."

Part V
SEPTEMBER

53

At home, 1109 Westbrook Terrace

Labor Day passed without much fanfare. The major event in our household was that school started. I thought we might look forward to a period of normality for our son's senior year at Amarillo High. But Tuesday at the dinner table, after the first day of classes—when Bretta had gone out to eat with friends and we three remaining members of the Wright family took our chairs and began our meal—Brent made a startling announcement.

"Mom, Dad," he said, "I've decided to drop band."

Jenny gave me a look. Over the years I'd learned to respect that special, feigned gesture of indifference, the facial expression that appeared to communicate a *who cares* attitude, but in reality signaled a warning like *sirens for a nuclear attack*.

"More spaghetti?" she asked as she passed the serving bowl.

I nodded, took it, and piled an additional, generous amount on my plate. "Brent?" I asked, and held up the rest of the spaghetti.

He shook his head. "I'm not very hungry tonight."

"Garlic bread?" Jenny asked. Beyond her calm and composed face, I could see a storm brewing.

Again, I took an additional slice, and Brent declined.

"I've got a lot of homework this evening," Brent said. "Excuse me." Without giving us a chance to reply, he abruptly pushed back from the table.

Jenny locked onto my eyes. Puzzled by Brent's behavior, I tried to read her for a clue.

"You're excused," Jenny replied, her voice flat, non-expressive.

Brent, already standing, bounded up the stairs to his room.

I started to call out to him, but Jenny held up a staying hand, shook her head, and gave me "the look" again. I waited a few moments, until I thought Brent was in his room and out of hearing. "What's going on?" I asked, keeping my voice low, just in case.

"Betty Sue Brown called me this afternoon," Jenny said, her eyes suddenly reflecting a defeated sadness. "The Browns have two kids in band."

I nodded. "Luke and Lucy. They're both my patients."

"Betty Sue said the band had a visit by an abortion protest group during rehearsal this morning. This was outside, on the street, by the marching band's drill field."

I tensed. "Good grief. Why would they stage a rally around high school music students?"

"Betty Sue says it's because of Brent. And the worst part is, they plan on staging another one tomorrow."

Her words stunned me. A dull anger gathered at the back of my mind as I tried to sort out the implications. "Brent hasn't done anything," I mumbled, my voice barely a whisper.

"True. Except that Brent has a father who's an abortionist."

The full realization of what my wife was saying surged through my veins like fire.

"The school should have called the police," I said with force, my voice no longer hushed.

"They did."

"And what happened?"

Jenny gave me a long detailed narrative about how Charles Hackler, the band director, had complained to the police. But the protesters were across the street from the band's drill field, and since they were not on school property, the police couldn't do anything.

"I'll go by and talk with Mr. Hackler in the morning," I said.

The first thing Wednesday, I went to Amarillo High School, arrived thirty minutes early, and found the band director in his office getting ready for rehearsal.

"My son tells me he wants to drop band," I said.

"Really hate to lose him," Hackler replied, shuffling through some sheet music. "He's first chair, our finest trombone, and one of the best musicians in the band. I know his sister got a scholarship to Juilliard. You have very talented children."

I deflected his compliment by changing the subject. "What's this I hear about an abortion protest group?"

He carefully placed the stack of music in a folder and then eyed me squarely. "Yes, they came yesterday morning. Small group. Lots of signs. It really bothered Brent. I called Amarillo PD. Two uniformed policemen came and tried to get the protesters to leave."

"And?"

"The police told me that the protesters were and are within their legal rights. There's nothing they can do."

"What about my son? Doesn't he have rights?"

"Look, Dr. Wright, I'm on your side. I *want* Brent to stay in band. I think it's terrible what happened yesterday."

"Surely there must be something we can do," I said, struggling to withhold the rage from my voice. "This is devastating to his mother and me."

He studied me for a moment, and I sensed his reluctance to speak.

"Perhaps—" He looked away.

"Go ahead," I said. "Perhaps what?"

"Perhaps if you spoke to the protesters—made a personal plea?"

"Sure." I looked at my watch. "When and where?"

"We meet out on the drill field," Hackler said. "Rehearsal starts in fifteen minutes."

Students were coming in—getting their instruments and music. The cacophony of 200 students warming up for rehearsal created a din that made it impossible to continue conversation. I followed Hackler outside and down to the field, to where the band was lining up.

The protesters were there, too, across the street. I recognized the person who appeared to be their leader.

Dennis Smith—my *favorite* hospital security guard.

54

Amarillo High School

Dennis carried a huge sign, one that could almost have passed for a small billboard. White cardboard with bold black letters, it featured a skull and crossbones with the words STOP THE KILLING printed so huge it could be read easily from a hundred yards or more.

More than a half dozen additional, smaller signs, hand-painted, and carried by others, gave a variety of pro-life rhetoric: ABORTIONS KILL BABIES; ENDING A LIFE IS NOT A CHOICE; ABORTIONS ARE ILLEGAL; NO MORE ABORTIONS; AMARILLO SUPPORTS HB27; STOP THE ABORTION DOCTOR. Two of the protesters carried a replica of a baby-sized coffin, draped with black-and-white streamers.

As I approached the group, Dennis saw me right away. A distinct feeling of futility came over me.

"Good morning, Dennis," I said.

"Dr. Wright," he nodded. "What are you doing here?"

"Maybe I should ask you the same question."

A mirthless smile spread across his face. "Read the signs," he said. "Unlike you, we're telling everyone why we're here."

"Come on, Dennis, we both know you're here to harass my son."

"We're trying to make sure you, and other people like you, don't kill any more babies," he protested, his face coloring.

"So you admit it," I replied. "This little demonstration *is* aimed at me."

A woman carrying a sign that read, "Amarillo Supports HB27," worked her way between us. "We're trying to get *everyone* to obey the law," she interrupted. "If you'll do that, we'll go away."

"The law says I have the right to appeal."

An Amarillo PD cruiser drove up, its blue-and-red lights flashing. It stopped at the curb about ten feet away. Two uniformed policemen got out and walked toward me. I recognized one—the officer I had spoken with yesterday.

"Good morning," I said.

"What's going on?" he asked.

"We're exercising our right of free speech," Dennis replied, his legs spread and firmly planted, sign held high.

A white Ford SUV—"Amarillo Globe-News" painted on the door—pulled up. A man and a woman got out and started our way. The man carried a large, professional Nikon camera with a flash attachment. She held a clipboard and a small electronic device that looked like a tape recorder.

Dennis, brandishing his monstrous sign, turned to greet them. The camera flashed, several times.

"Thanks for coming," Dennis said. "The abortion doctor is here, trying to harass us. I called the police."

The photographer zeroed in, his flashgun repeatedly showering us with brilliant streaks of white light.

Charles Hackler, the band director, joined us. Amid the blaze of red-and-blue police lights and the illumination of white strobes from the newspaper's camera, he made a plea.

"Please. We're trying to rehearse."

I looked at the faces of the fifteen or so people gathered around. No one seemed concerned about Mr. Hackler or his students.

I turned and walked away.

55

Offices of Levy and Cox, Attorneys at Law

Isaac Levy poured two cups of coffee and handed one to me. "So what is it you want?" he asked.

"I want the pro-lifers to leave my son alone and let him attend his classes without harassment," I replied.

"What is it the other side wants—the pro-lifers?"

"Who knows?"

"Come on, Joe, help me out. What are they after?"

I thought about his question a moment, studying the coffee in my cup. "Retribution, I guess. They're mad because I've appealed, and I'm still practicing medicine while my case works its way through the courts."

He shook his head. "Close, but no cigar," he said.

I sipped my coffee and thought about Isaac's enigmatic question. It seemed clear. Dennis Smith and his extreme rightwing conservatives wanted *me*. And they thought the way to pressure me was through my family. Obviously, Isaac had a different perspective.

"Okay, tell me," I said. "What's the cigar?"

"I think they're after the hearts and minds of the people."

"Same thing."

"No—not exactly."

"I'm listening."

"Let's take the moral high ground. Is it right for people to interrupt the education of our children?"

"Of course not."

"Let's play the game of *what if*—"

I looked at my watch. "How long is this gonna take?"

Isaac smiled. Poured coffee refills. Ripped open his usual pink package of sweetener and stirred it into his cup.

I waited.

"What if," he continued, "the SAT test was next Saturday, and the pro-lifers' daily demonstrations at the high school interrupted student preparation for this important exam?"

He'd piqued my interest. "Go on."

"What if this affected student test performance to the point that our children's test scores were lowered? What if they couldn't meet college admission standards?"

I nodded. I could see where he was going with this.

"Or, what if these demonstrations were interrupting daily football practice, and, as a result, we lost the game next Friday night against Lubbock High?"

I laughed and almost spilled my coffee. "Now *that* would end these pro-life demonstrations. People wouldn't stand for it."

Isaac relaxed back into his chair. "I take it Mr. Hackler thinks the pro-lifers are interfering with rehearsals?"

"Yeah," I said. "You should have heard him this morning, defending his students' practice time. He was really angry."

"I believe the band parents have an organization."

"I can take it from here," I said.

The next night Charles Hackler called an emergency meeting of the AHS Band Parents Association, and—of the 200 students—almost 90 percent of the families sent one or both parents. Over 300 people packed the band's rehearsal room. Mr. Hackler asked me to say a few words.

I kept it short.

"Yesterday morning," I began. "I met with the protesters to ask if they would find some other way to register their disapproval of me," I said. "They refused."

The room got very quiet. I continued.

"My son Brent has offered to drop band. However, he loves his trombone, and I hate to see him give up his music. Mr. Hackler has suggested an alternative, and I'd like you to hear his plan. It might make it possible for my son to continue his music."

I deferred to Hackler, and not wanting to stick around, I left.

When I got home, Jenny was on the phone with her friend Betty Sue Brown. I listened to one side of the conversation.

"Wow!" Jenny said.

She paused.

I waited.

"Call me in the morning, and I'll meet you at Starbucks." Jenny hung up. "The band parents are meeting in the morning at the high school with signs," she said as she greeted me with a hug.

"Really?"

"And they're contacting all the area TV stations."

56

My office, the Medical Arts Building

Friday morning I arrived at the office before eight o'clock. My head nurse, Virginia Cotton, brought a cup of coffee to my desk. "Thanks," I said.

"Your first patient isn't scheduled until 8:30," she said. "I thought you might be over at the high school this morning."

"How'd you know about the stuff at the high school?"

"Everybody knows," Virginia replied. "It's on all the local TV morning shows."

"Really? What're they saying."

"It's a protest against the protesters."

"Go on."

"You know—hell, everyone in Amarillo knows—we've had a small group of pro-lifers with signs at the high school every morning this week. If the protesters had stayed at the school entrance, probably no one would have reacted. But they took their signs out to the band's drill field."

"Because a certain abortion doctor's son plays trombone in the group—"

"Obviously." She looked at me with a silly grin, a way to acknowledge that she knew that I knew that we were talking about me. "So this morning, the band parents staged a rally against the signs."

"And you think the band parents are pro-choice?"

"No, they're just pro-band. But they're asking that the demonstrators cease and desist—that students be left alone and allowed to rehearse without political distractions."

"Sounds reasonable."

"Not to the pro-lifers."

"Good grief. What do they want?"

"Freedom of speech."

"And the band parents?"

"Freedom from harassment."

I sipped my coffee and then, for an instant, our eyes locked.

I wanted to tell her it wasn't that simple. And, unfortunately, confrontation in our little part of the Texas Panhandle could never be reduced to just words, or to the annoying circumstances that Virginia had now summarized in her statements about freedom. For a brief moment I thought about taking our conversation to the next level of ideology. Instead, I glanced at my watch.

Virginia, too, checked the time. "Patients are waiting," she said.

A moment later, she ushered my first case of the morning into the examination room—a man in his mid-50s with hypertension who'd come for his annual physical. While I was anxious to know the result of the conflict that currently permeated Amarillo, it seemed impossible without interjecting myself. I had to stay out of it and, obviously, the best way to do that was to just continue to see patients one at a time. So, I took this man's blood pressure three times—standing, sitting, and lying down, and then prescribed a stronger medication for high blood pressure.

The next patient arrived—and then the next—and one after another, the day passed with me focusing on my work.

That evening, Brent put on his uniform and went with the band to the Lubbock football game to march at halftime.

The weekend slipped by without incident.

Monday morning, no protest group appeared at the band's drill field.

Each morning during the next week, I expected the protesters. But no one came. Gradually, day by day, it became apparent that I had won.

A small victory in the eyes of the world.

A biggie for my son.

57

The Medical Arts Building, two weeks later

I looked out the lobby's front window and winced. Perhaps I had won the battle at Amarillo High School—won a battle but not the war. Across the street, Dennis Smith carried a sign. It didn't mention me by name, but the fact that he selected the street corner across from my office for a McCormack rally, and that his sign, STOP THE ABORTION DOCTOR, was the largest of those displayed by the protesters, left no doubt about his target. Dennis resented his defeat by the band parents. And he blamed me.

Unfortunately, Dennis had a powerful ally.

The "McCormack for President" campaign was picking up steam. And now, thanks mainly to the hard work of Dennis Smith and his local associates, Reggie McCormack was coming back to the Texas Panhandle and working to build his political support by bashing me. It was a variation of the plan he had used so successfully last summer—mobile sound trucks cruising the town all day, mini-rallies to build attendance, and the big climax, a nationally televised speech from the Amarillo Civic Center.

So I watched, along with the entire staff of the Adams-Campbell-Wright Clinic. Bretta came over to stand by me at the window.

"You going over like you did the last time?" she asked, and I could see the anxiety in her face—hear it in her voice.

"I don't know," I answered. "What d'you think I should do?"

"I'll go if you'll go," she offered.

Her words shocked me. The farthest thing in my mind was that my daughter would ever have to confront the man who was making her private medical circumstances a public political cause. I pondered what to say. A long minute passed as we stood together at the window and watched the protesters do their thing.

"Earth to Joseph Wright," Bretta chided, elbowing me playfully in the ribs. Her anxiety had apparently passed.

"Uh—I'm thinking."

"Let's walk over there, stand in the front row."

"Bretta, that might not be such a good idea," I warned.

She put her arm through mine. "I remember a father who once told me it was better to confront our problems than to avoid them."

"I think there's also a saying about leaving yourself open for potshots."

"What can he do to us that he hasn't already done?" she asked.

"For starters, he can use those video cameras." I gestured toward the television crews down on the street.

"So what about them?" she shrugged.

I didn't have an answer. I kissed her on the forehead. "Okay, let's roll."

As we headed for the clinic entrance, I tried to think of something humorous, some way to relieve the tension hanging over the staff.

At the door I stopped, turned to face everyone, and said the only thing I could think of. "Call 911 if this turns into a riot."

That did it. The staff unleashed a barrage of facetious remarks. "Go get 'em tiger." "No rotten tomatoes." And a dozen other teasing remarks. As we went out the door, everyone clapped and cheered for us.

McCormack started his stump speech while we walked across the street. Bretta led. She elbowed our way into the front row and immediately the television cameras zoomed in. To his credit, the candidate never missed a beat. It was a speech I'd heard before, and my guess was that it had become so routine he mouthed the words without thinking.

I thought about how different this was. Same location, same platform, same McCormack, but the dynamics had been radically altered. This time he recognized me. And this time I had my daughter standing beside me.

Suddenly, McCormack's speech took a different course. In an uncharacteristic way, he stammered. "We, uh . . . we . . . we have two unexpected people with us this morning." He paused, apparently unsure of what to say. "I'd like to invite Dr. Wright and his daughter to join me here at the mike." He waited.

Somewhere, in the foggy recesses of my brain, a small voice warned me. *No, don't go into his territory.* I squeezed Bretta's hand, leaned over, my mouth close to her ear, and whispered, "No."

McCormack waited, and as he did, the rally's confrontational energy ebbed. I could sense the crowd shifting, waiting for something to happen. Apparently, he could, too. Silent, passive indecision was the last thing anyone wanted at a political rally.

Then McCormack made a major mistake. He took the mike off the stand, carried it over to the edge of the platform, and knelt, trying to get as close as possible to Bretta and me. "Dr. Wright, this is your opportunity to tell your side of the story, to tell folks how you justify killing your own grandchild." He held the mike out toward us.

I knew the television cameras were on Bretta and me. I put my arm around her and pulled her close.

"Or, Miss Wright, perhaps you'd like to tell us how it feels to have an abortion?"

I squeezed her tight.

The cameras continued to roll. A big fat tear streamed down her cheek.

Sometimes the most elegant response is to say nothing. This was one of those times, and the poignancy of the silence brought the political rally to a screeching halt. McCormack's tactics had backfired, and for a few seconds—a long, embarrassing moment—he didn't know what to do.

Finally, our silence forced McCormack to take the only course of action left to him—he took his mike back to the lectern—all energy now drained from his pep rally. Neither Bretta nor I had said a word. But, with his political momentum destroyed, it was obvious to all that the candidate had crossed the line.

He had shown himself to be a bully.

58

At home, 1109 Westbrook Terrace

That night, dinner ended with an argument. Jenny, Bretta, and Brent didn't want to watch the McCormack special. I told them about Isaac Levy's admonition that I needed to become familiar with my opponent's attack, but nobody budged.

So, in the end, I went upstairs to the bedroom television to watch McCormack by myself.

A few minutes later, Jenny joined me.

McCormack's legendary voice came across at its finest. Deep bass, with a pronounced Southern accent, he used his verbal prowess to "sell" his message to the television audience. He did it well. But five minutes into his stump speech, just as I was expecting his attack on the "misguided doctor" in Amarillo, Texas, he surprised me. McCormack switched his focus to Columbia, South Carolina, and started talking about *his* university.

The linchpin of his success as a television evangelist started with the founding of a small college ten years ago. He named it RQM University, and it had enjoyed astounding growth. The concept of a small, Christian institution of higher education that emphasized moral values, one that provided guidance for youth at the most critical time of their formative years, made a hit with the extreme right. And the money rolled in.

RQM University was rapidly becoming one of the best-endowed colleges in America.

A central feature of RQMU was the Prayer Tower. A huge, steel-and-glass structure, modeled after the Eiffel Tower, it dominated the campus and became the symbol of both the university and the McCormack ministry. Tonight, as Jenny and I watched his "McCormack for President" broadcast, the video switched to an impressive, panoramic view of the tower. With McCormack's voiceover, we watched an aerial view—probably taken from a helicopter—that began with the Columbia skyline. Gradually, over the next several minutes, the camera drew closer and circled around. Then it changed to shots taken from the ground, and shifting to time-lapse photography, it worked from daylight to a night view, with spectacular lighting. From the ground, the scale of the tower looked enormous.

"Wow," Jenny said. "That's impressive."

I pressed the mute button. "Maybe Brent would like to enroll there."

Jenny punched me in the ribs.

"Ouch, that hurt," I complained.

"Serves you right, making jokes about our son's future."

"Maybe Brent could audition for a trombone scholarship."

"That's not funny." She drew back and raised her hand in a fist, looking for a vulnerable spot.

I rolled over, pinning her hand to the pillow, my lips on hers.

I kissed her, and she kissed me back. The fight went out of her and her body went limp.

I had the vague impression that McCormack was somehow connecting his university to his presidential campaign and trying to convince the country that he could use this same successful approach to build America.

But I missed it.

With McCormack's muted face on the screen, I made mad, passionate love to my wife.

Part VI
OCTOBER

59

At home, 1109 Westbrook Terrace

September eased into October as fall came to the Texas Panhandle. A crisp, twenty-degree morning brought color to the leaves, freshness to the air, and a welcome end to allergy cases at my office. Normally, this would be the time of year I loved.

But this wasn't a normal year. It was the year a presidential candidate chose to make me his *cause célébre*. So, kicking and fighting, I reluctantly decided I'd better watch his campaign commercials and his TV appearances to become familiar with what he was saying about me.

I hated it.

But after awhile, I found tracking McCormack's campaign amusing. So, on Friday night of the first weekend in October, a time when both Bretta and Brent went "out" with their friends, Jenny and I found ourselves at home alone with the television and another McCormack campaign special.

However, this one was organized around a different format.

McCormack's campaign handlers had wisely joined forces with other pro-life activists and presented the program as a panel discussion. His guests included the president of the National Women's Union, the chairman of the American Right-to-Life Committee, and Dr. Lawrence Pope, noted author and minister of a prominent Baptist church in Florida. Pope was a popular pro-life activist and McCormack supporter.

The three panelists took turns bashing an infamous Texas abortion doctor—me.

And they looked for every opportunity to praise their pro-life presidential candidate.

The whole forum seemed over the top.

"I think Reggie wasted his money," I said, as I punched the remote and the screen went black.

"Who would watch any of that obviously biased crap?" Jenny asked on her way to the wine cabinet. She opened a bottle of Pinot Grigio and poured two glasses.

"Good question." I took the glass she handed me and sipped.

"I'm Catholic, pro-life, and I thought it dull and boring," she said.

"You say you're pro-life, yet you support your husband and your daughter."

"That's an entirely different thing."

"Remember, I'm the evil abortionist," I said, mimicking the sonorous bass voice of the presidential candidate. I thought I did a pretty good impersonation. Apparently Jenny didn't.

"Cut that out," she replied, her voice stiff, her face contorted into an angry scowl.

I didn't want to upset her further, so I kept silent and sipped my wine.

She sipped hers.

Silence hung between us like an icy Canadian cold front.

Finally it became apparent that I would have to be the one to end our standoff.

"Basically, I'm pro-life, and I think my views are very much like yours," I said, finally.

"You are?"

"Well, I'm against abortion on demand," I said. "How about you?"

"Of course," she replied. "But what do you mean, *basically*?"

"In medicine, there have to be exceptions. Our daughter's a good example."

"Rape?" Jenny questioned me in tone, eyes, and posture.

I nodded and took another sip of wine.

Jenny finished her glass, came over, and kissed me. It was a slow, tender kiss. "If only McCormack knew."

"But he needs me." I grinned. "Where would he be without me?"

She laughed, and then she poured us each a second glass.

We talked for a while. We laughed together. Then, with the kids gone, the evening warm and mellow, a philosophical mood came over me, and I let my thoughts unwind.

"A woman must not be forced to become a prisoner of her reproductive system," I said.

"Joe, where'd that come from?"

"When a woman has been gang raped—when she has fought off her attackers as best she can and yet ends up pregnant—it would be an injustice to require her to endure the result of the attack."

"When it's our daughter, I can see what you're saying."

"And there are other exceptions."

"Many of our friends at St. Mary's Church won't agree."

I thought about my list of exceptions for a minute or so. Jenny was right, many of our Catholic friends would not agree—in fact, some would not accept *any* exceptions. The clock struck ten. "It's probably best to let someone else decide the legal issues."

I started up the stairs.

Saturday passed uneventfully. And I started thinking of some time away from conflict. I even talked with Jenny about taking a few days to go quail hunting. But the Sunday morning papers changed everything with an alarming, front-page story. An Associated Press news release announced that the US Supreme Court would take up, as their first case, *Texas v. Wright*.

The scheduled date would be announced the first Monday in October.

Tomorrow.

60

The Medical Arts Building

Isaac called. He was so excited I could hardly understand him. He kept saying, "Monday this . . . Monday that," and then, "Next Monday—the big day," and, finally, "Monday's our best chance."

"Whoa," I shouted, overpowering his burst of rhetoric. "One thing at a time."

He paused, momentarily, his breathing labored.

"Pick one word," I said into the telephone, "and say it slowly, distinctly, so I can understand you."

He said two. "Supreme Court."

"Yes, I heard," I answered. "They're going to hear our case. We expected that—eventually the court would hear it—didn't we?"

I heard a rush of air—an exhale of exasperation. "Damn it, Joe, this is not six months from now. They're going to hear our case *next* Monday. The Supreme Court of the United States is going to hear *Texas v. Wright*, six days from now."

"I know," I said, my voice calm, exposing my ignorance of the implications. "What do you think's the big rush?"

"Who knows, but we have to make some important decisions—this morning."

"Such as?"

"Such as, who's going to represent you?"

"You are, of course. You're my lawyer."

"No," he said, and I could picture him shaking his head. "The lawyer who argues your case has to be a member of the bar—the Supreme Court Bar."

For a moment I thought about what he was saying. Obviously, this was out of my league, and I didn't have a clue about what to do or say. "So what do you suggest?"

"We've already had calls from six different law firms. Everybody knows this is a big case. For sure the biggest of the year—maybe of the decade or even the twenty-first century."

The first thing that popped into my mind was money. "How much is this going to cost me, Isaac?"

Again, I sensed Isaac's frustration. I could visualize an enraged look on his face as he vigorously shook his head. This time the timbre of his voice went up when he spoke. "Joe, I'm trying to tell you, this is a famous case. Don't think about money. Think about how we're going to win it." He paused for a moment, and then added. "Big, prestigious firms never quote fees in their initial contact, but it could be expensive."

I didn't respond right away. I couldn't. Instead, my thoughts turned to our family budget—Jenny's and my very limited financial resources. It seemed unfair that the government provided the lawyers for their side, yet public citizens like me had to bear the burden, personally.

"We've had a pro bono offer from Planned Parenthood."

I thought about the Evelyn Jones hearing last August and the opposition's female lawyer in the dark suit—the expert in feminist rhetoric. "What's her name?"

"Her?"

"I assume it's the same woman we heard when we attended the confirmation hearing in the Senate Office Building. She represented Planned Parenthood."

"Just a minute," Isaac replied. The sound of rustling papers came over the phone. "Teresa Sawyer. She's a big-time, expensive attorney from one of the largest firms in New York City. But for this case, she's free."

"How much time do we have?"

"Hours. We've got to start work on this immediately."

"I don't want Sawyer," I said. "But I can't afford an expensive litigator, either. You pick the best lawyer you can find for little or no money, and I'll trust your judgment."

We left it at that, and I went back to seeing patients.

Later that afternoon, Isaac called and left a message. Terry Sawyer would be our lead lawyer and would meet us at the Washington Hilton on Friday morning.

The last thing I wanted was an extreme left, feminist ideologue. I picked up the phone and started dialing Isaac's number. Halfway through, I stopped—time, money, and Supreme Court rules dictated our choice. Confronting Isaac wouldn't help. Slowly, I put down the phone.

61

My office, in the Medical Arts Building

At the end of the day, just as I finished with my last patient, the phone rang. "Joe, things are happening fast," Isaac Levy said.

"Yeah. I got your message about Sawyer."

"The court has added a special session just for us."

I laughed and thought of several things I could say about "special" circumstances, most of them negative. Instead, I asked, "Tell me, how are things coming along for our presentation?"

He hesitated, and I could hear his breathing.

I waited, thinking the news must be bad.

"Too early to say," Isaac answered, finally. "We expect the Texas lawyers will present pretty much their same case. If so, this will be the third time I've heard it."

"Yeah, and they've won every round," I reminded him.

"This time we'll be doing something a little different."

"You want to change our presentation?"

"A bit, yes. We now have five attorneys. And, as you and I agreed, Terry Sawyer from Planned Parenthood will be our lead. I'm second chair. The other three are helping us prepare."

I felt a wave of resentment at the mention of Sawyer's name. She wasn't an attorney who inspired confidence. "Any new ideas?"

"Some."

I waited.

Several seconds went by. For some reason Isaac seemed reluctant to converse openly and freely. I could have made it easy for him and broken the silence with something innocuous, but I didn't. Instead, I waited, letting the pressure force him to respond. Finally, he gave me three words:

"Joe, I'm worried," he said.

"Tell me why," I replied. "If the news is bad, it's better to get it sooner than later."

"The three new judges bring a whole new dimension to this case."

"So?"

"So we know how the others stand. Three will continue to support *Roe v. Wade*. The other three are going to vote to overturn."

"Everyone in the country knows where Evelyn Jones stands," I said. "She's a firebrand pro-lifer."

"Which leaves Alto and Robertson," Isaac replied. "And that's why I'm worried."

My thoughts whirled. "Both appointed by a Republican president," I stated flatly.

"Exactly. And both are playing their cards close to the vest. Like I said, neither has opened his mouth. We don't have a clue which way they'll tilt."

"Will they listen to your presentation—to your arguments?"

"Of course. This is the United States Supreme Court."

"Then you need to give them a hell of a presentation."

"And we will, but—"

There always seemed to be a but. *But* if Bretta hadn't walked home alone on the night of May 6. *But* if the Texas Legislature had passed HB27 in a different year. *But* if McCormack hadn't been running for president. *But* if we lived in any one of the *other* forty-nine states.

"Joe, you still there?" Isaac asked.

"Yeah."

"I apologize. I shouldn't have brought this up. Terry's a terrific lawyer. She's going to wow everyone."

As Isaac's words made their way into the gray matter of my brain, I thought back to the Senate hearing for the Jones appointment. In my opinion, she hadn't wowed anyone. For sure, she had the opposite effect on my thinking. But I didn't want to go into all that with Isaac right then, so I changed the subject. "You want me to go to Washington with you?" I asked.

"Yes, absolutely. With so many reporters and cameras, we'll need your physical presence to bring a personal quality to the hearing."

"What can I do?" I asked.

"Catch a plane on Thursday. Meet with us on Friday morning. Also Saturday and Sunday."

"I mean, what can I do on the day of the presentation?"

"Sit in the front row. Show the world that you're a good father as well as a doctor."

I chuckled. "The token patriarch?"

He didn't laugh. Instead, he asked a question, his tone edgy. "Will you do it?"

"Of course," I replied. "I'll fly to Washington on Thursday evening."

We said our goodbyes and hung up.

Isaac the worrier. But this time I thought he justified his nickname. The rush to get ready precluded a good, well-prepared case. Worse yet, our lead lawyer was a pro-choice zealot who antagonized others. And, worst of all, the court appeared stacked against us.

I thought about "throwing in the towel."

62

At home, 1109 Westbrook Terrace

The news coverage of the Supreme Court proceedings overwhelmed me. I thought we'd seen all of the left and the right—and the *gray* in between—about abortion issues. Starting with the Texas Legislature's passage of HB27 almost seven months ago, followed by McCormack's rise in the polls as a pro-life presidential candidate, it didn't seem possible that a hearing by the high court could surpass such widespread coverage.

I've been wrong before. But never like this.

Texas v. Wright was a big story. So much so that its bigness became *the* story—a legend in and of itself. I watched as television commentators scrambled to show the massive number of remote crews gathered around the famous building in Washington—on the street and on the steps of the old marble structure.

CNN gave it continuous coverage and, not to be outdone, the other networks ran hourly updates about the court and their forecast of what was yet to come.

Then, on Wednesday morning, just when I thought the media circus had grown beyond all possible limits, things got worse. The television networks and the national news associations sent camera crews, newspaper feeds, and even foreign news services to Amarillo. The result came like a spotlight focused on me, on my house, on my family—on the most miniscule and mundane details of my life.

In my bathrobe and slippers, I went out to get the morning paper and found dozens of media representatives with their cameras and microphones at the ready, eager to pounce. Reporters yelled questions.

"Dr. Wright, are you going to Washington?"

"What are your chances?"

"Would you like to tell us your side of the story?"

I didn't know what to do or say, so I picked up my *Amarillo Globe-News*, waved to the crowd, and retreated back inside the house.

I thought they might go away. And in a way, that's what happened. They moved downtown and set up on the street outside my office at the Medical Arts Building.

I called the Amarillo PD.

"Officer, what can I do?" I asked. "I'm afraid this mob is going to intimidate my patients."

"We can ask that they move across the street," he replied. "Want me to send a couple of uniforms?"

"Yes, please."

A few minutes later I looked out the window to see two policemen pushing the crowd to relocate to the other side of Polk Street. I watched a sea of angry faces, and though I couldn't hear their comments, it was obvious that the police were receiving a flood of griping and profanity.

After about fifteen minutes, the two officers got back in their cruiser and drove away.

I thought everything was settled and returned to my examination rooms to see patients. A few minutes later, my head nurse, Virginia, came to me.

"I think you'd better take a minute and look outside," she said.

"What's happening?" I asked, a sinking feeling creeping over me. "What now?"

"Your friend has arrived with his PA system."

I excused myself and went to the front window to find a panoramic view of Dennis Smith and his pickup. He had loudspeakers mounted on the vehicle's roof and was blasting a running commentary about me. I watched as dozens of media people maneuvered to record, film, and photograph him. He had the volume turned up so loud, I could hear him through the glass.

"Dr. Wright is on trial in the United States Supreme Court," he boomed. "I urge you not to trust your medical care to a physician who is under indictment."

Harvey Adams, one of my medical partners, came and stood beside me.

"That's libelous," Harv said. "We can sue the pants off him for statements like that."

I nodded. "I suppose we could."

He started toward the door, "It's going to give me great satisfaction to tell that stupid son of a bitch how much money we'll take out of his hide."

"Wait," I cautioned. "I'm the one he's yelling about. Let me confront him."

Harv looked at me with disappointment, but he stopped. "You tell him if he doesn't quit, immediately, I'll have every damn lawyer in the

Texas Panhandle suing his ass."

I walked out the door and crossed the street. I could see the TV cameras turning to zoom-in on me. A red flag waved inside my brain, and I could imagine big letters on it spelling out the word *caution.* I knew I had to be careful. Our experience at the AHS Band's drill field had proved that Dennis would not listen to logic. The approach had to be subtle, and it had to let Dennis think he was making the decision.

"Morning, Dennis," I said.

"Dr. Wright," he said, his voice broadcasting loudly over the PA. "Killed any babies this morning?" He held the microphone out, a few inches from my lips.

I placed my hand on the mike, pulling it gently toward me and asked, "May I?"

Then Dennis made a mistake. "Be my guest," he said, and he removed his hand, effectively handing me his microphone.

I unplugged it, and handed the cord back, the mike still in my hand.

"Hey," he yelled, "that's mine."

"I'll return it," I said, "but let's talk for a minute."

"No," he snarled. Television cameras moved closer.

"I'm trying to help you, Dennis. It'll only take a moment."

He looked around at the cluster of reporters and TV equipment. Several cameras flashed. I could see he was having second thoughts.

"My partners, Dr. Adams and Dr. Campbell, tell me that what you're doing is against the law. And if you don't quit, they're going to sue you for libeling our clinic."

His face turned red, his expression a mean scowl. "They wouldn't dare." His voice came at me as a loud growl filled with malevolence.

I handed him his mike. "Don't say I didn't warn you." I gestured to the TV cameras. "And Dennis, as you can see, we'll have plenty of documentation."

I turned and walked back to the clinic. Inside, I stopped to look out the window.

Harvey Adams and I watched as Dennis slowly got into his pickup and drove away.

Score one for the good guys.

63

Rick Husband International Airport, Amarillo

Thursday afternoon I grabbed my bag and headed for the airport. Good news: The electronic display showed American 3843 to be on time. Bad news: The line going through security clearance was the longest I'd ever seen.

The minutes ticked away as people inched their way to the scanner. Once there, I pulled my laptop out of its bag, dropped both the computer and the bag into plastic trays, removed my coat and shoes, put them in another tray, emptied my pockets into a small plastic bowl, and scooted everything onto the conveyor belt. My motions were both quick and efficient. I felt good—expecting to pass security in record time.

Standing at the scanning portico, the TSA agent motioned me through.

"Beep, beep, beep," sounded the alarm.

Two agents, a man and a woman, directed me to stand aside.

The man frowned and asked, "Let's see your belt."

I pulled it off and handed it to him. "It's never been a problem before."

"Walk through again," he said. The scowl on his face indicated frustration with both the heavy crowd and me—especially me—the fact that I was holding things up.

"Beep, beep, beep." To my ear, the alarm sounded louder than ever. People stared. The TSA guy's expression turned to anger.

"You have something hidden on you?"

"No, sir."

"See those footprints painted on the floor?"

I nodded.

"Stand on them. Spread your arms."

I did.

He took an electronic wand and waved it up and down my legs. Then he passed it over and under my arms. Under his breath I could hear him cursing the extra time and trouble.

Finally, he scanned my back—hips up to my neck.

"Turn around," he groused.

I did, and he passed the wand over my front, starting with my crotch and moving upward toward my face. When he reached my upper chest, the gadget chirped.

The agent raised his voice. "What've you got under your shirt?" He didn't exactly yell the words, but he spoke them loud enough that everyone in the area turned to look. The edge to his tone implied that I might have a 45-magnum hidden in my clothing—trying to sneak it onto the plane.

Then I remembered—the St. Jude medallion that Bretta had given me.

I unbuttoned my shirt, lifted the chain over my head, and handed it to the agent.

"Sorry, I forgot."

"Back through the scanner," he motioned.

I walked through a third time. Nothing happened.

The agent handed me the medallion. With impatience, he waved me toward a table where someone had piled my shoes, jacket, laptop, computer bag, and the small plastic bowl with my keys, watch, and change.

I reassembled myself . . . everything back like it was except the St. Jude medallion. I carried it in my hand and walked to the gate.

At Gate 32, I arrived just as the agent announced that our plane would be about twenty minutes late. I took an empty seat next to a young man wearing an army uniform.

We introduced ourselves and shook hands.

I had the medallion in my hand and started to put it on—to lift the chain over my head and tuck St. Jude inside my shirt. For some reason I hesitated. I studied the image and thought about Bretta, of how much she meant to me. As my mind replayed her words—back to that night when she handed the medal to me in the little box—my hand trembled and I almost dropped it.

"Is that what caused all the commotion at the security gate?" the soldier asked.

His question snapped me out of my reverie. "Say again."

"Us army folks are sensitive about security." He smiled. "When the alarm went off, I stopped to look and saw you take off the medallion."

I showed it to him. "It's St. Jude, the patron saint of impossible causes."

"Really," he said. "You have an impossible cause?"

"Not exactly."

He waited.

I wondered how much to say to this stranger.

"Sorry, I didn't mean to pry," he said.

"It was a gift from my daughter. She's been through some tough times recently, and I helped her." I put the chain around my neck, dropped the medallion inside my shirt, and re-buttoned the top button. "We're very close, so this has special meaning."

He pulled out his wallet and showed me a photo of two teenage girls. "I have two daughters. When I was in Afghanistan last year, I looked at this picture every day. It kept me going."

An announcement interrupted. The agent asked everyone to line up at the jetway for boarding.

The soldier stood, put his hand on my shoulder, "You're lucky. Sounds like a wonderful daughter." He picked up his bag and joined the line.

I looked away, embarrassed. I didn't want him to see the wetness gathered in my eyes.

64

The Washington Hilton

On Friday morning, when I first met our new team of lawyers, I felt a little encouraged. Teresa Sawyer—Terry as she asked everyone to call her—seemed much different from the stern-faced, rigid attorney I remembered at the Evelyn Jones hearing last August. In the formal atmosphere of the Russell Senate Office Building, I'd seen her as a narrow-minded, monolithic, pro-choice advocate of the radical left.

But here in a small hotel conference room—with me, Isaac, and three other lawyers—she came across as much more relaxed and down to earth. Wearing jeans, sneakers, and a Harvard Law School sweatshirt, she brought a casual leadership to our highly charged meeting. Even though she left no doubt about her pro-choice views, her persona exuded much less belligerence than at the hearings in the Caucus Room. I slowly warmed to her legal strategy and began to think, maybe, she wasn't such a bad choice after all.

"Each side has thirty minutes to present its case," Terry said. "Here are copies of the two briefs." She passed out the two documents—theirs and ours. For the next hour we read.

I read the state's presentation first. As Isaac had predicted, it rehashed their material of the previous trials. The linchpin of their argument was that human life begins at conception, and from that basic, undeniable fact, it should follow that any event which ends life was murder and subject to all penalties of law. The brief held a lot more material, most of it directed against pro-choice rhetoric about viability of the fetus in the early stages of pregnancy. I had to admit, it was hard to argue against ending life, no matter at what stage it occurred.

Our material was somewhat different. It backed away from *abortion on demand*, the extreme-left, feminist position that Sawyer had pushed at the Jones hearing—with, I might add, disastrous results. Instead, she led with *reproductive freedom* for women and the thesis that, "Otherwise, women become vulnerable slaves to their biology." She used Bretta as an example to make the case. Here was a young woman who had been brutally gang-raped and should not be forced by law to carry the unwanted pregnancy of an unknown father—a result from the attack. I thought it projected a powerful legal argument.

One by one, as each of the six of us finished our reading and study, we drifted from the conference table to the coffee pot located on a bar at the east end of the room. Isaac got there first. I joined him in whispered conversation.

"What'd you think?" I asked.

He smiled and gave me an affirming nod. "She's good."

Terry Sawyer came over, poured a cup of coffee, and stood by us.

"Congratulations," I said. "You've crafted a strong presentation."

"Thanks," she answered. "I'm having some regrets about it, though."

"How's that?" Isaac asked.

"*Roe v. Wade* is based on a woman's right to choose. Abortion on demand—period. The brief you just read concedes that very important freedom for women and, instead, falls back to specific circumstances, reasons that have to be justified and therefore proven. I don't like it."

"I'm against abortion on demand," I said.

A chill wafted across the room.

Stone cold silence.

I was afraid to look up, so I stared at the floor.

I heard someone clear their throat. It sounded masculine, and it came from Isaac's direction.

An angry feminine voice responded. "Then we have a problem." There was only one woman in the room—Terry.

I looked up, and her eyes locked with mine for a moment. Her face was red, and she glared at me. It was an expression I'd seen from my wife when, many years ago, after a heated argument, she had threatened divorce.

"Maybe we'd better return to the table and talk about this," Isaac suggested.

"Or maybe we should let Dr. Wright find another lawyer," Teresa Sawyer replied.

65

The Washington Hilton

Isaac Levy earned a new sobriquet—compromiser. It started immediately after my gaffe on Friday morning. Isaac asked me to leave the room. Then, while I cooled my heels in the hotel coffee shop, he spent an hour with the four lawyers from Planned Parenthood. I don't know what he promised them, but it was probably more than I would have, if I had been party to the negotiations.

When Isaac joined me in the coffee shop, he came at me with a vengeance.

"Damn it, Joe, are you trying to wreck our case?"

"No," I answered. "Just want everyone to know where I stand."

"Let me tell you where I think you stand—just inches away from becoming history's all-time most stupid, ignorant, foolish, dim-witted, obtuse chump."

I chuckled, "Don't hold back. Just tell me what you really think."

Isaac turned red in the face. The crimson flush began at his shirt collar and rose gradually to his hairline until a vein, just above his right temple, visibly throbbed. I pictured steam coming out his ears.

Obviously, this wasn't the best direction for our conversation, and I held up both hands in a gesture of surrender. "Sorry, I just couldn't resist."

"This isn't funny," he said.

"No, but it isn't the doomsday that Sawyer and her three cohorts are making it, either," I countered.

"Joe, listen to me," Isaac implored, his voice on the rise. People in the restaurant turned to look. "Monday's hearing isn't a Justice of the Peace Court in the Texas Panhandle."

I held a finger across my lips. "Shhh," I hissed, gesturing at the people who were staring at us.

Isaac slumped back in his chair, shaking his head, speechless.

"I apologize for ticking her off."

Isaac looked at me like I was an errant child.

"What is it you want me to do?" I asked. "Kiss her feet?"

At first he didn't say anything. He looked around the room. Then he leaned forward, put his hands together, elbows on the table, and in a whispered voice said, "I want you to think and act realistically."

"Realistically?"

"The reality of our situation is that we need Sawyer."

"I agree, but—"

"No buts."

We stared at each other for a long moment. "You want me to say that I support abortion on demand when, in truth, I don't."

"No," Isaac replied.

"Then what do you want me to say?" I asked.

"Nothing. Just keep your damn mouth shut."

I thought about that and lowered my gaze to the floor. "Okay."

He sat back, relaxed in his chair. When I looked up, he smiled. It wasn't a big, heartfelt smile, just a little softening of his lips, of the anger that, until now, had dominated his face. "Let's go back to the room and see if we can find a way to let these lawyers help us."

So we did.

And I spent three days of difficult conciliation, of dancing on eggshells while we tried to put together our strategy for the Supreme Court presentation. One of the things that made it possible for me to do this was Terry's knowledge of procedures. She explained that, even though we had enough presentation for the entire thirty minutes, we wouldn't get to use it.

"We'll be lucky if we actually present three minutes of our prepared material," she said.

"What happens to the other twenty-seven minutes?" I asked.

"Questions. One of the justices will interrupt, probably Scully, and then, before I've fully answered, there will be a question from the other side."

"Other side?" I asked.

"Historically, Scully, Thompson, and South have been pro-life. Whereas Galesburg, Kennison, and Bayer vote pro-choice."

"What about the new justices—Robertson, Alto, and Evelyn Jones?"

"We know where Jones stands. But Robertson and Alto have been conspicuous with their silence. We'll all be watching for their questions."

At that moment it struck me that the interpretation of law, even at its highest level, came down to a personal level. Bias—a personal predisposition. If so, then my fate was a foregone conclusion. It was a sobering thought and caused me to withdraw into an ascetic meditation for the next three days. Like a scared tortoise who pulls his head back into the shell, I let the lawyers debate their differences and, for the most part, I only listened.

On Sunday we practiced questions. Terry stood at a lectern, gave her speech for about three minutes, and then we peppered her with questions for twenty-seven minutes. We did this six times, each time with new and different questions.

Terry was good. Damn good. And I congratulated her.

"Thanks, Joe," she said. "And I promise not to compromise your position about abortion on demand."

I smiled and suggested she get a good night's rest. We parted on surprisingly good terms.

I went back to my hotel room and tried to sleep. Couldn't. Ended up watching a 1930s movie. And finally fell asleep wondering—

What the hell *are* our chances?

66

Monday morning, the United States Supreme Court Building

We took two cabs from the hotel and arrived at the Supreme Court Building a little before seven-thirty. I looked at my wristwatch and calculated the time—two and a half hours until our scheduled ten o'clock presentation.

The east side of the building was already crowded with demonstrators. While circumstances made it impossible to count, I estimated the number of people at several thousand. A line waiting to get into the building stretched from the steps, across the plaza, down to the street, and then south as far as the eye could see.

The pro-life demonstrators struck me as better organized and more active. A recognizable group of at least a hundred stood on the steps with duct tape over their mouths, the word "life" written on the tape. Signs, mostly hand-written, were everywhere. But one stood out because it was printed—and must have numbered in the hundreds. In bold black letters it read, "Repeal *Roe v. Wade*."

On the other side, pro-choice supporters marched in a circle and joined in a chant that they repeated over and over:

"One-two-three-four, we won't take it anymore.
Five-six-seven-eight, separate the church and state."

One woman carried a huge, black replica of a coat hanger, probably four feet in length, with a sign, "We won't go back to illegal abortions."

Terry led and the five of us elbowed our way through the two crowds to the police line at the building entrance. Isaac held a letter identifying us as litigants, which he handed to the policeman in charge.

"Wait here," the policeman said. Then he turned away and started conversing on a walkie-talkie.

While we waited, I looked out over the crowd and listened to the rhetoric.

"Hallelujah, praise the Lord, in the name of God, protect the innocent," yelled a big, bearded evangelist in a black suit, his voice so loud he could be heard above the noise of the crowd.

"Women have the right to choose. Pro-faith, pro-family, pro-choice," came the voice of a woman with a bullhorn, carrying a huge sign that read, "Drive out this president. Keep abortions legal."

Terry and Isaac carried on a conversation. I listened.

"How many of these people are going to be inside?" Isaac asked.

"See the line?" Terry responded, pointing. "Only the first fifty in that line."

"What about all these other people?" he asked. "Do *they* know that?"

"Probably," she answered. "But they don't care. They're here for the publicity."

I looked out across the demonstrators and could see television crews, photographers, and reporters mixing with the crowd. The most visible media coverage centered on the waiting line where dozens of pro-life protesters were lying on the ground, many in the fetal position, forcing those in the queue to step over them.

"Come with me," called the policeman who held our letter.

We followed him up the steps and into the building. He handed our letter to a uniformed policewoman who led the way to security screening. Much like an airport surveillance procedure, we had to remove our shoes, hand over our briefcases, and walk through a metal detector. I remembered to remove my St. Jude medallion and drop it in the tray. On the other side of the security area, we were handed off to a big, tall, muscled guy in a black suit. He wore an earpiece and I could see a bulge under his left arm.

We followed him into a spacious, ornate, high-ceilinged room—the United States Supreme Court.

67

The United States Supreme Court

A courtroom, any courtroom, carries a certain aura—a statement of importance or what I've heard described as an impression of history. It communicates a sense of awe to those who enter, and the expectation that respect and reverence are demanded. After all, this is the site of decisions that direct the course of human endeavor. I've entered a number of courtrooms—some more impressive than others—but never one that compared to this.

The chamber was enormous.

We followed our guide to the front of the room and took our places at two tables, a smaller one with two chairs next to the lectern for the presenter—Terry and Isaac sat there—and another with four chairs for our other lawyers and me. I took the next few minutes to look around the room and breathe in the ambiance.

Our seats at the two tables faced the east where a dais with nine oversized, high-backed chairs looked out over the courtroom. I guessed the room's dimensions to be seventy feet square with a vaulted ceiling, probably thirty or forty feet high. Each side featured eight mammoth, marble columns of Greek design, which provided the building's support. A bronze fence about three feet high separated the spectators from the front of the courtroom. I counted the seats in one section and estimated space for an audience of 400 or more. Thick carpet and heavy velvet drapes soaked up the sound and gave the room an overall hushed atmosphere.

At eight o'clock, two hours before the hearing, I expected the room to be empty. It wasn't. Security people were everywhere, as well as a crew of electronics technicians who were engaged in checking the microphones. Lawyers for the State of Texas took their tables opposite ours. Gradually the room filled with clerks, marshals, members of the Supreme Court Bar, and the press corps.

High up on each of the walls, four huge, federal-style clocks ticked off the minutes. At exactly ten o'clock the clerk of the Supreme Court, who sat at the left of the bench, rapped his gavel and announced, "All rise." The justices filed into the room and took their seats, after which the clerk commanded, "Be seated. The United States Supreme Court is now in session."

For the next five minutes or so, Chief Justice John Robertson conducted business. Several lawyers came to the lectern and read names of attorneys to be admitted to the bar. Then he called for the State of Texas to present its case.

"Mr. Chief Justice, and may it please the court," the state attorney general said. "We ask that you consider House Bill 27, passed by the Texas Legislature on February 27 of this year."

Before he could continue, Justice Ruth Galesburg interrupted. "Sir, this legislation contradicts established law. Do you have any new circumstances that would provide the basis for change?"

"Yes, Justice Galesburg, we can cite more than two dozen instances where state legislatures, and even the United States Congress, have passed laws that ask for changes to *Roe v. Wade*. In 1995, Congress passed a nationwide ban on abortion, and—"

"And it was vetoed by President Clinton in 1996," Galesburg interrupted, her voice harsh with an edge that cut through the room.

"We can also cite," the Attorney General replied, "cases that originated in New York, California, and Nebraska—in 2003—where legislation banning abortions was passed and would now be law if it were not for multiple suits filed by Dr. Leroy Carhart and other doctors, on behalf of Planned Parenthood Federation and its member affiliates."

Justice Bayer cut in. "But those suits to block implementation were upheld by this court because they lacked provisions to protect women's health."

A new voice came over the PA system. "How does Texas's HB27 make provision for this?" Justice Scully asked.

"Our brief, on page four, paragraph two, states the following: *Corrective surgical procedures to end the pregnancy are allowed when two or more licensed physicians sign affidavits stating that it is necessary to save the life of the mother.*"

"But this doesn't answer the question," Justice Kennison broke in. "What about the mother's health?"

"A matter of health is very subjective," the attorney general replied. "The common cold is a threat to our health. Does this mean that every woman who has a cold can use this as a reason to justify an abortion?"

"That is exactly the problem," Justice Thompson stated. "An exception that allows the ending of a baby's life, at any stage, must have definitive guidelines. Saving the life of the mother is a clear line."

The room became very quiet. Justice Clarence Thompson, noted for his quiet reticence to speak out on issues, seemed to momentarily halt discussion. Then Galesburg asked a question, followed by a dozen more from Bayer, Scully, South, and Kennison.

Robertson, Alto, and Jones remained silent.

"The red light is now on," the attorney general said. "I'd like to close with a short statement."

"Go ahead," Chief Justice Robertson said.

"The people of Texas, through their elected government, have clearly expressed their wish to end abortions in our state. We respectfully ask this court to honor that request."

He sat.

I looked up at the clock on the north wall. Exactly thirty minutes had passed.

Our attorney, Teresa Sawyer, stood and made her way to the microphone.

68

The United States Supreme Court

Teresa Sawyer said, "Chief Justice Robertson, and may it please the court," her voice remarkably feminine. In this room, where for the past thirty minutes we had been listening to voices of a mostly masculine, argumentative timbre, Teresa's words floated out over the public address system with a calming, soothing effect. Without thinking, I relaxed, and I sensed that those around me eased back in their seats also.

"We are considering this morning a matter of utmost concern, a subject that affects the most personal aspect of a woman's biology—the circumstances that govern her reproductive freedom." Then Terry paused. It was a moment of quiet that surprised me, and, I think, everyone in the room. It seemed inevitable that one of the justices would take the opportunity to break in, to ask a question. The fact that none did created an elegance to Terry's opening statement. It was as if she had just won a major point.

I sensed that the attorney general, seated at his table less than ten feet to my left, shifted uncomfortably in his chair.

"Perhaps we are not far from agreement," Terry continued in her soft-spoken manner, "and that, if a way could be found to determine an evaluation for what we call the *health of the mother*, the court could find an interpretation for legislation to resolve this conflict in Texas Law."

"Do you have a suggestion?" Justice Scully asked.

"Not this morning," Terry replied. "But I have an example of *what not to do.* On May eleventh of this year, a twenty-three-year-old woman was brutally raped by three unknown men in Canyon, Texas. For weeks she lay at death's door, but due to the efforts of an outstanding local medical staff, including her father, Dr. Joseph Wright, they saved her life. However, when this young woman began to recover and realized she was pregnant, she took a coat hanger and tried to abort herself."

I didn't know that Terry was going to use these intimate details of my daughter's case. In our practice sessions at the hotel she'd never mentioned them. But as an answer to Scully's question, it was dynamite. No judge, even a justice of the United States Supreme Court, would argue with it.

Terry continued. "This graphic example, a rape victim impregnated by unknown attackers, a young woman so desperate she was willing to risk serious personal injury to gain freedom from her own biology, should give us pause to consider the need to provide a legal, safe alternative to HB27."

I marveled at Terry's sense of timing. She knew when to press and when to let up—to savor the point well made. Again, for the second time, she waited.

As each nanosecond of silence slipped by, it added substance to Terry's point.

"You've not yet offered a suggestion for how to evaluate the *health of the mother*," Justice South stated. "Does this mean the term is so subjective that our only alternative is to disallow it as a reason for abortion?"

"No, Justice South," Terry replied. "That's what HB27 does. And the example I've just given shows the injustice of that approach. A way can and must be found to consider the mother's health."

"Suppose I agree with you," Justice Scully interrupted. "How do you see that impasse being resolved?"

"The American medical system is considered the best in the world," Terry shot back. "I suggest that litigants who want to overturn *Roe v. Wade*, and who now realize that an exemption to protect the mother's health will be a factor in the potential success of any proposed legislation, must work with the medical community to develop a comprehensive definition and procedure."

"On the other hand," Scully interjected, "why not accept HB27 and let those who want the *health of the mother* added as an exemption, have that responsibility."

"Several reasons," Terry replied. "*Roe v. Wade* is settled law. Any change should be considered only if it provides a viable alternative. And we've just analyzed an example that shows HB27 is not acceptable. Health of the mother is a difficult, contentious issue, and it may prove to be irresolvable. In that case, *Roe v. Wade* may be the best answer."

Scully leaned forward in his chair and his voice boomed. "Since 1973 there has been considerable feeling *that Roe v. Wade* is not the answer. *That* it was a mistake. *That* something must be done by this court to correct the injustice it has created against young life."

I sensed that Terry had gone too far. The audience in the courtroom reacted, and I could hear movement as people shifted uneasily.

Justice South asked the next question. "Are you proposing abortion on demand?"

It was a stark, pointed question, and it caught Terry by surprise. I could see, for a second, that she wanted to say yes. To her credit, and perhaps in deference to me, she didn't.

"No," she said, "I'm not advocating abortion on demand. But I am presenting the argument that it is better than Texas's HB27."

At that point I thought the case was over. It continued for another fifteen minutes, but the exchange only amounted to a rehash of the same questions and statements.

Finally, Chief Justice Robertson, in a loud stern voice, said, "The case is accepted." He rapped his gavel loudly. The nine justices stood, turned, and left the room.

I didn't know if we had won or lost.

69

The Washington Hilton

We took a cab back to the hotel and assembled in our little conference room for a final meeting with our lawyers.

"Good job," I said to Teresa Sawyer, meaning it. I thought she was brilliant.

"I was mighty tempted to say yes," she said, the big, gleaming smile on her face leaving no question that she was mocking me. I knew exactly what she was referring to, and I grinned back.

"When Justice South asked if you were proposing abortion on demand?"

She nodded, still smiling. "Yep."

"But you said no," I answered with a chuckle, returning a smile as big as hers.

She shrugged. "Maybe they'll drop the ball, and that's what we'll get."

"I wouldn't count on it," I replied. "But let's talk about the future.

What do you think?"

She set her briefcase on the table but left her hand on the handle as though ready to walk out the door. "Before I give you my opinion, I'd like to hear what the others think." She turned to the other three lawyers. "Isaac?"

He shook his head. "I wish I could be optimistic, but it looks like the deck is stacked and not in our favor. It's probably a six-to-three vote to overturn. But they'll wait until the end of the term to announce."

Terry looked at her other lawyers. One by one, in solemn voices, they answered.

"I agree," said the first.

"Yes," added the next.

"It was a long shot, and nothing happened that changed the odds," replied the third.

Terry looked at me. "Joe?"

"I'm the client," I answered. "I don't think I have a vote."

"But you have an opinion, and we're interested in what you think."

I shook my head. "I thought when you brought up Bretta's circumstances, that you touched an emotional response. But at the end it didn't seem to affect their thinking, or at least the direction of their questions. I guess it's a toss-up."

Terry fidgeted a little, which was uncharacteristic. She moved her briefcase slightly and changed hands. "I wish I could say that with dynamic statements we presented such a brilliant case that we swayed legal sentiment and changed the course of history." She left off the usual *but.* It didn't matter—I could hear it loud and clear anyway.

I looked from face to face around the room, waiting for one of the four lawyers to speak. No one did.

"You did your best," I said. "And I appreciate your efforts."

"We all expected the six-to-three vote was a foregone conclusion," Isaac reiterated.

Terry lifted her briefcase and turned toward the door. "I guess we'll have to wait until they're ready to tell us."

"Next June?" One of the other lawyers asked.

"It'll be the last decision of the term," Terry answered. She turned, shook hands with Isaac and me, exchanged words of goodbye, and walked out the door.

The other three lawyers followed like a reception line.

Isaac picked up his briefcase. "Ready?"

I followed him to the elevators. We agreed to meet at the taxi stand in front of the hotel with our suitcases.

Later, in a cab on the way to Washington's Reagan Airport, Isaac had his thoughts and I had mine. Silently I counted the months—November, December, January, February, March, April, May. The Supreme Court would probably announce their decision in early June.

If I wanted to avoid being arrested, the Wright family probably had seven months to move to another state.

70

At home, 1109 Westbrook Terrace, Amarillo

I don't know what I had expected, but it certainly wasn't the cloud of failure that met me at our home. Seated around the breakfast table, my family hit me like a three-barreled shotgun.

"I thought we had a chance," Jenny groused. "If it was an inevitable decision, and the justices had already made up their minds, why go to Washington? Why hire a roomful of lawyers and spend all that time and effort? Why bother with the Supreme Court?"

Bretta joined in. "And why does it take a year for them to announce their decision if everyone already knows what it is?"

"Who cares what a bunch of old geezers think?" Brent complained. "We should be pushing law enforcement to go after the bastards who attacked Bretta."

There were no answers. I didn't even try.

Bretta and Brent finished breakfast and left. An unhappy aura lingered as Jenny poured the two of us a second cup of coffee.

"Susan Vernon called Monday night," Jenny said. "We had a long talk."

"Susan who?" I asked.

"Susan Smith, my roommate at Texas Tech. She married Gerald Vernon."

I remembered. "Yeah, every time I see Gerald at medical meetings, he always asks me to come to Alaska and go deep sea fishing. How are Gerald and Susan?"

"You know he opened a family medical practice in Juneau."

"Yes, but it's been twenty-five years since we left medical school. Out of the blue she calls you Monday night?"

"She and Gerald had read about you in Juneau's *Capitol City News*. They talked about us. Gerald asked her to call me."

I picked up a pink package of sweetener and dumped it into my coffee. "About what?"

"About whether or not we'd be interested in moving to Alaska."

I laughed. "Alaska is the last place on earth I'd think about moving to."

"Joe, we need to be thinking about plan B. What's going to happen to us when the Supreme Court announces their decision?"

I stirred my coffee. In both our minds we figured things weren't about to go our way. Jenny was right—we needed to think ahead.

She handed me a small note. "Here're his numbers—home, office, and cell. Susan suggested you call him."

I finished breakfast, drove to the office, and found that I had a light schedule. Bretta had not expected me to return from Washington so quickly and had not scheduled any patients. After seeing a couple of walk-ins, I called Isaac Levy and asked if he could meet me for lunch. He agreed, and we met at the Dave's Bar-B-Q at noon.

Isaac greeted me with celebrity status. "The infamous Dr. Wright of *Texas v. Wright,*" he said.

"The case that overturned *Roe v. Wade*?" I asked.

"That's what everyone is predicting," he answered.

A waitress came, and we ordered "The Special," a barbeque beef plate with coleslaw and baked beans.

"I need some legal advice," I said. "What's going to happen when the court announces its decision?"

"Well, obviously, it'll be one of two things. If the court rules Texas's HB27 is unconstitutional, then *Roe v. Wade* prevails as established law, and we all go back to our everyday lives."

"And the other alternative?"

"All hell breaks loose."

Isaac's words startled me. I knew that if HB27 prevailed, it would be a big deal. But until that instant—when those four words came from his mouth—I had never felt the full force of how big. Suddenly, the enormity of it gripped me, and I found it difficult to speak. With a shaking hand, I lifted a glass of water to my lips and took a big draw. It helped.

"Are you okay?" Isaac asked, pausing, his expression serious.

"I'm fine." My voice sounded squeaky, high pitched. I cleared my throat and tried a second time. "What I want to know is," I cleared my throat again, "what happens in Texas, and more specifically, what happens to me if the court overturns *Roe v. Wade*?"

"This was your case, so you're probably first in line. They'll arrest you, but if you're lucky you'll be allowed to post bail. The state will immediately take your medical license, and you'll be facing five years in prison for illegal medical practice."

This came as no surprise. I remembered talking about it months ago when the possibility seemed remote. Today, when circumstances made it appear much more likely—perhaps a certainty—it hit me like a dagger to the heart. I steeled myself and began thinking like a fugitive.

"How much time between the court's announcement and when the consequences come down?"

"Probably not much," Isaac answered.

The waitress brought our food.

Isaac immediately picked up his fork and took a big bite of barbequed beef. I looked at mine with my stomach knotted and felt my appetite evaporate. For the next few moments, Isaac chewed while I tried to calm my nerves.

Isaac continued, apparently oblivious to my discomfort. "The biggest factor in all of this will be the media. I'm guessing that your mug will be plastered on the cover of every newspaper and magazine in the world."

"And the media will come to the Texas Panhandle?"

Isaac set down his fork, leaned back in his seat, and cocked his head as though that was the most stupid question he'd ever heard.

"What do you think?"

71

In the car, driving back to the office

When I'm in the car, driving by myself, I like to keep the radio on. And I've found three local stations that broadcast continuous news—ABC, CBS, and NPR.

The news of the day focused on early voting for the current presidential election. Apparently, a downturn in numbers, reported nationwide, alarmed the political pundits and supplied grist for today's broadcast media.

"In the United States, the period for early voting varies between four and fifty days prior to election day," the commentator said. "In the last presidential election, over 30% of all votes were cast early."

A second commentator, a woman, asked, "With less than two weeks until election day, how do the numbers add up this year?'

"Terrible," the first said. "If we use last election numbers to compute percentages, less than 1% have gone to the poles as of last night. Of course, we still have almost two weeks to go. But even if the numbers double—or even quadruple—we'd only have 4% voting early?"

"Why so much angst? Who cares if people vote early?"

"You're right. We don't care if people vote early or vote on election day. But the early vote is a harbinger of the turnout for the election. If numbers are down for early voting, numbers will also take a nosedive on the day of the election."

"Give me some idea of what the experts are predicting. How big is the drop?"

"In the last election, the United States reported 211,731,000 eligible voters. Of these, 121,745,000 voted, or 57.5%.

"Hey, skip all the minutia," she said. "Give me the bottom line. How bad is this?'

"We may have the next president elected by just fifty million people. That would be less than 25% of all registered voters—the worst since we started keeping records in 1828."

72

The next day, my office, The Medical Arts Building

I called Dr. Gerald Vernon in Juneau, Alaska. As expected, he was with a patient. I left my name and number. Five minutes later he called back. "Gerald Ray, is that you?" I asked.

"Joe, you sonofagun, good to hear your voice," he replied. "How are you?"

"To be honest, I've been better. But Jenny said Susan called. Said you might need another doctor?"

"We're killing ourselves—both of us working day and night. Joe, we're desperate. Can you start tomorrow?"

I chuckled. "Maybe we should talk about this face to face. How about I come to Juneau?"

We talked briefly about a visit to his clinic, about meeting his medical partner, and, most of all, about bringing Jenny for a tour of the city. He wanted me to come immediately. I promised to make arrangements soon, probably in the next week or so. It was interesting that we didn't talk about abortion. Perhaps it didn't matter.

I had barely put down the phone when my head nurse, Virginia, knocked, cracked the door, and stuck her head in my office. "Sheriff Jack Richards is here and wants to talk with you. He says it's important."

Remembering Isaac's words at yesterday's lunch, a chill rippled down my spine. *They'll arrest you, and if you're lucky, you can post bail.* I had a mental picture of being hauled out of the office in handcuffs.

"He also asked if Bretta was available," Virginia added.

"Show him in," I said. "Ask Bretta if she could join us."

I looked at my watch—fifteen minutes behind schedule, patients waiting. We needed to make this quick.

Jack came in with an air of authority and shook my hand. "Finally," he said, "we have a lead."

It took me a second to realize that he was talking about the rape investigation. "That's great news," I answered.

"I'd like Bretta to hear this."

I nodded. "She's coming."

We sat in awkward silence while we waited for Bretta. Jack fiddled with his radio. Then, after a few moments, he broke the mood.

"Saw you on TV," he said. "When are you gonna hear from the Supreme Court?"

"You know as much as I do. Isaac Levy thinks it may be next summer."

Bretta came into the room. Jack and I stood. They embraced.

"I think we have new facts that will break open the case," Jack said.

Bretta and I looked at him, waiting.

"Maybe we should sit to talk about this?" Jack asked.

All three of us took our chairs.

"Do you know Melissa Jorsky?" he asked.

I shook my head.

"I do," Bretta replied. "She's a chemistry major from Dumas. Blonde, a year behind me, she'd be a senior this year."

"Melissa was assaulted last weekend," Jack informed us. "In an incident like the attack on you, three guys grabbed her late at night."

I looked at Bretta. Her face had turned white, and I could see fear in her eyes. She sat rigid in her chair, her hands gripping the arms.

"But they had some bad luck," Jack continued. "After they forced her into their car, they ran a stop sign at the corner of Long Boulevard and 4th Avenue."

I leaned forward in my chair. That intersection was only a few of blocks from the library.

"They ran head-on into a street sweeper, and the driver immediately called police. The bastards ran and left Melissa in the car. Except for the fact that she escaped unharmed, the kidnapping was very similar to Bretta's incident last May. We took Melissa to the Emergency Room, and she's going to be all right.

"Thank God," I said.

Bretta didn't—or couldn't—respond.

"We traced the car to a guy named Oliver Mackenzie and took him into custody. With Melissa's descriptions of the other two, and by asking around campus about Mackenzie's friends, we've identified Frank Underwood and Hector Garcia as the other suspects." Jack turned to Bretta and lowered his voice. "We'd like to see if you could identify them as your attackers."

Bretta reached over and took my hand, squeezing it hard.

"I've been waiting almost six months for the opportunity to do this." she said, her voice strong, clear, and without a trace of hesitancy. "How soon can we do it?"

73

My office, The Medical Arts Building

Bretta agreed to go to the Randall County Jail at five o'clock for a lineup—to see if she could identify the three who had attacked her. I said I would go with her for support. Sheriff Jack Richards thanked us, gave Bretta a parting hug, and left.

"How about I take you to lunch today?" I asked.

"Dad, you don't have to worry about me," Bretta replied. "I can do this."

"And I'd like to invite Isaac Levy to join us."

"I don't need a lawyer."

"I know you don't. But—"

"But you're going to invite him anyway?"

"It won't hurt anything. And it might help." I stood, held out my arms. "Give your old Dad a hug."

We embraced, and I held my daughter tight, aching for her, wishing that these terrible things had not happened. Standing there, holding her, a wave of emotion broke over me—an unfamiliar combination of deep concern and heart-stopping fear. I wanted to protect her from the brutality of testifying, yet it seemed imperative that I not get in the way.

In the firmness of her grasp, I found myself frozen with a vision of Bretta as a much older person. Then, like a bolt of lightning, a flashback of images came roiling through my senses—the small child, the teenager, the young college freshman. And suddenly, somewhere in my subconscious, a feeling compelled me to believe in her resilience, in her ability to cope with these difficult circumstances. It gave me a vision that she would barrel forward like a locomotive, armored with her own momentum, made indestructible by her intense motivation.

I adored her. She was my pride and joy. She had made my life almost unbearably full, euphoric and, at times, miraculously hers. When she eased her grip, we parted, and it came naturally to repeat the gesture that had defined our relationship over the years—I kissed her on the forehead.

"Thanks, Dad," she said.

"You know you're number one."

We locked eyes for a brief moment, and then she glanced at her watch. "You're running thirty minutes behind schedule. Maybe we'd better skip lunch?"

"Let me handle it," I insisted.

I shooed her out and called Isaac. He agreed to meet us at the Burger Barn at 12:30. Then Virginia and I started seeing patients. We rushed through the morning and made it to the restaurant only ten minutes late.

Bretta apologized for us.

"I'm used to it," Isaac replied with a smile of understanding. "Doctors are always late, so I went ahead and ordered for the three of us."

Bretta and I took our chairs as a waitress brought three large, red baskets filled with hamburgers and french fries. I thanked him for going ahead. He asked about Jack Richards and what we knew about the lineup and the guys who had been arrested. I gave him the names and details.

"Oliver Mackenzie's bad news," Isaac said.

"You know him?" Bretta asked, surprised.

"Only by reputation," Isaac replied. "Mackenzie's been in and out of the courts since he was a teenager."

"How old is he now?" I asked.

"Mid-twenties." Isaac turned to Bretta. "How much do you know about rape trials?"

"Nothing," she answered. "But I know the bastards who attacked me. I'll never forget their faces." Her words carried an edge that filled the air between us with an unbridled fury.

Isaac reached over and took her hand. "Good for you."

Bretta teared up. She reached for her purse and a Kleenex.

"Today will be easy," Isaac continued. "You'll be behind a one-way glass, and the police will ask you to pick out the rapists from the lineup of men."

"Just like on TV," Bretta said as she dabbed the moisture from her eyes and cheeks. "I can do it."

"But this is only the beginning," Isaac cautioned. "Later there will be a trial and you'll have to testify."

"Isn't there some way around that?" I asked, my heart thumping.

"Unfortunately, no," Isaac answered. "And that's why lots of rapists get away with it. It's hard on the victim. Many women would rather let the SOBs walk than go through the ignominy of having to testify in open court."

"I want these monsters to get what's coming to them," Bretta said, her voice steeled with anger. "Just tell me what I have to do."

"It won't be easy," Isaac said. "They'll have a lawyer, and he'll cross-examine you about your testimony."

"I'll just tell the truth. I want the whole world to hear what these guys did to me."

"But their lawyer will try to discredit you. He'll say that it was consensual—that you wanted to have sex with them."

"And that I asked for a broken leg, for two dozen cuts that required 163 stitches, and that I wanted to get pregnant by three guys that I didn't know."

Isaac stared at her, his gaze benevolent but serious, then asked. "You're sure you want to do this?"

"Absolutely," Bretta replied. "I couldn't be more sure."

"The lineup's at five o'clock," I said. "Will you come, Isaac?"

"I wouldn't miss it," he replied.

"And will you be with us at the trial?"

"Of course."

The waitress brought our ticket. I grabbed it before Isaac could.

74

Wednesday afternoon, Randall County Jail

The lineup went quickly. Isaac and I stood in the back of the darkened room and watched as Bretta, without hesitation, picked the three rapists. Then we returned to the lobby where we met Melissa Jorsky, the other victim. Bretta and Melissa embraced and had a teary reunion. While they were talking, I spotted Jack Richards and walked him down the hall to a water fountain.

"What'd you think?" I asked Jack, hoping he'd give me a straight answer.

"It went well," he said.

"Can you tell me more?"

He hesitated, and then said, "In separate lineups, both Melissa and Bretta identified the same three suspects. We couldn't ask for better."

"That's good to hear," I replied, relieved. We had to depend on Jack to make the case. But if he was pleased, then that was good news.

"Joe, we need to be careful with this information," Jack warned. "If the media get it, the publicity might give the defense an angle they could use at the trial."

"May I tell my family?"

"Only if you're sure they won't blab."

I nodded. "I'll swear them to secrecy. And you know our main concern is for Bretta. We won't do anything to jeopardize your opportunity to nail these guys."

"I told you we'd get 'em," he said, a look of unmistakable pride in his face.

"And you did."

We shook hands, and he walked on toward the jail. I went back to the lobby and found Isaac and Bretta. We said our goodbyes, and Isaac left. As Bretta and I drove home, she called her mother to say that we were on the way.

After a brief conversation, Bretta handed the phone to me. "Mom wants to talk with you,"

"Finally," I said, "we have some good news."

"Let's make dinner a family celebration," Jenny said.

"How about I stop by the liquor store and pick up a bottle of Dom Perignon?"

Jenny laughed. "That'll go great with my tuna noodle casserole."

So, a few minutes later, we gathered in the kitchen and, with our best wine glasses, the Wright family circled to toast the good news. Bent—still a month shy of his eighteenth birthday—had a glass filled with 7-Up. But he joined us in the spirit of festivity And it felt good, really good, to have something to celebrate. As I sipped the expensive Champagne, I hoped our troubles would take a turn for the better, and we'd find a way to put this all behind us—to get on with our lives. But while we were waiting for dinner, we made a mistake—we watched the evening news. And the lead story delivered a bombshell that shook our family to the core. The newscaster said, "The United States Supreme Court gave a date for their decision on *Texas v. Wright.*"

It would be released on Friday, October 31.

Standing there in front of the television, I counted—

Today was Wednesday, October 29. That meant the release date was just two days, maybe less than forty-eight hours away.

Everyone, and I mean *everyone*, had predicted the court would not render their decision for many months, probably not until June. Suddenly, our future in Texas appeared to be, at best, a very short time.

"Joe, what'll we do?" Jenny asked.

"Let's have dinner, and then I'll call Gerald Vernon," I said.

So, with an ominous cloud of uncertainty hanging over us, we closed ranks as a family.

We toasted the good news.

We discussed the bad.

Bretta and Brent took it all with surprising maturity. The possibility that their father might go immediately to another state was just a fact of life—something they would have to adjust to.

Jenny tried to make a joke of it. "If you move to Alaska, does this mean I'll get a fur coat for Christmas?" she asked.

"Of course," I said, and I tried to laugh, to support my comment with a chuckle. Unfortunately, my effort failed—miserably. It wasn't a laughing matter.

Going up the stairs to use the phone in our bedroom, I thought about something else. Friday, October 31, was just four days before the election.

I couldn't believe the timing.

75

At home, 1109 Westbrook Terrace

Before I tried to reach Dr. Gerald Vernon, I checked the time. If it was 7:30 in Amarillo, Texas, it would be 4:30 in Juneau, Alaska. I thought it would be a good time to reach him at his clinic. I dialed the number.

A receptionist informed me the doctor was with patient. I left my name and number.

In five minutes, he called back.

"Joe, you Texas buckaroo, when're you coming to Alaska?" he asked.

"How about tomorrow?"

"Really?" His one-word question betrayed his disbelief. "Are you serious?"

"That's not the question," I replied.

"Oh?"

"The question is—how serious are you about adding another doctor to your practice?"

We talked briefly about a visit to his clinic, about meeting his medical partner and staff, about bringing Jenny for a tour of the city—he sounded enthusiastic. I said we'd catch the first flight tomorrow morning. He went into a long spiel about seafood and the four of us going to dinner. Again, we didn't talk about abortion.

So Jenny and I went upstairs to pack. I pulled two suitcases from the closet and set them on the bed.

"Oh, no," Jenny said, "I just remembered."

"Remembered what?" I asked.

"Mother's coming tomorrow. We're supposed to meet her plane at 6:25 tomorrow evening."

"Brent or Bretta can go to the airport," I said. "Katherine loves it when the grandchildren come to meet her."

"Let me go see if they can do it," Jenny said. "If one of them can pick her up, I'll call Mother."

Jenny left the room. I packed. And I thought about how lucky I was to be going to Alaska. Maybe this move to the north wasn't going to be so bad after all. Hunting. Fishing. Fewer visits by Katherine.

Jenny came back. "Bretta said she would meet the plane. She's not so happy about us leaving her to babysit her grandmother."

"But she'll do it?"

"Yes."

"Might be good training for the future."

"How's that?"

"You know, for when she gets a mother-in-law."

"Joe, that is open, blind, unmitigated, utter, absolute, unadulterated . . . prejudice. All mothers-in-law are not difficult.

"Okay, give me an example.

Jenny turned away, obviously thinking.

After fifteen or twenty seconds with no response, I thought I had scored a victory. "See, all mothers-in-law are—"

"How about me?"

"You're not a mother-in-law."

"I will be. When Brent marries, his wife will call me," Jenny paused for effect, "her mother-in-law."

I may be a dumb, ignorant, male, chauvinist pig, but I'm smart enough to know that any response to that example was a no-win situation.

"That's different," I said. Time to bail. I know when I'm licked.

"How is it different?"

"I think I'll pack a lot of clothes," I said. "I may not be coming back to Texas."

"Hey, you're changing the subject," Jenny said. "I want us to settle this mother-in-law thing."

"Did you hear about the pharmacist who was arguing with his customer?" I asked.

Jenny looked at me like I was out in left field. "Where did that come from?"

"The pharmacist—yes or no?"

"No."

"So the pharmacist tells his customer, 'In order to buy arsenic, you need a signed, medical prescription. A picture of your mother-in-law just isn't enough."

Jenny didn't laugh. In fact, she didn't even crack a smile.

Sometimes our humor doesn't seem to follow the same track.

76

Alaska

Early the next morning, we took an American Eagle propjet from Amarillo to DFW, a big American Airlines 777 to Seattle, and a small Alaska Airlines jet to Juneau. Gerald and Susan Vernon met us at the tiny air terminal in Alaska's capitol city. Gerald looked good, just like I remembered him in medical school, but with glasses, a few wrinkles, and a touch of gray.

Susan didn't. The twenty-five years had added at least a hundred pounds, probably more. In fact, I wouldn't have recognized her had she not been with Gerald. But she laughed a lot and gave me a big hug—fat and jolly.

The Vernons dropped us at Juneau's most famous hotel—The Baranoff—and arranged to meet us for dinner in the hotel's dining room at seven-thirty. We all ordered Alaska King Crab. The wives had white wine. Gerald and I ordered the local beer, Alaskan Amber Ale. It was wonderful—delicious food coupled with lots of laughter and stories of medical school.

Jenny and Susan talked about the kids. The Vernons had four, about the same ages as our two, but closer together. Their oldest was now in Texas Tech Medical School, the youngest a senior at Juneau-Douglas High School. And a surprising coincidence, their senior—like our Brent—played trombone in the high school band.

So Jenny told the story about the AHS band parents and their confrontation with Amarillo right-to-life protesters.

"I can see you're really into the pro-choice movement," Susan commented, responding to Jenny's conversation.

Jenny shook her head. "Actually, I'm a member of the Panhandle Crisis Care Center, a pro-life political group."

"Really?" Gerald asked, clearly surprised. Susan seemed a little startled herself. He turned to me. "I heard you did a D&C on your daughter and that started the Supreme Court case."

We spent the next hour trying to untangle the politics, sharing our views and opinions with each other. It pleased me to learn that the Vernons views paralleled mine. Gerald stated that he rarely did abortions and, as far as the citizens of Juneau knew, the clinic was moderately pro-life.

"And what about today's headlines? The big announcement tomorrow?" Susan asked.

"We expect that the court will overturn *Roe v. Wade*," I answered. "Which means that it will uphold Texas's HB27, making it illegal to perform abortions in the state."

"Where does that leave you?" Gerald asked.

"Subject to arrest, loss of my medical license, looking at a five-year prison sentence."

"Good God," he said. "All because you performed a D&C on your daughter after a gang rape?"

I nodded. "That's why we're here in Alaska. I'm trying to figure out how best to negotiate a future for Jenny and me."

Gerald smiled, lifted his glass of beer. "Here's to HB27, Texas's loss, Alaska's gain." The four of us clinked our glasses and took a sip. As I joined in the toast, a disturbing uneasiness settled over me.

"What do you think the effect will be if I join your medical practice?" I asked. "What if a bunch of pro-lifers organize a demonstration against your clinic?"

"No way," he replied. "Our community image is that we don't do abortions."

"But that impression could change if you add an infamous abortion doctor to your staff."

Gerald leaned forward, hands together, elbows on the table, and lowered his voice. "How many abortions do you *plan* to do?"

"Zero," I replied. "Same as I *planned* to do in Texas."

He relaxed back into his chair. "Just like my partner and me. But if we think one is needed, we do it quietly."

"Safe, legal, and rare?" I asked.

"We don't quote Bill Clinton in this state," Susan said.

"But that happens to be our view and our practice," Gerald added.

"Suppose I join your clinic and the pro-lifers start demonstrating against you?" I asked.

"No way," he replied. "This is Alaska, the state where everything is laid back. Way back."

"But *what if*?" I persisted.

"Hey, we've got too many patients now. Might be a good thing if we had demonstrations and they drove away a few. But it's a moot point. I still don't think that will happen."

We finished dinner, paid the tab, and walked to the lobby. Conversation returned to politics.

"What about Reginald McCormack?" I asked. "How's he doing in Alaska?"

Gerald and Susan laughed.

"Why is that funny?" Jenny asked.

"Alaska is mostly voting Republican these days," Susan replied. "And we have a fairly strong Democratic minority. But I hardly ever hear of anyone who is thinking about voting for an independent. McCormack isn't even a blip on the radar."

I felt a light elbow jab in my ribs and turned to see Jenny smiling ear to ear.

We said our goodnights. The next day I'd go with Gerald to the clinic, and Susan would pick up Jenny for a tour of Juneau.

On the way up in the elevator, my wife had an interesting question.

"I wonder what effect the Supreme Court's announcement will have on Reggie's campaign."

"I couldn't care less," I said.

It was a remark I would live to regret.

77

Juneau, Alaska

Gerald Vernon picked me up at 7:15 a.m. It surprised me to learn he'd already been to the hospital and made rounds. "Aren't you getting a little old for this kind of grind?" I asked. "Only a little past seven and you've finished with hospital rounds?"

"Just a normal day," he replied. "We have to open the clinic and start seeing patients at eight o'clock or we'll be stuck there into the night."

"Sounds like you have quite a thriving practice."

"Yeah, we're victims of our own success." Then he proceeded to give me a running commentary about his clinic, about starting early and working late, not having time for golf, for vacations, for Christmas, for family.

I thought about what I was getting into, *about* the money—which would be good—*about* the circumstances that made it difficult to recruit doctors to Alaska, *about* the culture shock of moving my family to one of the most remote parts of the country. But what choice did I have? We couldn't stay in Texas. One fact loomed as more and more important—I was lucky to have a friend like Gerald Vernon.

We arrived at his clinic and parked in back. I checked my watch and noted it was only 7:30 a.m. when we walked in the back door. The red brick building was beautifully furnished and busy. Gerald introduced me to his partner and members of the staff. When he indicated that I might be joining them as a new doctor, everyone reacted the same—a big smile and a warm welcome.

If anyone had heard of *Texas v. Wright*, they didn't connect me with the news.

By eight o'clock their medical practice was in full swing. I peeked out into the patients' waiting room and found it full. A TV for patient viewing blared away with CNN. After watching for a moment, I learned that the Supreme Court would announce their ruling at two o'clock eastern time—nine o'clock Alaska time—less than an hour from now.

This could be a place to come and learn my fate.

For the next hour I toured the facility. Throughout it bustled with activity—much busier than our clinic in Amarillo. I thought it an impressive, smoothly run operation and ended up back in Gerald's office.

He stuck his head in the door. "How about consulting on a case?" he asked.

"Sure," I replied. "What'cha got?"

"A fisherman with extreme facial pain."

I followed Gerald to an examination room and he introduced me to his patient. "This is Fred Reynolds, age fifty-seven. Fred, I'd like you to describe your symptoms to Dr. Wright."

Fred ran his hand along the left side of his face. "Hurts like hell," he said. "I've been to two dentists and an oral surgeon. One of the dentists drilled a tooth to see if there was a cavity. The oral surgeon called it TMJ syndrome."

"Do you know what that is, Fred?" Gerald asked.

"Well, sorta," Fred affirmed.

"Temporal-Mandibular Joint," Gerald replied. "Where the lower jaw connects to the skull, the temporal bone. TMJ syndrome is widely recognized as the cause of head and neck pain."

"Okay if I touch your jaw?" I asked.

Fred nodded.

I placed my hand along his lower jaw and ran it back to a point under his ear. "The pain is only on the left side?"

"Yes, Doctor," Fred answered.

"Since there is no pain from the TMJ on the right side, I think it unlikely that it's related to the joint." I turned to Gerald. "Did you notice the swelling in the neck under the left jaw?"

Gerald ran his hand along the jaw, as I had done, and then repeated my examination under the ear. "You're right. There is a slight swelling."

"Do you remember Tic Doloreoux?" I asked.

Gerald smiled. "The anatomy quiz with a question on nerve root causes—our second year in medical school?"

"Yeah. Everyone in our class missed it. And we sent a petition to the dean, complaining that our professor, old Whatzisname, was unfair because he included a question about obscure French neuralgia."

"Joe, you sonuvagun, how do you remember stuff like that?"

"I had a case, just one, in Amarillo. I treated it like Shingles."

Gerald turned back to his patient. "Fred, I'm going to give you a prescription for Zynoxin. It's a salve for nerve inflammation and should get rid of that pain." He scribbled out the prescription on a notepad, tore it off, and handed it to his patient.

Fred beamed. "Thank you, Doctor," he said. Then he looked at me.

"Will there be any extra charge for the consultation?"

"No," I replied with a smile. "Your insurance with Dr. Vernon will cover it."

After Fred left, Gerald started an embarrassing shower of praise about my diagnosis, about how they needed to add an experienced doctor to their clinic.

I looked at my watch—it was 8:55.

"I'd like to catch the nine o'clock news," I interjected. "CNN is supposed to announce the Supreme Court decision."

"Sure," Gerald replied. "There's a small TV in my office."

We walked the short distance to his room, and he closed the door.

"This will be a big deal if they overturn *Roe v. Wade*," Gerald said.

"No *if* about it," I replied. "It'll be a *very* big deal. I predict a six to three decision. I was there and heard the presentation of the case."

"Really?"

"Galesburg, Kennison, and Bayer will vote to continue the status quo. They're well known for their pro-choice views and support of *Roe v. Wade* as settled law."

"Go on."

"But Thompson, Scully, and South will vote to overturn. You could tell from their questions and discussions that they haven't changed their pro-life positions."

"Who does that leave?"

"The three new justices—Robertson, Alto, and Jones," I replied.

"Evelyn Jones is from Texas," Gerald said. "Everyone knows about her pro-life viewpoint. What have you heard about Robertson and Alto?"

"Both were appointed by a Republican president. Everyone expects they will vote to overturn. However, they've been very quiet, so nothing's for certain."

"You think this could go the other way?"

"There's a chance."

The television interrupted our conversation. CNN switched to their coverage of the Supreme Court. A reporter named Rolf Brewster stood on the steps on the east side of the famous building, holding a bulletin. "We have the announcement," he said. "It's a six-to-three vote."

Gerald nudged me. "Guess you were right."

Brewster continued. "The majority opinion was written by Evelyn Jones."

"It figures," I said.

The newsman looked up at the camera. "Just a minute. I want to re-read this." He studied the announcement, a look of consternation clearly showing on his face.

"Come on," I said. "Quit stalling."

"The vote is six to three to *uphold* Roe v. Wade."

78

Gerald Vernon's office, The Juneau Family Medical Clinic

The Supreme Court ruling seemed to have stunned Rolf Brewster. The TV's sound stopped as Brewster clasped one hand over his ear. He looked away from the camera, down at the paper in his hand, argued with someone, then lifted the bulletin, and faced the camera squarely.

"I'll read this word for word," he said, his voice loud and his face steeled with determination. "The United States Supreme Court," he paused, "in a majority opinion written by Justice Evelyn Jones," again he paused, "voted six to three to uphold *Roe v. Wade*. I repeat, the press release clearly uses the word 'Uphold.' This means the Court has ruled as unconstitutional a Texas statute known as House Bill 27, and that, in the recent contentious case titled *Texas v. Wright*, the court has approved Dr. Joseph Wright's appeal."

Brewster eyed the camera, apparently taking instructions through his earpiece.

"We'll be back in a moment," he said.

As a commercial for hemorrhoids filled the screen, the phone on Gerald's desk rang. He answered, turned to me, and said, "It's for you—Isaac Levy."

When I put the receiver to my ear, I heard a flood of incomprehensible gibberish. This didn't surprise me, because I had now come to expect Isaac's excitable nature. He kept repeating the word "won."

"Won . . . holy crap . . . Terry won . . . we did it . . . we won . . . can't believe . . . Joe, you won . . . Goddamned miracle . . . won."

"Stop," I said loudly.

He rattled on with more variations of "won."

"Isaac," I shouted, trying to get a word in edgewise.

He continued, unabated.

"I'm going to hang up," I warned.

That did it. He stopped.

"Congratulations," I said, doing my best to control the rush that surged through me.

"Terry did it, not me," Isaac countered.

"Hey, I'm the one who didn't want her," I said. "You picked her. You coached her. It was your strategy that pulled this off."

He paused.

And I enjoyed a moment of delicious silence.

Isaac broke the quiet. "Ain't it grand?"

"Something must have happened with Evelyn Jones," I replied.

"She's agreed to an interview on PBS tonight. Hopefully, we'll find out what turned the tide."

"That'll be a blockbuster, and I hate to miss it, but Jenny and I are flying home."

"I'll record it for you," he answered. "How about coffee tomorrow morning at the Donut Shop? Eight o'clock?"

"Eight?"

"We've got a lot to talk about." Isaac hung up.

Gerald and I exchanged our goodbyes. He said a few cuss words when I told him we wouldn't be moving from Texas. But he had patients waiting, so Susan drove Jenny and me to the airport. We went standby to Seattle, first class to DFW, and then found regular seats on a half-empty propjet to Amarillo. It was almost midnight when we pulled into the garage at home.

Surprise. Bretta, Brent, and Katherine had stayed up to greet us.

"We're not moving to Alaska," I assured them.

"But I was thinking about enrolling at the University of Alaska next year," Brent said.

"And I was looking forward to moving away from all this controversy," Bretta added.

"I knew you weren't," Katherine said. "Alaska would be like living in a wilderness. Texas is far enough from civilization."

I motioned for my family to come close. We circled up with our arms around each other. "It's a free country," I replied. "Brent, you can go to any college or university you want. And Bretta, why not reconsider your thinking about Juilliard?"

"Let's talk about this in the morning," Katherine said, stifling a huge yawn.

I turned to my kids and gave each another hug. "Did either of you watch the Evelyn Jones interview on PBS?"

"We all did," Bretta said. "She gave a personal interview with a woman reporter named Margaret Warmer. And we recorded it for you."

"Dad, Evelyn Jones sounds just like you," Brent said. "She's against abortion on demand, but she insists that any new law regulating abortions must make provision for the health of the mother."

"Amen," I said. "And I guess I'll have to take back all those criticisms of her bias."

"But that's not all," Bretta continued. "In another news segment Jim Lowher reported that Evelyn Jones felt so strongly about this, she convinced Robertson and Alto to vote with her. That's where the six-to-three vote came from."

"Good for her," I said. "God bless Evelyn Jones and the Star Spangled Banner."

Bretta turned and saw the emotion I couldn't hide, "My God, Dad, you're crying."

"Good night, all," Katherine said. She turned and went upstairs.

Brent started doing "high fives," and we followed him around in circles. Then Bretta wanted to do hugs, so we did hugs all around, again.

Finally, Jenny picked up her suitcase and started up the stairs. "You three will have to sing "God Bless America" without me. I'm going to bed.

Brent and Bretta went to their bedrooms with the biggest smiles I'd seen in many months.

I carried the rest of the suitcases up to our bedroom, slipped into my pajamas, and fell into bed, exhausted.

But I couldn't sleep.

So I went back downstairs to the liquor cabinet, poured myself a double scotch, and turned on the TV recording of Evelyn Jones and her PBS interview.

79

1109 Westbrook Terrace

I frequently watch the PBS news, and as the recording started, I recognized the set and the reporter, Margaret Warmer. The interview started like a hundred others. "You're a renown jurist with a history of pro-life views," Warmer said.

"Yes, I consider myself pro-life," Evelyn Jones replied. "I'm very much against abortion on demand."

"Last August, when the Senate held hearings for your appointment, political pundits were extolling your nomination because it seemed so predictable that, if given an opportunity, you would vote to overturn *Roe v. Wade.*"

"Yes, that's true."

"Correct me if I'm wrong, but didn't *Texas v. Wright* give you that opportunity?"

"Almost." Evelyn Jones shifted in her seat.

"Am I missing something? Please, explain."

Justice Jones told a heavy story—her niece had been raped in an incident like Bretta's. It amazed me to hear her describe the trauma—of a young woman who had become pregnant by a gang-rape, of the emotional distress her niece had faced as a prisoner of her biology.

"The rape itself was hideous, so repulsive she may never recover. The prospect of having to endure the resulting pregnancy came as such a repugnant factor, I think it would have destroyed her."

"Health of the mother?" Warmer asked.

"Absolutely," Jones replied. "Any new legislation must consider it. Texas's House Bill 27 failed because it did not."

"Everyone thought Alto and Robertson would vote the other way."

"They play their cards close to the vest. No one really knew how they would come down on this issue."

"I've heard that you were the one who convinced them."

Jones smiled, knowingly. "You give me too much credit."

"But, they selected you to write the opinion."

"Yes, quite an honor."

Margaret Warmer's gaze dropped down to her notes for a moment. When she looked up, she said, "We have less than a minute. Could you speculate briefly about where this issue will go from here?"

Evelyn Jones shook her head. "I don't know, and I don't think anyone does. The country is confused by all the recent publicity. Last summer, at the time of my appointment, I thought *Roe v. Wade* would be overturned, that it was only a matter of time. Now I don't know. Some of my colleagues, other justices, have talked with me about the difficulty of defining 'health of the mother.' Personally, I think it *can* be defined. I think it *must* be."

"Thank you for taking the time for this interview," Warmer said. "And especially, thank you for your candor."

"We owe it to Bretta Wright, the young woman whose ordeal brought this case to the court. My heart goes out to her."

"Mine, too," replied Warmer.

I shivered—involuntary, tiny, emotional ripples that gripped my physical self and caused me to swell with emotion. In my lifetime I've felt elation and pride for my daughter, but never more than at that moment.

Part VII

NOVEMBER

80

Saturday morning, November 1st

The damned alarm woke me at seven-thirty. I showered, shaved, and cursed Isaac for scheduling an early morning meeting on a Saturday. But I dressed, got in the car, and backed out of the garage with the car radio tuned to NPR.

Surprise.

NPR's Scott Simpson was interviewing someone—a representative of a polling service—about me. He mentioned my name just as I pushed the remote button for the garage door opener. It's not often one hears your own name on a national news broadcast. I stopped to listen.

"How important do you think this case, this decision—*Texas v. Joseph Wright*—will become?" Simpson asked.

"It's already big," the guest replied. "And it's going to get bigger. Some of my colleagues are already calling it 'top ten,' one of the ten most famous decisions in Supreme Court history."

"As big as *Roe v. Wade*?"

"*Roe v. Wade* is generally regarded as number one, the most widely known case. And if the decision on *Texas v. Wright* had gone the other way, if the court had allowed it to overturn *Roe v. Wade*, then it would, most likely, have become the number one case."

"A big, big story—" Simpson continued.

"But there's another—a parallel story—that is even bigger," the guest said.

"The election?"

"The *size* of the vote in the forthcoming election." He paused. "The size."

"The size?"

"Everything points to a new record—the lowest percentage of registered voters, ever."

"Yeah, we've been reporting that for several weeks. Early voting is down, way down."

"That's old news," the guest said. "That was before yesterday's decision on *Texas v. Wright*."

I looked at my watch. I could see I was going to be late for my meeting with Isaac. I decided to drive and listen. I backed out of the driveway, turned and headed toward the Donut Stop.

"Okay, what's the *new* news?" Simpson asked.

"Three things," he answered. "Confusion, apathy, and the independent candidate."

"Maybe we should take these one at a time," Scott Simpson said. "We've always had apathy—let's start with that."

"In the last presidential election, the United States had 211,731,000 registered voters. Of these, only 121,745,000 voted, or 57.5%. Political writers called this voter apathy because, when compared to other countries, America was near the bottom."

"Can you give me a few comparables?"

"You know the old joke about statistics? We have, in ascending order, three levels: lies, damn lies, and statistics."

Simpson laughed, and I did, too.

The guest continued. "There's some truth to that old saw, because you have to be careful when you use comparable numbers. You have to delineate the basis for the comparison."

"Okay," Simpson said. "Do you have some carefully drawn, accurate examples?"

"Yes. In the most recent elections, when voting for the country's chief executive, the percentage of registered voters who voted was 90% in Italy, 85% in Germany, 80% in Israel, 76% in the U.K., 74% in Canada. Is that enough? I could go on."

"No. I think our listeners get the message. Our 57% looks pathetic by comparison."

"And some pollsters think, next Tuesday, it may only be half that number."

"Half?"

"Suppose only 25% of registered voters turn out for this year's presidential election?"

"Surely not." Scott Simpson sounded appalled.

"That's the number I am predicting," the guest said. "And I think most of those who go to the polls—over half of this year's record, miniscule, voter turnout—will cast their ballot for McCormack."

"Wow," Scott Simpson exclaimed.

"Big story," the guest said.

"So big, it takes your breath away," Simpson replied. "But you said three things. We've talked about apathy and McCormack. Was the third topic 'confusion'?"

"The Supreme Court should have waited to announce their decision on *Texas v. Wright*. Their announcement on Friday, just five days before a presidential election, has created massive voter confusion."

"You think the fact, that the court did not overturn *Roe v. Wade*, discourages voting?"

"Yes and no," the guest replied. "No, McCormack voters are not discouraged. In fact, he is using the Supreme Court decision to motivate his followers. He's using it very effectively with the extreme right—to get them to the voting booth and support him. But that's the *minority*. Just the opposite for the majority, that big silent *majority* we hear so much about. Yes, they are confused about the *Texas v. Wright* decision. And, yes, *confusion* discourages voting."

"You said earlier that McCormack's people were already highly motivated to vote."

"That's true, but with America's voter apathy—we just went over the percentages—you can never have enough motivation for getting people to the voting booth."

Yes for some, no for others. That was enough for me. I killed the engine—which turned off the radio—and went inside The Donut Shop looking for Isaac.

81

The Donut Shop, Amarillo, Texas

It was a few minutes after eight o'clock when I found my lawyer, brimming with enthusiasm, seated at a table by the window with coffee and donuts for us both. "You sonofabitch," I growled, plopping into the booth opposite him, "why couldn't we be doing this at noon?"

Isaac chuckled and came back with a question of his own. "Have you checked any broadcast media or looked at any morning headlines?"

I settled in, took a bite of donut, and nodded my head. "A little. I had the car radio tuned to NPR on the drive from my house."

"You're the man of the hour. CNN called you the winner in the biggest David and Goliath story since the Bible."

"Good for them. But NPR talked more about the likelihood of a small turnout in next Tuesday's election."

"You don't get it, do you?"

"Get what?"

"The two are related. The two biggest stories of the day are inexorably intertwined."

"Well, golly, gee whiz, I don't really care."

"You're famous, Joe. Everyone wants to interview you."

"Fine. Have them call me on Monday, after I've had a good night's sleep."

Isaac laughed—a big Texas cackle.

"Isaac, for Christ's sake, you're embarrassing me," I told him when he kept laughing.

Finally, he quit and then, with a serious face, he switched on his lawyer persona and started giving me advice. "I think you should pick one network for an interview and insist they share with the others."

"Whatever you say." I took another bite.

"How about PBS?"

"Sure," I said. "I love PBS. Jim Lowher is my favorite newscaster."

He pulled out a card filled with phone numbers and dialed one on his cell phone. I listened as he introduced himself as my lawyer and representative. The conversation went on and on, much longer than I thought necessary. I went to the counter, purchased two more donuts, and refilled our coffee cups.

When I returned Isaac punched off and gave me a big smile. "You're on."

"On? On what?"

"A reporter, probably Judy Woodruff, will interview you on the *PBS News Hour*. They said you can do it as a remote from Amarillo."

"When?"

"Monday."

Isaac chomped down on another donut. I sipped my hot coffee.

A thousand thoughts raced through my mind. What to say? What questions would they ask? How should I prepare?

A light rain was falling as I walked to my car. Someone honked. I looked up to see one of my patients pulling into the parking lot. She smiled and gave me a "thumbs up."

As I reached out to open my car door, I heard another horn. It was a high school kid, one of Brent's friends from the trombone section. He stopped, rolled down his window, and yelled. "Hey, Dr. Wright." He smiled, a big mouthful of white. "Way to go!"

82

Saturday morning at home, 1109 Westbrook Terrace

The phone rang off the wall. At first, I thought the whole experience exhilarating. Call after call of good will, best wishes, heartening encouragement, and congratulations. The hospital called to tell me they had reinstated my privileges. Sheriff Jack Richards asked if there was anything his office could do to help me. Nurse Elsa Jennings called to say she was returning to duty in the ER.

It was all good news.

But after a while, the celebrity got old and I asked Jenny to take over. She answered a couple, but then Isaac called. "It's your lawyer," Jenny said, handing me the phone.

"Isaac, what's up?" I asked.

"Are you sitting down?"

"Uh oh. What's up?"

"If you've got a chair handy, I suggest you take it. I've got some news that's gonna knock your socks off."

I sat. "Okay. I'm sitting."

"PBS has changed their mind," he said.

"That's fine," I answered, assuming they wanted to cancel the interview. "That'll save me a trip to the TV station."

"No," Isaac continued. "They want to schedule a special—a thirty-minute interview with you and Jim Lowher."

"Really?" My heart began pounding. Jim Lowher? This sounded like big stuff.

"Yep. They want to do it primetime, Sunday evening."

Nearly speechless, I barely managed, "What do you think I should do?"

"I've already told them you'd do it."

"Isaac, damn it. I wish you'd ask me first before committing—"

"Hell, you know you'll do it. This is a big deal. No way you could pass this up."

I didn't know what to say. Thirty minutes on national television seemed like an eternity. I couldn't imagine what Lowher could ask to fill that much time. Then a hollowness in my chest made it difficult to breathe as I thought about sitting under hot lights, cameras rolling, and me . . . speechless. Just like I was now.

The silence became too awkward for Isaac. "Joe?" he asked. "You still there?"

"Yeah, I'm here." I took a slow deep breath. "But I can't do this. You'll have to call them back and decline."

"Hold on, Joe. Let's not do something you'll regret."

"Isaac, I'm telling you, I don't want to do it. There's no reason for me to do it."

"Yes there is. Have you been listening to the news?" Isaac asked.

"No, I've been on the phone."

"The Roper Poll has just released their latest results. They predict that McCormack is going to win."

"So?" I said. "That has nothing to do with me."

"Wrong. Roper's Poll says the reason McCormack's numbers are surging ahead is because of you."

"Me? How could that be?"

"Backlash."

"No."

"Yes," Isaac countered. "Roper's data indicate that the Supreme Court's decision has energized the pro-life movement and that McCormack's supporters are going to carry the election. McCormack's using you as his battle cry, and he even has a new campaign slogan."

I had a sinking feeling in the pit of my stomach.

"You want to hear it?"

I didn't. But no matter, Isaac was hell bent on giving it to me anyway.

"The Wright decision was the wrong decision. Vote for the *right* candidate—vote McCormack and let me correct it."

83

Saturday evening, my home, 1109 Westbrook Terrace

Isaac came to the house. Jenny invited him to have dinner with Bretta, Brent, and me. The five of us were digging into Jenny's lasagna when Isaac's cellphone rang. He left the table for a long time, but we could hear him in the hallway—his side of the conversation bubbling with enthusiasm. When he came back to the table, he wore an ear-to-ear smile.

"That was CNN," he said.

"And what did they want?" I asked.

"And they want to carry your interview with Jim Lowher."

"Good God, I hope you told them the interview was off."

"Not exactly."

I can smell a rat. Jenny says I have a sixth sense that gives me ability to do it better than anyone she's ever known. Isaac wouldn't look at me—a dead giveaway that he was hedging on my demand to back out of the interview.

"Give me the PBS number," I demanded. "I'll call them."

"And CNN?" Isaac asked, his face a glowing, mischievous, ear-to-ear grin.

"Hell, yes," I growled. "Give me both numbers."

He handed me a three-by-five card filled with phone numbers. "I've also got Reggie McCormack's number. You want it, too?"

"Don't be absurd," I answered. "Why would I call McCormack?"

"To congratulate him. To tell him you're handing him the election."

"Isaac, I'm not going to let you lay a guilt trip on me. First, I think you're wrong. Dead wrong. Nobody gives a rat's ass what I think about this election. And second, I don't care about McCormack. Have you ever heard the term *laissez-faire*? For Christ's sake, you should know by now—I'm neutral."

Isaac's cell phone rang. He looked at the caller ID. "Excuse me," he said and walked out to the hallway again.

"Dad, Mr. Levy might be right," Bretta said. "Maybe you should try to explain to people how our family has had to deal with all of this."

"That's not what Isaac has in mind though, Bretta."

"What does he want, then?" Jenny asked.

"He wants me to take sides in the abortion debate," I said.

"He's pro-choice?" Brent asked.

I thought about it and realized that I'd never heard Isaac express his personal opinions on the abortion issue one way or the other. "Sorta," I answered. "He defended me, so at least I assume so."

"But you always deny that you're pro-choice," Brent said.

"That's right. I am *not* pro-choice."

"All the more reason to go on TV tomorrow night and correct the impression that you are," Brent argued.

I sighed. This was a seventeen-year-old who was challenging my politics. "It's not quite that simple," I said. And as the words came out of my mouth, I felt as though I was backing myself into a corner.

Isaac returned to his seat at the table. "Big news," he said. "That was the producer for PBS's *News Hour.*"

"Did you tell him I'm backing out?" I asked.

"No."

Now at the end of my patience, I exploded. "God damn it, why not?"

"Joe, what about our agreement not to use profanity in front of the children?" Jenny piped in lightly.

"Well golly, gee-whiz, I think this may be a darn exception."

Bretta and Brent laughed.

Jenny rose from her chair, came around to my side of the table, leaned down, and kissed me. "No exceptions," she scolded.

Isaac chuckled. "I think Joe's right. This news merits an exception."

Jenny stood beside me, her hand on my shoulder. "Okay, tell us your *exceptional* news."

"First you have to recognize, it comes from the top, the chief of PBS broadcasting." Isaac stopped, looked around the table, and made eye contact with each of us.

"Quit stalling," I groused. "Tell us."

Isaac smiled, a twinkle in his eye. And I remembered the look. It was the same egotistical smirk I had seen last August when he'd confronted the principal at Texland Elementary over Bretta's teaching position. Like a poker player who held the winning hand, he was stringing us along, deliberately holding back information that he knew would carry the day.

"I don't care what PBS says or does," I repeated. "I'm not going on national television and make an ass of myself."

"The news is that ABC, CBS, Fox, and NBC also want to carry the interview," Isaac said.

"Wow," Brent said, obviously impressed.

A moment of silence fell over our kitchen.

Isaac's cell phone chirped.

This time he took the call at the table. "Hello," he said.

The four of us stared at Isaac and listened.

"Really?" Isaac yelped, his face reflecting surprise.

We waited.

"Good," he said. "That'll help."

I shook my head with an increasing realization that, as the stakes grew, I held the losing hand.

"Okay, I'll tell him. Two o'clock at the KACV studio." Isaac punched off.

"So what now?" Jenny asked, and I could see she was practically holding her breath.

"The NFL has agreed to delay Sunday Night Football for thirty minutes."

"Double wow," Brent shouted.

"And Jim Lowher is flying to Amarillo tomorrow morning," Isaac continued. "He wants to do the interview in person."

The room came alive with conversation. Isaac, Brent, and Jenny all talking at the same time. Jenny went back to her chair, excitedly expressing her views about tomorrow.

Only Bretta and I sat quietly—our eyes locked. Then she stood, came around the table, and sat on my lap.

Bretta put her arms around me and kissed me on the forehead. "Dad, do this for me." Then she held me tight. "Please."

84

The next morning at home, 1109 Westbrook Terrace

In my pajamas, robe, and slippers, I went out to get the Sunday morning paper and found a media circus gathered on the street in front of our house. Amarillo PD had sent two police cruisers. Even Jack Richards, in his sheriff's uniform, was there. He picked up my newspaper and handed it to me.

"Morning, Joe," he said, greeting me with his usual smile.

Taking the newspaper, I glanced around, embarrassed to be caught in my PJs. A barrage of camera flashes went off as I said, "Jack, what are you doing here?"

"Yeah, that's what the Amarillo cops have been asking. But I thought maybe some personal protection might be helpful."

"Thanks, but do I really need any special help from law enforcement?"

"You driving to the Amarillo College TV studio?" he asked, changing the subject.

I nodded. "Isaac Levy's picking me up right after lunch. Jenny and the kids are following us in my car."

"I've called the Texas Highway Patrol," he informed me. "We'll provide a police escort."

"Jack, that's not necessary," I objected. Sirens and flashing lights were the last thing I wanted.

"Listen, we can't afford to let anything to happen to you. Whether you like it or not, you're stuck with us."

I could see it wouldn't do any good to argue. We shook hands. "See you about one o'clock." Then I waved to the crowd, and—with television cameras rolling and newspaper strobes flashing—ambled back into the house.

The headlines in the *Amarillo Globe-News* tried to anticipate the details of my interview with Jim Lowher. Just as I had feared, this story was growing to preposterous proportions.

Jenny fixed Belgian waffles, a family tradition for our Sunday morning brunch. And I read every word of every election story in the morning newspaper. Especially, I studied the articles about the pollsters. Apparently, there was now a schism among the three leading political polls. Roper picked McCormack to win—a reaction to the Supreme Court's decision. Gallup foresaw a revolt against the abortion question and that either the Democrats or the Republicans should win. *USA Today* pollsters thought the voters were turned off by all the confusion and would boycott the election. If so, the election was up for grabs and impossible to predict.

I picked at my waffle—taking small bites, trying to make it last—and switched to reading statements from the three leading candidates. The Democrat expressed regret that the Supreme Court had chosen this time to release their *Texas v. Wright* decision. She didn't name me specifically, but the implication was certainly there that I was mostly responsible for the confusion.

The Republican didn't mince words—he blamed my appeal as the cause of all his problems with voter apathy.

Reggie McCormack took a different approach. He welcomed the Supreme Court's timing and the subject of my appeal as good for American politics. He wanted to praise God and to "thank me personally" for bringing the abortion problem into the spotlight. He felt sure it was only a matter of time until *Roe v. Wade* would be overturned, and he looked forward to leading the forces that would bring this about.

After a second reading of all the articles, I could see it was time to shower and get ready for the trip to the TV studio. Under cascading water, my thoughts roiled with possible election outcomes. As the hot water ran out and I turned off the shower, two ideas came to mind that I could discuss in the Lowher interview:

Confusion among the voters.

McCormack's use of religion to bolster his platform.

Jenny had laid out my best suit. She sat on the bed and watched me tie my tie. I noticed that she was wearing her newest and prettiest dress.

"You look nice," I said, meaning it.

"Wait until you see Bretta and Brent," she replied. "They're dressed to the nines."

I finished tying my tie. "I'm having second thoughts about the broadcast," I told her.

Jenny's smile faded. "Honey, there's no way to back out now. This has become a national event."

"No," I said, looking in the mirror and straightening my tie. "That's not what I meant. I'm beginning to think this might be a good thing."

"Really?" The surprise was unmistakable in her voice.

"You've heard the old saw—that a passionate minority wins over a passive majority."

She nodded. "I've heard that all my life."

"Bretta has convinced me it may not be true in this election. She wants me to speak out against the radicals."

"The pro-life extreme right?"

"Yes, and the extreme left—those who want abortion on demand."

"Can you do that?" she asked, flashing me a doubtful look.

The phone rang. Jenny answered.

After a brief exchange, she held out the receiver to me. "It's McCormack. He wants to talk with you."

85

At home 1109 Westbrook Terrace

"Dr. Wright," came the familiar, booming voice.

"Reverend McCormack," I answered. "To what do I owe this honor?"

"Several things. Do you have a few minutes?"

"Yes, a few." I glanced at my watch. "What can I do for you?"

"First, let me congratulate you on winning your case with the Supreme Court. That was quite a victory."

I wondered where this was going, but I had to say something. "Thank you," I mumbled.

"However—" he continued.

Uh oh, here it comes, I thought, and I braced myself.

"Enlightened thinking is that *Roe v. Wade* will be overturned," he continued. "It's only a matter of time, you know."

A hundred responses flashed through my mind—all of them confrontational. I bit my tongue and remained quiet, waiting him out.

"And I'd like to discuss this with you sometime, but right now I have a business matter to present to you." He paused, obviously expecting me to respond.

I didn't. And for a few seconds his words lay between us, waiting for a direction. But as the seconds ticked by, a tension developed with an unmistakable feeling of hostility.

"You still there?" he asked.

"Yes," my one-word answer carrying a negative emotion.

"I'd like to offer you a cabinet position in my administration."

Of all the things McCormack might say to me, I couldn't imagine anything less likely. His offer was so bizarre it floored me.

"Secretary of Health and Human Services," he added. "We need a doctor—a respected and capable person with a medical background—to look after the health of the nation."

"Uh, isn't this a bit premature?" I asked, trying to intimate that he'd not yet been elected.

McCormack laughed, a derisive chuckle. "You've been busy, and I'll bet you haven't read Roper's poll, have you? Let me save you the time. Roper predicts that I'm going to win, so I'm making a few calls this morning to get a head start on naming a cabinet. How about it? Would you take HHS?"

"I . . . I . . . I don't know what to say."

"Don't say anything," McCormack replied, his voice carrying a magnanimous resonance. "Just think about it and about the good you could do by leading the health initiatives of our country."

"But we've been on opposite sides," I countered. "Are you sure you'd want someone in your cabinet who has openly opposed your pro-life rhetoric?"

"I've heard that you're against abortion on demand."

"Yes."

"So am I," he said. "We share common ground. We can start there and build on it."

"And how will we do that?"

"We can join forces. For instance, in this evening's television session with Lowher, you could do wonders if you stress the reasons why you're against abortion on demand."

The light came on. All of a sudden I could see what was behind McCormack's call. The offer of a cabinet position was a bribe—a not-very-subtle offer to win my support for his presidential bid.

"I've got to go," I said. "I'll get back—"

"One last thing, this'll just take a minute," he replied, cutting me off.

I looked at my watch. It was time for Isaac to pick me up for our drive to the TV studio.

"God will forgive us our sins if we seek his forgiveness."

Sometimes McCormack's logic came at me like a curve ball. I had no idea why he would say that. "I agree with you, Rev. McCormack, but I have a feeling you want to make a specific point. What, exactly, do you mean?"

"God will forgive you for taking the life of your grandchild."

"Ah." Now I understood perfectly.

"All you have to do is ask."

"And you'd like me to do that as a part of the interview this evening?"

"I pray on television all the time," he said in his most conciliatory tone.

"Reverand McCormack, people are waiting on me."

"Dr. Wright, it's been pleasant talking with you. Just think about what we've discussed, and I'll get back to you right after the election."

I said goodbye hung up.

"What did he want?" Jenny asked, her expression telling me she was dying to know.

"When I tell you, you won't believe it," I replied and headed down the stairs.

"Try me," she pleaded as she followed along, a couple of steps behind.

We reached the entry. I kissed her and pulled open the door to find Isaac sitting in his car with the motor running and the police escort waiting.

86

In Isaac's car, driving to the television studio

Amarillo's PBS station, KACV-TV, is located on the campus of Amarillo College. I've made the drive from my home to the Washington Street site hundreds of times. Driving the speed limit, it usually takes fifteen to twenty minutes. I had counted on this traveling time to consult with Isaac—to get his help in preparing for the interview.

But a police escort makes a difference. A big difference. We didn't stop for red lights, other traffic moved out of our way, and it immediately became apparent there would be precious little time for the two of us to confer. If I told Isaac about McCormack's call, I knew it would dominate our conversation. I decided not to bring it up.

"What are your ideas about the interview?" I asked.

Isaac pointed to a packet with my name on it, lying on the console between our seats. "E-mail from PBS," he said.

He drove. I opened the manila envelope.

The PBS staff had prepared three pages of briefing: (1) Overview, (2) What makes good television, and (3) Suggested questions.

I skipped to the questions and read with concentration. All were numbered, and each had a rating scale for me to indicate my interest as high, moderate, or low. While we followed the Texas Highway Patrol troopers across town, I quickly scanned the material. At the end they asked me to "star" three questions that I thought would make a good opening. PBS would choose one as a "First Question" to start the interview. Then I discovered a fourth page filled only with blank lines and a heading marked "Additional Questions." I hurriedly added one I wanted to discuss: "What would you like to see implemented that would help Americans resolve the abortion debate?"

I went back and looked over the first two pages.

The "Overview" gave the producers' reasons for broadcasting the interview and what they wanted to accomplish. While there was nothing new or unexpected, I found it helpful to see their goals spelled out. It was reassuring that their objectives paralleled mine.

"Good Television" read like a page from the textbook for Television 101. "Avoid long answers. Look at Lowher, not the camera. Don't use clichés. Speak slowly and clearly. Try to avoid ehs and ahs."

When our car slowed, I looked out the window and saw that we were arriving on campus. "I take it you've studied these pages?" I asked.

Isaac nodded. "And helped write them."

"Any suggestions for me?"

"Knock 'em dead."

I smiled. "And how do you propose I do that?"

"You've read the page on good television?"

"I hurriedly scanned it."

"Try to follow those suggestions."

"But what about the meat of the message? What do you suggest?"

Isaac followed the trooper into a parking lot. An Amarillo College policeman indicated a reserved space near the studio's front door. Isaac parked and killed the motor. He turned to me, his expression the most serious I'd ever seen from my friend.

"Joe, I can't help you there. Through a quirk of circumstances, you've been handed a rare opportunity to influence history. People are interested in you, your family, and your innermost thoughts. They want to know where you stand on one of the most controversial topics of our time. The only advice I can give is—whatever you say—it needs to come from the heart."

"Of course," I replied. "Why would you think otherwise?"

"Because I've seen you hold back."

" Isaac, you're being unfair. That's hitting below the belt."

His lips formed a slight smile. It was a small gesture, one I could easily have missed. But in the front seat of Isaac's car, in the emotionally charged discussion about a nationally televised interview, the smile came at me like a warning, alerting me to expect words I wouldn't like.

"As recently as yesterday afternoon," he said, "I remember a guy who didn't want to do this interview. So, no, I think I've made a fair assessment."

He was right. But my immediate response was to defend myself. "That was different," I countered. "I didn't want to do this interview for lots of—what I thought at the time were—very good reasons."

"I call it holding back."

"You remember the Senate hearing for the Jones appointment? And how poorly my testimony compared to McCormack's?"

He nodded.

"That's why I didn't want to do this. I am *not* a public speaker."

"But here you are."

"Yeah. Here I am. Trapped."

"No, not trapped. Not at all. Analyze yourself. Think. What changed your mind."

"Well, for one thing, you kept needling me."

"Bullshit. All my pleading was falling on deaf ears, and you know it."

I took a deep breath and held it for a second while I thought about answering his question. Slowly, as I released air from my lungs with a light hissing sound, it seemed important to verbalize a credible response. One that Isaac could genuinely embrace.

"Bretta," I said. "I couldn't say no to her."

Isaac shrugged. It was clear he acknowledged my answer as *the* moment of truth.

We looked at each other.

Then he nodded. "Someone has to speak for the Brettas of the world. Who better than her father?"

A uniformed policeman rapped on my car window and said, "Dr. Wright? They're waiting for you in Studio A."

87

PBS Station KACV, Amarillo

Filled with anxiety, I entered Amarillo's PBS station. It brought back memories of my last time on national television—the Senate hearing for Evelyn Jones—and my bumbling, amateurish appearance that ended in total failure to block her confirmation. I felt my stomach churn.

All of that changed in ten minutes. The reason was Jim Lowher.

Instead of the confrontational atmosphere of the Senate Caucus Room, of a dais filled with unsmiling faces asking difficult questions—accusatory interrogations designed to frustrate my testimony—I found a courteous, supportive, friendly interviewer, a professional who immediately put me at ease. Jim Lowher was wonderful.

The emotional climate eased with his greeting. He shook my hand, and with a warm smile said, "Let me introduce our people." He led me around the room, and I shook hands with the producer, the director, the camera operators, the sound technicians, the makeup woman, and some

PBS executives whose titles sounded impressive. I introduced Isaac as my lawyer. Lowher suggested we adjourn to a conference room.

"I'd like to be on a first-name basis with you," he said. "May I call you Joe?"

"Yes, Jim, I'd like that," I said and really meant it.

Five of us sat around an oval table with coffee: Lowher with his producer and director on one side, Isaac and I on the other. Isaac and I had our briefing papers. Lowher and the two PBS guys worked from notebooks. The director took charge of the meeting.

"Joe, on behalf of PBS, I want to thank you for giving us this opportunity."

"It's an opportunity for me, too," I said. "Thank you for having me."

"Let's do what we can to help our country," he continued. "I see you have the prep sheets. You've studied our e-mails?"

I explained that I'd only just read them in the car. The director asked about an "opener," and we took five minutes to arrive at a consensus. After we agreed on three choices, and he discussed them with Lowher, he asked about my ideas for additional questions. I gave him my one suggestion, and everyone wrote it down. Lowher thought they should use it as the closing question.

Time passed quickly.

At 4:30 we took a break, and then, at five o'clock assembled in the studio for a run-through. Much like a dress rehearsal, we did the opening and then some random questions. Lowher explained that they didn't want to lose the feeling of spontaneity, so these might not be the exact questions they'd use.

Then we rehearsed the closing. We went through it several times with the producer holding a stopwatch. When he was satisfied, we broke for makeup. I was to be back in my chair at 6:45.

Isaac followed me to my dressing room.

"How'd I do?" I asked.

"I haven't the foggiest," he replied. "I'm just a hick, small-town lawyer."

"And I'm just a little country doctor you hornswoggled into doing this broadcast."

"But I do have an opinion from an expert."

"You do?"

"I asked the producer. He thinks you'll do great."

"Really?"

"Yeah. He especially liked your idea for the closing question."

Though I was relieved to hear the producer had given me a thumbs up, I thought about what Isaac was saying. He was my best friend, my advisor, my closest confidant. I debated whether or not to share with him my innermost thoughts, because I didn't think he'd welcome them.

Isaac could read me. "Listen, you idiot, don't try something stupid."

"Might be a good thing," I replied.

"You're thinking of changing your answer to the last question, aren't you?"

I nodded. "How'd you guess?"

"Because I know you. Because I remember the night you did Bretta's D&C. Because I know Joe Wright takes chances."

"And?"

"And I don't want to know what your harebrained idea is."

I smiled.

He smiled back.

The PBS director knocked on the door. "Fifteen minutes."

88

Studio A, KACV, Amarillo

Tension mushroomed as airtime drew near. We had all heard the rumors about a record audience of over 200-million viewers. As the director gave a five-second count in my earpiece, the interview started with an atmosphere of high-stakes drama.

"Welcome, Dr. Wright," Lowher began. "We appreciate your willingness to participate in this interview."

"Thank you for having me," I replied. And even though I knew what his first question would be, a feeling of excitement surged through my veins. I leaned forward in my chair, eager to respond.

"Where do you think our country stands on the question of abortion?" Lowher asked.

I had my answer ready. "That's the problem—no one knows."

With uncertainty about what his next lead would be, I listened carefully.

"The Supreme Court says they know," Lowher continued, his voice smooth and even, "and they've just told us when they voted last Friday to uphold *Roe v. Wade*."

"That's just their opinion." The words popped out without any thought on my part. "And I think we'll never have a true consensus if we look to government for answers. We've got to get this decision out of the courts and let the people decide."

"Not an easy thing to do."

"True."

"Some would say impossible."

"Maybe," I said. "But in the course of this interview, perhaps *we* could come up with a suggestion for the country."

Lowher looked at me in surprise. We had not rehearsed any questions about *letting the people decide.* He quickly changed the topic. "You've been criticized for performing an abortion on your own daughter."

"Yes, that's true."

"You admit you have done abortions?"

"Rarely. For the most part, I'm against the practice." Then I gave him a stern look and tried to make a point by speaking a bit louder. "I support the sanctity of life."

Unflappable, Lowher came right back with the next question. "Let's make it more pointed. Do you consider yourself pro-life or pro-choice?"

"Neither."

He chuckled. "People who are watching this interview are not going to like that answer."

"But that's the essence of the problem," I replied. "When it comes to a woman's right to reproductive freedom, there are no absolutes."

Lowher's brow wrinkled with doubt, and he shook his head as he spoke. "You'll have to explain that to our viewers."

"Let's take the basic concept that life begins at conception," I said.

"Even though I know some would disagree."

Lowher nodded, waiting for me to continue.

"Add to that the widespread conviction—which I personally support—in both the sanctity of life, and that it is wrong to end life at any stage."

Again, Lowher nodded.

"And yet, we must find some way to reconcile this conviction with a conflicting belief in, and compassion for, reproductive freedom for women."

"Polls show that there is great concern for that ideology by both men and women," Lowher interjected.

"Last May my own daughter was brutally gang raped by three vicious, cruel young men. When she found she was pregnant, her emotional distress was so great that she took a coat hanger and tried to abort herself. It was both dangerous and stupid. If she had punctured the uterus, she could have been left sterile or dead."

"I'm sorry to hear that," Lowher said with sincerity. "My condolences to your daughter."

"Yet, extremists in some pro-life groups fail to see the need to support women who have been raped, or who need to end pregnancy for legitimate reasons to protect the health of the mother."

"We're always going to have extremists," Lowher replied.

"Yes, but history shows that we can mute their disruptive force in society."

"And how do you think that can be done?"

"By letting the people decide," I replied. "Take the abortion decision out of government, out of the legislatures—*especially* out of the courts. Present it state by state, and let people vote."

The interview went on for the next several minutes with discussion about how abortion decisions might be taken out of the courts. Lowher asked pointed questions, and I did my best to answer them.

In my earpiece I heard the director tell us we had less than five minutes. "Time to wrap it up," he said.

I saw Lowher relax. Then he asked the closing question. He rattled it off, word for word, exactly as I had written it. "What would you like to see implemented in the future that would help Americans resolve the abortion debate?"

"A vote."

Lowher looked at me, speechless. That was not the answer we had practiced and so carefully timed.

89

Studio A, KACV, Amarillo

Jim Lowher stared at me with laser-sharp intensity. And I sensed that the cameramen, the audio technicians, and everyone else in the studio were about to come unglued. This was national television, with one of the largest audiences—perhaps *the* largest—in television history. Not a time to be improvising.

But I did it anyway.

I turned and looked directly into the camera.

"Our country is divided," I said. "What is needed is a vote of the people, a mandate on the abortion question."

The camera's red light glowed brightly. I knew they were continuing to film me.

"You, the television audience, know that I am not a political leader. I hold no office nor do I have any authority. I'm just a father, a parent like you, who wants the best for his child. However, I happen to be a doctor, and as fate would have it, I recently became personally involved in the most intimate details of a brutal gang-rape in which my daughter was the victim."

The camera moved up, closer.

"Picture this with me—a beautiful twenty-three-year-old woman, talented, intelligent, about to graduate from college with a bright future. Now imagine that she is kidnapped by three thugs, taken to a remote area, stripped, spread-eagled, and made into a plaything by these evil men. When she attempts to fight back, one of her attackers vents his anger with a baseball bat, breaking her leg in three places. And after they have all raped her, they use her for target practice. They throw beer cans at her—both empty and full—hitting her so hard it tears the flesh. Finally, they urinate on her, their parting denigration of a raped, beaten, broken body . . . left to die."

A thought flashed by—Isaac's words: Speak from the heart.

"Rape is worse than murder. With murder, the victim is gone and not forced to deal with what happened to her. Yes, I know, the family must deal with it, but not the victim. That's why rape is so much worse. The victim, the primary person, is condemned to a lifetime of coping, of trying to understand. Every hour of every day, the victim thinks of the rape and asks herself a thousand questions. She relives it, step by step, minute by minute, and it never goes away."

I leaned forward, allowing my voice to rise.

"Perhaps the most horrible crime of all is gang rape. A woman raped by a one man has an evil person on whom to focus—the rapist she can blame. But in a gang rape, that focus becomes diffused, and, worst of all, it is supplanted with feelings of worthlessness, of being nothing more than a piece of meat. The humiliation escalates and destroys self-worth. I have found it so destructive, I regard it the ultimate in human depravity."

Instinctively, and without a conscious decision, my speaking voice became quieter.

"I didn't want to do this program, but my daughter asked me to do it. She wanted someone to speak on behalf of rape victims like herself. I'm almost finished, there are only seconds left. Here's what Bretta and I want you to do."

I took a breath and said the next word with my most intense fervor.

"Vote."

At that point I knew I was taking Lowher's time. He had planned a closing statement. But I had the camera. I went ahead.

"We have an opportunity as a nation to speak out, to express our views. Next Tuesday, if you think that Reginald McCormack is right—that abortions must be banned in *every* case, that no exceptions will ever be allowed—then join the extreme right and vote Independent. And there is another option—the extreme left. If you think abortion on demand is every woman's right, then make a write-in vote. Write 'none-of-the-above' if you wish to register your support for the extreme left feminists who believe that ending life is merely a whim to which each woman is entitled."

I paused to take a breath. I knew only moments remained, and that I needed to make my last few words count.

"But if you favor a moderate approach to the question of abortion, then vote for one of the two remaining candidates—the Republican or the Democrat."

Slowly, and with every fiber in my body, I urged.

"Vote."

Louder.

"Vote this Tuesday."

I pleaded.

"*Your vote* will never mean more."

I relaxed, turned back, and faced Lowher.

"Thanks for letting me speak my views."

A look of relief washed over his face. "And we thank you, Dr. Wright."

The red light on the camera clicked off. The PBS logo flashed on the monitor, and an announcer's voice came over the studio's speakers.

"This concludes our special broadcast. We now return to regular programming."

90

Monday morning, at home, 1109 Westbrook Terrace

I lingered over breakfast with two concerns—an empty coffee cup and a disturbing headline in the morning paper. Jenny brought her carafe over to the table and offered to fix the first.

"Just a half," I said. "I've been consuming too much caffeine."

"Drink what you want," she said as she topped it off. "Why so glum this morning? You should be ecstatic over your interview with Lowher."

"McCormack," I said. "He never gives up."

I laid the *Amarillo Globe-News* flat on the table so she could see the headline and the customary oversized photo of Reginald Q. McCormack.

MCCORMACK'S RESPONSE TONIGHT

The headline spanned the top of the page that—in massive, bold letters—extended from margin to margin. The huge photograph, right under the headline, covered almost a fourth of the page and featured

Reggie at his photogenic best, a big show of teeth, and both arms above his head with fingers in "v" gestures of victory.

"He reminds me of Nixon," Jenny said as she sat beside me with her cup of coffee.

I laughed, picked up the paper, and read the article aloud to her.

"In an unprecedented move, presidential candidate McCormack has purchased three hours of prime time on the major networks to rebut Joseph Wright's stinging criticism expressed in his Sunday interview with Jim Lowher. Tonight's evening-long special, reported to have set a new record in campaign expense, will air at seven o'clock central time."

I lowered the newspaper and made eye contact with Jenny. "Stinging criticism?"

She chuckled, shook her head, and added, "You didn't criticize—you just suggested the moderates vote for someone else."

"You think he's seen the possibility that people may do that?"

"Who knows?" She changed the subject and asked, "I saw a small photo of you. What does the *Globe-News* have to say about last night's broadcast?"

The photograph showed Lowher and me with a TV camera in the background. I read the caption aloud. "Local Doctor Urges Nation to Vote."

"That's all?" Jenny asked.

"There's a short article about the broadcast."

"Read it."

"For thirty minutes Sunday evening, the nation's political world was centered in the Texas Panhandle. In an historic interview with PBS newscaster Jim Lowher, Amarillo resident Joseph Wright answered questions about his recent appeal to the Supreme Court. Nielson Ratings Inc., the industry's watchdog for television viewing, reports a record 200-million people tuned in."

I lowered the paper to take a sip of coffee. "Amazing, ain't it?" I chuckled.

"That the *Globe-News* gives bigger and better coverage to McCormack than to you?"

I nodded. "I wonder how many people will tune in to the McCormack special?"

"Sweetheart, that's something we don't have to worry about."

"I am *not* worrying."

"Then why are we even talking about it?"

"Good question." I looked at my wristwatch. "Damn. Time is getting away, and I'm scheduled to make rounds at the hospital."

In record time, I brushed my teeth, put on a tie, kissed my wife goodbye, and headed the BMW down Elm Street toward the hospital. It was the first time I'd driven this route in over five months, and it felt good. I hadn't realized how much I'd missed the routine of morning hospital rounds.

Following my old habit, I left the car in "doctors parking" and entered through the ER. There I ran into Nurse Elsa Jennings who was heading home after an eleven-to-seven shift. She gave me a hug and a big smile.

Upstairs at the central nurses' station, I started rounds with Harvey Adams. He voiced opinions about which patients to turn over to me. Exhilarated about returning to the mainstream of Amarillo's medical world, I just smiled and nodded.

Back out in the hospital parking lot, I found Ed Garfield just coming to work. He greeted me like a long-lost cousin and practically shook my hand off. I promised to join him for a cup of coffee soon—maybe that evening after rounds.

Driving to the office, an unfamiliar sense of elation rippled down my spine. For the last five months I had been telling myself how nice it was to sleep in—not to have the responsibility of morning and evening rounds at the hospital. But the truth was, I'd missed it. A chunk of my medical life had been taken from me and, even though I had justified it to everyone, in my heart of hearts, to my inner self, I knew it was a lie.

Now I was back, a full-fledged MD once again.

As I neared the office I heard the sound of a Sousa march.

Parking in the rear, I walked from my car to the back door of the Medical Arts Building. And the music sounded louder.

Bretta met me.

"What's happening?" I asked.

She rolled her eyes and pointed to the front of the building.

I walked with her to the big window that looked out on Polk Street.

Loudspeakers mounted on Dennis Smith's pickup blared away with a military band playing *The Stars and Stripes Forever.* Atop the truck he had mounted a large sign that read, "McCormack's TV Special 7:00 p.m."

91

The Medical Arts Building, Amarillo, 8:30 a.m.

Bretta sized up Dennis Smith's operation, his huge sign, the earsplitting music, and asked, "Don't they ever stop?"

"It's a free country," I replied.

"But it's driving me crazy."

"So, what's the alternative?"

She looked at me with a blank face. The music changed to *Washington Post March.* She shrugged. "I . . . I guess there isn't any."

"Of course there is," I said. "Several. Most are bad, but there may be one that's good."

Just then my two partners Harvey Adams and Melvin Campbell joined us.

"Good God, Smith's back," Mel complained.

Harv shook his head. "Persistent, isn't he?"

My nurse, Virginia Cotton, came to the window. "Oh, joy. We get to listen to Sousa marches all day," she grumbled.

"Dad," Bretta asked, "what did you mean about one alternative that might be good?"

"Have you noticed how, sometimes, religious sects coexist peacefully?" I asked. "Whereas, at other times their differences escalate into all-out war?"

"Northern Ireland," Bretta replied. "Things have settled down between the Catholics and the Protestants."

"However, in the Middle East," Virginia added, "the Sunni and the Shiite Muslims are killing each other."

"It's my contention," I said, "that a major factor in the escalation of such ideological conflict is the role of government."

"What do you mean?" Bretta asked.

"In my opinion," I answered, "when government tries to legislate any kind of philosophical orientation—such as religion—people feel compelled to react. Reaction leads to violence."

Bretta thought about that for a moment. "You're saying that pro-life versus pro-choice is like religion?" Bretta asked.

"Not exactly. But attempts at legislating how people think—what to believe—certainly is."

Melvin Campbell turned from the window, a disgusted look on his face. "All I can say is that I'm sick and tired of harassment. And the next time this sonofabitch shows up with his loud music, I'm calling the cops." He stomped off toward his office.

"Joe, I think you're an idealist," Harvey Adams said. "Maybe in a perfect world you could find a way to let Americans vote on abortion, to let Muslims vote on religion, and to let the Irish vote on government." Before I could reply, he turned and followed Campbell.

I put my right arm around Bretta, my left around Virginia, and nudged them toward our office. "There are lots of things worse than being called an idealist."

To the sound of martial music we began seeing patients.

The day passed quickly, and we got used to the music. To my surprise, by midday people didn't even comment on it. What everyone talked about was the Lowher interview. Every patient mentioned it, each congratulated me on my part in it, and every single person stated that they intended to vote. Even at the end of the day, when I stopped at the hospital to see patients, the hot topic continued to be the PBS special. And I wondered if this was purely a local phenomenon.

As expected, the national news focused on tomorrow's election.

But unexpected, and almost as big, was the story about Reggie McCormack's airtime. Somehow, the McCormack campaign had managed to buy all the prime time on America's three major networks—ABC, CBS, and NBC.

I couldn't believe it.

But at a cost of untold millions, some said billions, the television evangelist had edged out the other candidates and soaked up the principal TV access into voters' homes on the eve of the election.

Both the Republicans and the Democrats complained bitterly.

Even "unbiased" news commentators expressed their displeasure.

"Who would want to watch that idiot for three hours?" Jenny asked.

I didn't say anything, but I wondered how McCormack could afford it. And despite all the negative talk, at seven o'clock we, my family and I, gathered around the television.

92

At home, 1109 Westbrook Terrace

McCormack for President was the message. Glitz was the messenger. And if an MGM-style musical extravaganza could win an election, then Reggie had it in the bag. His three-hour television special started with a chorus of bright young singers belting out a medley of happy, upbeat songs—backed by a full symphony orchestra. The choreography included signs, balloons, streamers, and tons of confetti. His opener went on for several minutes and gave a powerful image of political victory.

And just when I thought the production had reached its apex, it got bigger.

Reggie McCormack took front and center, his big smiling face filling the screen, metallic tinsel drifting down—tiny, highly reflective bits that sparkled as they mirrored the lights. It was a production designed to hype his message. I thought it very effective.

"Has anyone checked with Mister Roper?" McCormack asked.

The response—to invoking the name of a famous pollster—was loud cheering and clapping. I had no way of knowing, but I guessed it to be a mix of studio audience and a soundtrack.

"In case you haven't heard, the Roper Poll predicts we're going to win," he said, and this time the response was incredible—more cheering and clapping, but louder and longer. It sounded like a stadium full of people. I listened carefully and found it even more artificial than I'd first suspected.

"Thank you, America," McCormack said. "I appreciate your faith in me and the principles I stand for. So I've asked the McCormack Singers to give us a song. It's my way of saying a prayer for your continued support—Amazing Grace."

The mood softened.

An attractive young soprano sang the opening words, unaccompanied.

"Amazing Grace, how sweet the sound, that saved a wretch like me."

The contrast—between the opening of a full-blown stage production and a single solo voice—was compelling. I found myself pulled into the words. Next, she was joined by a tenor, and in harmony, the two soloists continued.

"I once was lost, but now am found. Was blind, but now I see."

The music modulated up a half-step, and they were joined by the entire chorus singing sotto voce, just a whisper. Soft, beautiful, emotional music.

"'Twas grace that taught my heart to fear. And grace my fears relieved."

Again the song modulated, and for the next verse the orchestra added a stunning, legato accompaniment. With each verse the music gradually swelled in both volume and intensity. I couldn't take my eyes off the screen.

"The Lord has promised good to me. His word my hope secures."

Jenny came over and sat beside me. "What does a hymn have to do with tomorrow's election?"

"Probably nothing, but you have to admit, it pulls at your heartstrings."

At that point the music peaked to a stirring climax.

"He will my shield and portion be. As long as life endures."

The song ended to wild cheering and clapping, more streamers and confetti. Then McCormack appeared at his pulpit, microphone in hand.

"Thank you. Thank you, friends. Thank you for your prayers. And God thanks you for your support of life."

Applause.

"Like the song says," McCormack continued, "He will be our shield—as long as life endures."

"Do we *have* to watch this?" Jenny grumbled. Clearly, she'd had enough of McCormack for one night.

"No," I replied. "We don't."

She punched the remote. The screen went black. "What's going to happen tomorrow?" she asked.

"Wish I knew."

"What about the pollsters?"

"Last week, after the Supreme Court decision, they quit."

"Quit?"

"They said this election's too volatile. Like marbles on a glass-top table. People keep changing their position."

"What about your interview?"

"What about it?"

"How much of an impact did you have? What do the polls say?"

"There haven't been any polls taken since Friday," I said. "That's what I keep trying to tell you. After the Supreme Court announced their bombshell, no one's willing to stick his/her neck out with a prediction."

"Meanwhile, McCormack hits us with all this emotional religious music."

I nodded. "He's spending an enormous amount of money."

"And blocking the other candidates," Jenny complained. "It seems so unfair."

"Yes, but—"

"But what?"

"But there may be others, like us, who react negatively."

Jenny looked at me. I could almost read her thoughts.

"You tuned him out," I reminded her. "I wonder how many others did, too."

She smiled the biggest smile I'd ever seen. "You think he may have spent all that money, only to have it backfire?"

93

Election Day

Driving to the hospital, I listened to the car radio. The NPR reporter droned on about a heavy, early turnout at polls in the Eastern Time Zone. At the nurses' station on the second floor, they welcomed me like a celebrity. "Saw you on TV this morning," one said.

"You were on *The Today Show*," another echoed.

"Wait a minute," I cautioned. "I've been right here . . . in Amarillo."

"They re-ran your Sunday night interview with Jim Lowher."

"The closing. Where you tell everyone to vote," an orderly added.

Another nurse came in and hung up her coat while we were talking. "Sorry I'm late," she said. "But I have a good excuse."

"So what's your *good* excuse?" the nurse in charge asked.

"The mob at the polling place. You wouldn't believe the line."

I interrupted. "You think McCormack's big TV special caused more people to vote?"

She smiled at me, a benevolent facial expression, the kind a mother gives to a toddler who has just asked an unanswerable question. "I think the pro-life zealots who were determined to vote for McCormack came and voted for him."

"But the big crowd?" I asked. "Did you hear any buzz about the turnout?"

"Sure. Everybody was talking about it. You wait in line for thirty minutes, and it becomes the topic of the morning."

"McCormack?"

"Nobody connected it to McCormack," she answered with a big grin. "I never once heard his name mentioned."

"What are they talking about?" I asked, suddenly excited as well as curious.

"About voting this time. About duty. About a name I heard mentioned over and over." She reached out and put her hand on my arm. "Your little speech on Sunday night really hit home. You're the reason I'm late to work this morning."

I started my rounds and found that everyone wanted to talk about the election—about my TV interview with Jim Lowher. Trying to hurry became an exercise in futility. Many were making special arrangements to leave the hospital just to vote.

Finally, I escaped and drove to the office with the radio on. The morning's big story continued to be voter turnout.

We had a light morning, and I took my time with patients. They wanted to talk about the election, so I let them. Every single one gave me an extended endorsement about my Sunday night pitch for voting. I thanked them, feeling a bit uncomfortable with all the praise.

Isaac called and wanted to meet for lunch.

Bretta came in and wanted to talk about the rape trial. "They've scheduled it for next Monday," she said. She told me this in a matter-of-fact tone, but I knew, that inside, the impending trial weighed heavily on her.

"Good," I replied as cheerfully as I could. "Let's get this behind us."

"I'll have to have the day off," she added with a brave smile.

"Of course," I said. "And I'll cancel all my patients. Isaac Levy will join us."

"Another thing," she continued. "I called Juilliard, and they said I could still have the teaching assistantship if I start in January."

"Bretta, that's wonderful!" I jumped up and held out my arms. "Give your old Daddy a hug. You've made my day."

She did.

And I sensed a special moment—a time when we came together with our arms around each other, emotions running high. "I'm so happy for you," I said.

Virginia came in and scolded me. "We're getting stacked up," she warned.

Bretta left, but the few minutes we'd had together generated feelings that remained. I worked my patients with happy energy and let my thoughts churn. We needed to get through this trial, but I worried about finding a way to do it without traumatizing my daughter. The fact that she wanted to return to music was a good sign—the best possible.

The morning rushed by, and then I drove to the Burger Barn for lunch with Isaac.

"You listening to the national news?" he asked the moment we settled into our booth.

"Not really," I replied. "I've had a hectic morning."

"Huge turnout at the polls. Everyone's predicting record numbers."

"Oh, that. Yeah, I've heard the buzz. You think McCormack's big special last night is bringing them out?"

"Maybe, but—"

"But what?"

"But that's not what the exit surveys are saying."

"I've never had much faith in exit stuff," I said. "And I need to discuss the trial with you."

Conversation switched to next Monday's trial and how Bretta should prepare for it. Isaac agreed to be present and sit with us.

Then we talked about Juilliard. Isaac surprised me with the enthusiasm of his response.

"Joe, that's the best news I've heard in months. Bretta needs to do something with all that talent. Lots of people can work in a doctor's office. Not many can have a professional career in singing."

He was right, of course. I thanked him, finished lunch, and went back to the office. The afternoon passed quickly without incident, and I drove to the hospital for rounds. Ed Garfield met me at the nurses' station.

"My wife and I are coming to the dinner party," he told me.

"Say again?" I asked. "What dinner party?"

"At your house," he said, as if I were daft. "I'm bringing a case of champagne." He looked at me funny. "You didn't know?"

I shook my head. "I guess Jenny forgot to tell me."

Ed's face turned red. "Damn. I think I've just ruined a surprise."

94

Northwest Texas Hospital

Two can play the surprise game. So I decided to hang around the hospital—to let Jenny sweat it out for a little bit. I went down to the ER and found Elsa Jennings. No patients—things were quiet. Elsa introduced me to two other nurses and a young MD who was doing his residency. But after a few moments of celebrity, I was glad to see them move on. Elsa poured two cups of coffee, and we sat at the front desk to chat.

"Big election," she said.

"So I hear."

"Your closing remarks on Sunday evening's TV interview really found a sympathetic response. Everybody's still talking about it."

"Let's just hope it does some good."

"Even Dennis Smith was impressed."

I chuckled. "What'd Dennis have to say?"

"He was talking with Kathy Thompson, the ER nurse." She paused.

"You remember Kathy?"

"How could I forget her? She testified against me about Bretta's D&C."

Elsa nodded. "Kathy told Dennis she thought your speech would motivate scads of people to vote."

I laughed. "Just what Dennis wanted to hear."

Elsa laughed with me. "No, the *last* thing Dennis wanted to hear. He got on his soapbox and lectured everyone within earshot about how misdirected your remarks were. He was so offensive that even Kathy couldn't stand it. She walked off and left him ranting."

I looked at my watch and saw that it was getting late, well past time for me to be home for dinner. I explained to Elsa that I needed to call my wife. When Elsa left, I pulled out my cell phone and punched up the stored number.

"Where are you?" Jenny asked, clearly perturbed.

"At the hospital," I replied. "It's been a busy day."

"Joe, we're waiting for you," she wailed.

"You and the kids go ahead without me. I'll be along as soon as I can."

"You don't understand. We're *all* waiting for you."

"Who's waiting?" I asked, pretending bafflement.

"It's a surprise, you idiot. *Come home.*"

I chuckled. "Jenny, you know I don't like surprises."

She sniffled, a mix between anger and crying. "Joseph Wright, don't be difficult. Look, I've planned a surprise party for you. An election watch. Catering, champagne, all our friends." She started crying.

"I'll be right there." I punched off. Feeling guilty, I could now see that my little prank had backfired and made me look like a jerk.

At home I found cars parked up and down the street. I had to squeeze into a spot two blocks away. When I walked in the front door, there were dozens of people, many of whom were gathered around the television: Harvey Adams and Mel Campbell and their wives, all the office staff and their spouses, Isaac and his wife, members of our bridge club, even Jack Richards in his sheriff's uniform.

Everyone clapped and cheered while I stood there feeling foolish.

Bretta started the singing: "For he's a jolly good fellow, for he's a—"

More clapping.

I shook hands, accepted words of praise, and made my way to the kitchen where I found Isaac.

"How's the election going?" I asked, selecting a cheese puff from an hors d'oeuvre platter and popping it into my mouth.

"Huge," Isaac replied, following suit.

Ed Garfield, standing near and manning the makeshift bar, handed me a glass of champagne.

95

At home, 1109 Westbrook Terrace

As Charles Dickens phrased it—"It was the best of times and the worst of times." The best was the election party at our house—a roaring success. The worst was the election we had expected to savor together—there were no results.

While it was exciting to witness an event predicted to go down in history, it was both disappointing and boring to learn that the massive numbers had overwhelmed the system.

Polls couldn't close with people waiting in long lines. Election officials worked frantically to push voting machines and election communications that were stretched beyond their limits. Reporters tried, with little success, to find trends on which to base predictions. People became frustrated. Tempers flared. Our party gradually wound down.

Finally, at 1:00 a.m., one state issued results.

Sort of.

Massachusetts, with twelve electoral votes, reported a Democratic win. However, the results were a dead heat between major parties, with the independent candidate trailing far behind. The totals—1,864,225 Democratic and 1,864,085 Republican, and a meager 10,924 for McCormack—guaranteed a recount and the very likely possibility that the numbers might not hold.

The only definitive result that could be reported was the paucity of votes for right-wing, conservative McCormack.

As television results languished and the tiny bits of information came at a snail's pace, our house guests departed, and the Wright family went to bed.

The next morning, we turned on the TV to find most of the same reporters on the major networks, now disheveled but still grappling with the closeness of the election. The uncontested states voted as expected: California went Democratic, and Texas went Republican—as did a handful of other "solid" states where the result, whether the turnout was large or small, was never in doubt.

But in Florida, Ohio, Michigan, and all the states that were up for grabs, the results remained elusive or, like Massachusetts where political experts had made the call based on razor-thin margins, subject to a possible change in status. "Too close to call," and "recounts likely" were common comments repeated over and over by television commentators.

So, while no one knew who won, the big news was "the loser."

McCormack.

He probably would receive zero electoral votes.

Unquestionably, the super-conservative, radical-right had been decimated.

And the really big news was the size of the turnout. The previous record, set in the last election with a total of 121,056,394, was now history. While the exact number of votes cast would not be known for several days, the current estimate of 150,000,000 was thought to be close and would surpass the old record by an amazing 24%.

As expected, Isaac called, and we arranged to have lunch together at the Burger Barn.

"What'd you think?" I asked, once we got settled and placed our orders.

"I think you're famous," he replied, grinning

"Aw, shucks, twarn't me," I laughed.

"Wuz too," he argued. "Everyone in America credits you with this massive election turnout."

"But it was the people," I protested. "They wanted to vote, and they did."

"I think it goes deeper than that," he said. Then he gave me a long philosophical lecture about America's Silent Majority, about the millions who—since 1973 when *Roe v. Wade* became the law of the land—had chosen to avoid the schism created by zealots and their division into the mutually exclusive factions known as pro-choice and pro-life.

"But you said we needed a vote that would give a convincing consensus on abortion," he stated, emphatically. Then he stared at me with a big lawyer's grin that mocked me and, at the same time, implied his support for what I had done. "Well, Dr. Wright, that's what we got."

I felt cornered.

He was right about some things. Yes, through a quirk in history, I was handed the opportunity to speak to millions of people, to offer my opinion on one of our country's most divisive topics, and because of the accidental trauma that had come to my family, people listened. But I honestly felt that the latent frustration of the so-called silent majority had nothing to do with me.

I tried again.

"Isaac, you've got this wrong. A record voter turnout on abortion was going to happen, with or without me."

"Dr. Wright, I'm trying to give you a compliment, and you're too damned stubborn to acknowledge it."

"Am not."

"Are too."

"Am not."

"I have an idea as to how we can settle this," he said. "Let's ask a neutral party, someone who will give us an honest, objective answer about how much your role in the election determined the result."

"Okay," I replied. "Who do you suggest that is both neutral and objective?"

Isaac paused. His expression went to that of a trial lawyer who had just won—a mouthful of teeth with a smirk that unmistakably projected superiority.

He said, "Reginald McCormack."

96

The Burger Barn, Amarillo, Texas

We had a good laugh. A big, old-fashioned belly laugh. And then I laughed at Isaac because he was laughing so hard. Tears came. And we laughed at each other because it was embarrassing and because people were staring at us.

Obviously, we couldn't contact McCormack. He was facing financial ruin. And Isaac was right—it was probably my fault. My thinking changed, and gradually I began to realize—it wasn't funny, it was tragic. I swiped the moisture away from my eyes as I thought about the irony.

"McCormack gambled everything and lost," I said, actually feeling a little sorry for the poor guy.

"Not just Reggie," Isaac continued, "the television networks that sold him air time on credit will be the big losers."

"On credit?" That seemed preposterous. "I didn't know they could do that."

"You're right," Isaac replied. "They usually don't. But this was an exception. Or rather, McCormack was the exception. He had a history of buying airtime, using it to raise money, and then covering his bills with the money he raised. But haven't we had this conversation?"

"Yeah, I remember, during the campaign." And I thought back to how McCormack had used me, used Texas's HB27, and used even the Supreme Court to build his political rise. Time and time again, it had worked—magnificently.

Until the bubble burst.

"How much was McCormack in for?" I asked.

"No one knows," Isaac said. "But I've heard guesses of at least a billion."

"Billion? With a *B*?"

Isaac nodded. "But remember last May? He was the dark horse with so little support he couldn't get his name on the ballot in many states."

"And in October," I shook my head as I remembered his incredible, meteoric rise, "Roper picked him as the frontrunner."

"The bigger they come, the harder . . . . "

"There's another cliché about playing with matches that's probably more on point," I said.

"Dr. Joseph Wright, the incinerator?" He chuckled. "You take lessons from Schwarzenegger?"

We finished up, paid the check, said our goodbyes, and I drove back to the office.

The afternoon passed quickly, and after the last patient, Bretta came to see me.

"Dad, the district attorney wants to meet with me about the trial," she said. "I was wondering if you'd have time to go with me."

"Sure," I replied. "Just tell me when."

"He said he would arrange his schedule to fit ours, but I suggested late afternoons, tomorrow and Friday."

"He wants to meet twice?"

"Yes," she nodded. "A couple of hours each day—four to six p.m. He said he needs at least that much time to prepare me for the trial."

"All right then. You set it up. I'll clear my schedule."

"Thanks, Dad." She kissed me on the cheek and left.

I closed the office, stopped at the hospital for rounds, and headed home. When I walked in the back door, I could smell garlic bread and pasta sauce. I checked my watch—time for the evening news. Brent and Bretta already had the kitchen TV on.

"The election is tied," reported the broadcaster.

Then we got a lesson on the American Electoral College. A total of 538 votes was set in 1961 with the ratification of the 23rd Amendment. The number is determined by adding 435—the number in the House of Representatives—plus 100 senators, and 3 for the District of Columbia. Election of the President required a majority—at least 270 votes.

I watched as NBC reported the current totals for this election.

Democrat—269.

Republican—269.

Independent—0.

Presidential electors would meet in their respective state capitals in December, 41 days following the election, at which time they cast their electoral votes. Thus, the electoral college never meets as one national body. Copies of the "Certificate of Vote" are signed and sent to Washington to await a joint session of the new Congress, where they are opened and counted. Candidates must receive a majority of the electoral vote to be declared *president-elect* or *vice-president-elect.*

If no candidate receives an absolute electoral majority, 270 votes out of the 538 possible, the new House of Representatives is required to go into session immediately to vote for president. The House votes en-bloc by state, that is, one vote per state, which is determined by the majority decision of the delegation from that state. If a state delegation is evenly split, a deadlock normally results, and that state is considered as abstaining. This vote would be repeated if necessary until one candidate receives the votes of more than half the state delegations—at least 26 state votes, given the current number, 50, of states in the union.

The House of Representatives has elected the president on two occasions, in 1801 and in 1825.

"Did you follow all of that?" Jenny asked, looking a bit confused.

"Sounds exactly like today's lesson in my government class," Brent replied. "We spent the whole hour on this stuff."

"So who's going to be elected?" Bretta asked.

"Doesn't matter," I replied. "The important thing is that we have a law that prescribes an efficient, fair way for the people to elect their leaders."

"But this isn't the people," Jenny complained. "It's electors or the House."

"Who are elected by the people," I countered. "So, if we've done our homework and voted wisely, we're in good hands."

"Pass the sauce, please," Brent said.

Obviously, my family was ready to move on, but I felt compelled to make a point. "What's important is that we, the people, make sure the system works. That we don't sit idly by and let some extremist minority use election procedures to thwart the will of the majority."

Brent handed me the pasta sauce. I held it for moment, waiting for a response. Looking around the table, Jenny and Brent were eating, Bretta smiled, rolled her eyes, and lifted her fork. That's the trouble with my wife's pasta and sauce—it's so good it kills all conversation.

Besides, the election was now old news. The topic of the day was the rape trial. But no one wanted to talk about that at dinner.

97

The District Attorney's Office, Canyon

For the rape trial, we switched to neighboring Randall County—different judges, different courtroom, and most importantly, different prosecuting attorneys. I can't say that I missed Billy Bob, Potter County's district attorney, but I felt an air of uneasiness as Bretta, Isaac, and I filed into the Randall County District Attorney's conference room. Randall's DA, Kenneth Parker, took the seat at the head of the table. Isaac and an assistant DA sat across from Betta and me. Parker passed out copies of his case overview.

"As rape cases go, this one's going to be messy," Parker said. "I suggest we all take a minute to read through the case summary."

I scanned the five-page document and felt my stomach tighten. Anger coursed through my veins. Parker had made a stinging criticism of the medical team, which "included the father of the victim," for not insisting that a rape kit be processed at the hospital. His summary was that, because of this bungling omission, the trial would boil down to a case of "she said" versus "he said."

I threw the summary down on the table and waited for everyone to finish reading. Parker looked up momentarily and then eased back in his chair, a sign of getting his defenses up.

"You make it sound like these bastards are going to get away with this," I grumbled.

"Easy, Joe," Isaac cautioned. "We're all on the same side here."

"It is a difficult case," Parker replied.

"Well, it shouldn't be," I countered. "Both Bretta and this other girl—Melissa —picked these guys out of a lineup."

"Melissa Jorsky," Parker said. "But these are two incidents separated by almost six months."

The assistant DA added, "And the Jorsky incident was *attempted* rape. Even if we win that case, the penalties are much less."

"And in Bretta's case there's no hard evidence," Parker added. "If only we had the results of a rape kit."

He made it sound like this was my fault, and that, due to my incompetence the night of the crime, we could very well lose the case.

"There's no question Bretta was raped," I protested. "You've damn well got evidence of that."

"Dr. Wright, I'm on your side," Parker continued, "but we have to anticipate the defense's strategy. They'll raise the possibility that Bretta had sex with someone the night before."

"But her injuries—"

"Bretta says it was Mackenzie and his pals, but we have only her word against theirs."

I shook my head in disgust. This should have been a slam-dunk. Now these guys were taking the word of three punks—three *rapists*—against that of my daughter.

"Why wasn't a rape kit processed?" Parker asked. He looked directly at me, his eyes flashing with accusation.

"Because we were trying to save her life," I shouted.

"Easy, Joe," Isaac cautioned, placing his hand on my arm.

"I suppose you'd be happier if we had let Bretta die while we processed the goddamned rape kit?" My voice remained elevated as I glared at Parker, a father's rage coursing through me. I looked at Bretta whose face had gone pale, and I knew she was reliving the horror of that night as we two men duked it out like adversaries.

Parker's face reddened with anger. I was sitting close enough he could have struck me, but Isaac intervened. "Gentlemen!" he shouted. "This isn't getting us anywhere."

Time stood still for several seconds.

"We'll have to find a way to use the facts we have," Isaac continued, his voice at conversational level, "to prosecute these bastards and win a conviction." He turned to Parker. "We can do it."

Parker looked away. I could hear his breathing—his continued anger obvious.

"Bretta, do you remember any conversation from the rape scene?" the ADA asked. "One of the most important things a victim can do is quote the words said by the rapists during the attack. It lends credibility."

The four of us turned to look at her.

Bretta shook her head. "It was just a blur of yelling and screaming," she said.

"Anything?" Parker asked, his voice now normal. "Even a word or a sentence?"

Bretta paused, as though embarrassed to speak.

"Go ahead," I said. "It's okay, honey. You need to tell us."

"Fucking hellcat," she said. "That's what he called me after I kicked him in the groin."

"Anything else?" Parker asked.

"No. He went to his car and got the baseball bat. The other two guys were holding me down, but I had my legs free, and I tried to kick him again. That's when he hit me so hard it broke my leg. Then I passed out."

"Which one of the men did this?" Parker asked.

"Oliver Mackenzie."

"You're sure?"

"Absolutely sure," Bretta said. "I'll never forget the smirk on his face when he came at me with that bat."

98

In the car, driving home from the District Attorney's office

Bretta leaned her head against the passenger-side window. I could sense her listless disappointment as she watched the landscape slide by. "Doesn't look good, does it?" she asked.

I didn't know how to answer, so I played for time. "You're a very brave person. I'm proud of you."

"You didn't answer my question," she said, turning toward me.

"We'll get the bastards. You'll see," I told her with as much conviction as I could muster.

"Dad?"

"Yes?"

"I've lived with you for twenty-three years. I can tell when you're avoiding the issue."

I smiled. "Your mother says you read me so well that you know what I'm going to say before I know I'm going to say it."

We both laughed. A good laugh, the kind that bonds a father and daughter.

"Mom's right," Bretta said. "I can, and I do."

"Okay, tell me. What am I going to say?"

"You're going to tell me to hang in there."

She was right, of course, so I didn't respond. Instead, I patted her arm, and we drove toward home in an emotional silence. A dejected quiet—one where feelings rather than words provided the means of communication.

My thoughts roiled. I wanted desperately to help. With my left hand on the steering wheel, my right hand went to the bronze medallion that hung from the chain around my neck. I didn't think about it; it just happened—an instinctive reaction.

Psychologists have a term for the actions we take without thinking. It's standard fare in TV crime drama. When the villain points a gun at his victim, how does the poor guy respond? He holds his hands in front as he yells, "Don't shoot." We all know that hands won't stop a bullet, but the victim does it instinctively—without thinking—just as a mother reaches out to protect her endangered baby.

As I fingered the St. Jude medallion, the thought that popped into my brain was "impossible cause." And the symbolism that Bretta believed in me, in my support, that I would be there for her. I had a thought.

"There's an example in a book I read several years ago that I want to tell you about."

She turned away. Her reaction surprised me, and I sensed she was crying. We keep a small box of Kleenex in the armrest that divides the front seats. With my eyes on the road, I lifted it out and pulled a couple of tissues for her.

"This example was written years ago when the two towers of the World Trade Center were new."

Bretta looked at me. "Is this about 911?"

"No," I replied, "it could be any two tall buildings."

She wiped her eyes.

I continued.

"In this example, two guys are on top of one of the towers, and someone has placed a telephone pole from the corner of one building across to the other."

"Dad, what does this have to do with me and the trial?"

"Hey, I'm trying to make a point." I gave her my best smile. "This will only take two minutes, maybe less."

She looked at her watch. "Do I have a choice?"

"The first guy looked at the second, our hero, and said, 'I'll give you a thousand dollars if you'll jump on that telephone pole and crawl over to the other building.'"

"Our hero, laughed, and said, 'No way'."

"A hundred thousand?"

"I wouldn't do that for a million dollars," replied the hero.

Then as the two men stood there, looking over at the other building, a toddler wandered out on the roof, and came perilously close to the edge.

"That's my daughter," yelled the hero. Then he jumped on the telephone pole and in seconds crawled over to the other tower to rescue his three-year old daughter.

Bretta looked at me. "That's the end of the story?"

"It's about values," I said.

"The guy wouldn't do it for any amount of money, but he would do it for his little girl?"

"You're my little girl," I said.

She reached over and kissed my cheek.

We pulled into the garage and I killed the motor. It seemed appropriate that I follow the script she had for me.

"Hang in there," I said.

She turned away. Her reaction surprised me, and I sensed she was again crying. I pulled a couple of tissues for her.

"Thanks," she said as she wiped her eyes.

"Want to tell me?" I asked, my heart breaking for her.

"Sometimes I'm not that brave person you expect me to be."

"None of us is," I said, aching to let her know I understood.

"Dad, I'm thinking about not testifying."

99

In the car, in the garage

Sitting there in the garage, just the two of us, Bretta and I had a heart-to-heart talk—the closest, most intimate discussion I'd ever had with my daughter.

We talked about rape trials, about national statistics, about the reports that say, "Half the rapists never have to face trial because it's too embarrassingly painful for the victim to testify." And if Bretta refused to take the stand—to point to Oliver Mackenzie and his two cohorts—and say, "These are the guys who raped me," this case would probably fall apart, and there was a likelihood the DA would not win a conviction.

"Dad, I talked with Mary Jo Harris, the girl who was raped last year."

"Yes, I remember reading about her trial in the *Globe-News*," I said.

"I called Mary Jo last weekend," Bretta continued, tears streaming. "She told me when the defense attorney cross-examined her, he asked about her sexual history. Was she a virgin? How many guys had she had sex with? How recent was her latest sexual encounter? It was horrible to sit in that chair and have to answer questions about the most personal aspects of—"

"Stop," I said. "You don't need to do this."

"Dad, it's not worth it," she sobbed. "Especially when it looks like these guys are not going to be convicted anyway."

"I agree." I reached over and put my hand on her shoulder—my fingers touching her cheek.

"You're not disappointed in me?"

"Sweetheart, the last thing in the world that I'll ever be . . . is disappointed in you."

I pulled my hand back. She wiped the tears and softly blew her nose.

We sat silently for a few minutes.

Gradually the tears subsided, and she smiled—a tentative gesture, forcing the corners of her lips to turn up.

"Thanks, Dad."

"Dinner's waiting." We looked at each other while another poignant moment passed. Then I said, "Ready to go inside?"

We got out of the car, and we embraced. The emotional exchange, the electricity of holding her in my arms, felt as though my daughter were three years old again.

Dinner turned out to be a downer. Jenny and Brent could see that Bretta had been crying—but neither said a word. What little conversation we did manage was forced. Bretta ate only a few bites and then went upstairs to her room and closed the door.

That night I couldn't sleep. I tossed and turned. Finally I got up, showered, shaved, dressed, and left the house. I went to Denny's, one of the few all-night restaurants in the Texas Panhandle, ordered breakfast, and read the morning papers. Just as the sun peeked over the eastern horizon, I called Sheriff Jack Richards and asked if he could meet me at his office.

"Sure," he replied. "What's up?"

"I need to discuss details of the case you filed against me last May."

"The illegal D&C? The brouhaha that started all of this?"

"Yes."

He paused. "Joe, it's 7:15. How about I meet you at the sheriff's office at eight o'clock?"

I reread the football predictions for the weekend, drank another cup of coffee, and drove slowly to Randall County Sheriff Headqarters. Then I waited on a bench in the lobby.

It was a brisk November morning. At 7:55 Jack came in, wearing a heavy coat. He greeted me and invited me back to his office.

"Okay," he said, hanging up his coat. "What do you want to know?"

"What kind of evidence did you have against me?" I asked, trying to keep the anxiety out of my voice. "I mean, regarding the D&C."

"The stuff Dennis Smith and Kathy Thompson brought."

"Which was?"

He went to a filing cabinet, pulled out a manila folder, brought it to his desk, and started leafing through the contents. "A bloody surgical instrument—a curette. They gave sworn affidavits that you used it—to perform the abortion on Bretta—to scrape the uterus."

"But you also had the embryo and surrounding tissue?"

Jack nodded and continued reading. "Dennis called it a fetus."

"Whatever. What happened to it?" I asked.

"Probably still in the evidence file. Normally we package medical evidence in plastic bags and freeze it."

Together we walked to the sheriff's evidence room, and Jack produced the curette, still carefully packaged and frozen. He held it up so I could see some blood and tissue—what might be a fertilized embryo—that I had scraped from Bretta's womb.

"What would be the procedure for obtaining DNA?" I asked.

"We send it to the state crime lab in Austin," Jack replied. "Usually takes ten days to two weeks."

"Could you use this to ID the mother and father that produced the pregnancy?"

The light came on.

Jack grinned.

"Probably," he said.

100

Randall County Courtroom

District Attorney Kenneth Parker asked for a delay. The judge granted it. The state crime lab processed the DNA. And two weeks later, on the Monday before Thanksgiving, we sat in the courtroom and watched as they swore in the first witness—one of the deputies who had found Bretta. Parker led the officer through his testimony—graphic details of how my daughter had been left to die—unconscious, bleeding, badly beaten, a broken leg.

Bretta sat stoically.

Not me.

Tears flooded my eyes. I pulled out a handkerchief.

Then I put my arm around Bretta and squeezed her tight. She laid her head against my shoulder.

Next, Parker called the EMT who drove the ambulance, and we began a second recounting of Bretta's condition. After the first few words of testimony, the lawyer for the defense objected.

"Your Honor, the defense will stipulate to the condition of Bretta Wright on the night in question. We don't need to hear this again."

"No," the judge replied, "I think we do. It could be important to hear the specifics—the medical details of her condition—from the emergency team that found her and took her to the hospital. Mr. Parker, please continue."

For the next ten minutes, we heard a retelling of Bretta's fragile situation. About the loss of blood, the critical level of her vital signs, the grotesque appearance of her broken leg, about the possibility of a punctured lung as they moved her onto a stretcher, and their doubts that she would survive the trip to the emergency room.

I studied the jury. Most, like me, were wiping their eyes.

Next, Parker called Peter Young, MD, the ER physician who was on duty that evening. Young's testimony was both carefully rehearsed and devastating. He spelled out the details of vaginal tearing, of bleeding and tissue damage, of bruising in the pelvic area, and his opinion that a multiple rape had taken place.

"Did you process a rape kit?"

"No, sir, I didn't."

"Don't you know that it's important to gather evidence if rape is suspected?"

"Yes."

"Well, Dr. Young, why didn't you?"

"Because we were trying to save the life of the patient," he answered, an edge to his voice.

"I think we'll have to have a more detailed answer than that," Parker said.

For the next thirty minutes, Peter Young gave a comprehensive accounting of that awful, terrible night in May, of the ER's response to Brenda's arrhythmia, renal failure, cardiac arrest, and *life or death* circumstances.

"She almost died," he said. "Her blood pressure and pulse—the cardio-pulmonary readings—were the lowest I have ever encountered in my medical career. The surgical world would call them unsurvivable. And when complicated by her numerous ancillary problems—the broken leg, the broken ribs and punctured lung, the multiple lacerations—this case defies any prognosis that the patient could be here with us, today."

"Did the question of whether or not to process a rape kit ever come up?"

"Of course," Young responded.

"How many doctors were treating the patient?"

"Four," Young replied. "Dr. Irwin, the anesthesiologist; Dr. Olsen, the orthopedic surgeon; Dr. Wright, her father—who was doing the sutures—and myself."

"You discussed this with these other doctors?"

"No, I didn't."

"And why not?"

"We were too damned busy. We were all frantically trying to save the patient's life," he repeated.

"How long did these doctors continue to treat the patient, to persist at—as you say—*trying to save the patient's life?*"

"Bretta was in the ER for twelve hours—a record for our hospital," Young said. "All four doctors and the entire ER staff were committed to her treatment during this time. Then she went to the RR, the recovery room, for twenty-four hours—another record. Dr. Wright was with the patient during the ER, the RR, and the next forty-eight hours in ICU. I continued to monitor her progress over her two-week hospital stay. The other doctors remained on call."

"You have anything else you'd like us to know about the medical details of this case?" Parker asked.

"Yes, sir," Young replied. "In my medical career, this was the most savage act of sexual brutality I've ever seen. Bretta Wright almost died."

"Your witness," Parker said, nodding to the table where the three defendants sat with their attorney.

The defense attorney rose, buttoned his jacket, and approached the witness.

"You say that Bretta Wright was raped?"

"Yes, there's no doubt about that."

"Wait a minute, we're talking about *proof*," the defense attorney said, his voice loud, almost a shout. "And before we send these young men to prison for life, we want proof, not just *your opinion*."

"It's not just my opinion. Ask any of the four doctors who treated Bretta."

"Move to strike," the defense attorney said. "There has been no proof from any witness that any of the accused has committed rape against Bretta Wright."

"Sustained," the judge said.

"That's all." The defense attorney returned to his seat at the table.

My stomach churned as the point struck home. No semen, no blood, no hairs—there was no evidence linking Bretta and her injuries to any of the three men who were accused of raping her.

101

Randall County Courtroom

"The prosecution calls Melissa Jorsky," DA Kenneth Parker said.

After Melissa was sworn in, Parker said, " Melissa, tell us about the events of Thursday night, October 24."

"I was walking home from the chemistry lab about midnight," Melissa said. "I had been working late, trying to finish an assignment, an experiment for Chem 305."

"You were alone?"

"Yes. I have an apartment at 806 Maple, and I was about a block from home when a car pulled up, and those three guys jumped out and grabbed me." She pointed to the defense table where Oliver Mackenzie, Frank Underwood, and Hector Garcia were seated with their attorney.

"You say they grabbed you. Be more specific. What exactly did they do?"

"I tried to run, but they tackled me, held me to the ground, put duct tape over my mouth, tied my hands, and then carried me to their car."

"They forced you into their car?"

"Well, they threw me onto the floor of the back seat."

"Then what happened?"

"They took off, driving fast, and ran the stop sign at Long Boulevard and Fourth Avenue."

"That's where the accident occurred?"

"Yes, sir."

Parker paused. He had the rapt attention of every person in the courtroom, and, like an actor on stage, he hesitated for dramatic effect. I found myself holding my breath, waiting for the next bit of information.

"Tell us about what happened next," Parker said.

"The accident saved me," Melissa replied.

"Objection," the defense attorney yelled. "That's only her opinion."

"Sustained," the judge said.

"Melissa, I should have said, tell us about the wreck," Parker said.

"He was driving too fast." She pointed toward Hector Garcia. "He ran the stop sign, and we crashed into the street sweeper."

"So this wasn't a little fender-bender?"

"No, sir. The impact totaled the car. We were probably going sixty or seventy when Garcia hit the sweeper."

"Were you injured?"

"No, sir. I was lying on the floor of the back seat."

"What about the others?"

"Garcia, the driver, had to be taken to the hospital. Mackenzie and Underwood were in the back seat with me. They suffered only minor injuries."

"And the driver of the street sweeper?"

"Not injured. That sweeper is huge. It's built like a tank, and the driver sits high. So—like me—he was lucky. We both walked away without a scratch."

"And what happened after the crash?" Parker asked.

"The driver of the sweeper called the cops. Almost immediately I could hear sirens. At first Mackenzie and Underwood tried to help Garcia. But when they heard sirens, they took off running."

"A few minutes ago you stated that you thought this accident saved you."

"Objection," the defense attorney shouted. "Your Honor, again, he's asking for an opinion."

"Goes to foundation, your honor. There may be facts that caused the witness to form an opinion about being saved. Saved from what? I think the jury should hear what's behind this statement."

The judge scratched his chin and then nodded. "I'll allow the question. However, I want to caution the jury that we have only an opinion from the witness. We do not know, for a fact, that this accident saved her."

Parker turned back to Melissa Jorsky, and, in a much softer tone, asked, "Why do you say this accident saved you? Saved you from what?"

"Rape," Melissa said.

"Objection," the defense attorney yelled.

"Your Honor, can we let the witness testify?" Parker asked.

"I agree. We need to hear the witness." The judge scowled at the defense attorney. "Let's hear what she has to say, and then we'll find out if this is just her opinion."

"Your Honor, the prosecution is trying to poison the jury with the emotional fears of this witness."

"I've made my ruling," the judge barked. "Now sit down. Let's hear her testimony, and then, if you think it's merely opinion, I'll consider your objection."

"But Your Honor—"

"I've given you my ruling. One more word, and I'll hold you in contempt."

The defense attorney sat, his face contorted with anger.

Parker continued. "Go ahead, Melissa. Why did you use the word rape?"

"Because, that's what they said they were going to do to me."

"Objection!"

"That's $500," the judge said. "And the next time it'll cost you twice that much. You'll have your turn to cross-examine the witness soon enough."

I had to admire Kenneth Parker. He had picked the perfect time to focus on the word "rape." It was a faultless trap, and his opponent fell for it. At this point I could feel sympathy—a tangible concern throughout the courtroom—for our side.

The defense attorney opened his mouth to protest, his face filled with frustration, but he managed to refrain from saying anything. Slowly, and with obvious reluctance, he sat.

Parker continued. "Melissa, who said they were going to rape you?"

"The three of them—Mackenzie, Underwood, and Garcia. After they put tape over my mouth and tied my hands behind my back, they laughed about me trying to kick Oliver. They compared me to Bretta Wright. Garcia asked Mackenzie if he'd brought his baseball bat."

"How did Oliver Mackenzie answer?"

"He said, 'No. No bat, because sex won't be as good if she's unconscious.' Then they all laughed."

"They were planning to rape you? You're certain?"

"Absolutely. Just like they raped Bretta."

"Except, this time, no baseball bat."

"That's what they said."

"Maybe they were just kidding. Mouthing off to scare you."

"No way!" She shook her head with a hard, firm look. "They didn't care if I was scared or not scared. They were laughing about it, like I was just a plaything. They wanted sex. And the only thing they were concerned about—the one thing they discussed—was they didn't want to have sex with a woman who was unconscious."

"Thank you, Melissa," Parker said. "I have no further questions for you."

"One more thing," she said, just as Parker started to turn away.

"Yes, go ahead," he said, turning toward the witness stand again.

"It was obvious they were going to kill me after they'd raped me," Melissa said, her voice high, thin, fearful.

Parker paused, but this time, I don't think he consciously did it. Instead he hesitated, as though trying to form his words. Then he asked, "Why do you say that?"

"After they shoved me into their car—Garcia was driving, the other two were in the back seat and had me on the floor with their feet on me—Underwood asked: 'Who would get rid of me?' Mackenzie said he would, because I'd seen their faces and could ID them."

"Oliver Mackenzie was going to kill you?"

Melissa gave a firm nod. "He said it, just before we hit the street sweeper."

"Thank you, Melissa," Parker said. Then he turned to the defense table, "Your witness."

The defense attorney grilled Melissa Jorsky for the remainder of the morning. He pressed her hard but couldn't shake her testimony. We left the courtroom for lunch. Isaac drove, and I sat in the front with him. Jenny, Bretta, and Brent took the back seat.

"What'd you think?" I asked.

"Melissa's testimony was devastating," Isaac replied. "No doubt about it."

"You think it's enough to convict?"

"Yes, for assaulting Melissa."

"But you heard her quote them about raping Bretta."

"In my opinion," Isaac said, "that's not enough to send them to prison for life."

102

The Burger Barn, Amarillo

Our group of five took the corner booth—a big round table away from the traffic of the cash register and front door. Bretta sat between Jenny and me. Bretta looked worried. Four of us—Isaac, Brent, Jenny, and I—ordered "the usual," a quarter-pound hamburger with fries.

Bretta just ordered a Diet Coke. "I'm not hungry," she told the waitress.

"You'll do better if you eat something," Jenny said. "How about a salad?"

Bretta shook her head. "I don't feel like eating, Mom. Okay?"

The waitress left.

I put my hand on Bretta's shoulder and pulled her close. "You don't have to testify. Those bastards are going to jail, no matter what." I squeezed her tight.

An awkward silence fell over our table. Bretta looked down, obviously trying to avoid eye contact. Jenny handed her a Kleenex.

I locked eyes with Isaac. Silently, I tilted my head toward Bretta, and he took it as a signal.

"Bretta," Isaac said, "your dad's right. You don't have to testify. In fact, you don't even have to go back into that courtroom."

Jenny reached over and patted Bretta's arm, her voice filled with a mother's concern as she said, "Honey, we're backing you. Just do whatever feels right."

"Sis," Brent added, "don't worry about me, the DA, or anyone else. You decide what you want to do and do it. We're all with you, no matter what you decide."

We made small talk for the next few minutes—an uncomfortable time for our family.

When the waitress brought our food, I had to take my arm away from my daughter's shoulder. Bretta held herself together and sipped her Coke.

I cut a tiny sliver off my burger and placed it on a napkin in front of her. "It would make your old dad feel better if you'd eat something," I whispered.

Conversation died. I sensed we all used our food as an excuse not to have to talk about the trial.

Bretta ate the little slice of my hamburger.

Isaac slipped out of the booth and paid the check. For once, I didn't argue.

In the end, Bretta insisted on returning to the courtroom.

We took our places in the front row.

District Attorney Parker called Sheriff Jack Richards as his first witness of the afternoon.

Parker carried a small Styrofoam container filled with dry ice over to the stand. White vapor wafted up out of the container as Parker, wearing heavy, protective gloves, lifted out a plastic bag containing a medical instrument and asked the policeman to identify it.

"It's a curette, a medical tool used for the dilatation and curettage procedure," Richards said. "It's used to scrape the womb in a D&C."

"An abortion?" Parker asked.

At the sound of the "A" word, the courtroom stirred. I heard a gasp from a woman on the jury.

As soon as the room quieted, Parker continued. "This particular curette has blood and tissue on it. Can you identify it?"

"Yes, it was brought to the Randall County Sheriff's Office on Wednesday, June 11 with sworn affidavits from Dennis Smith and Kathy Thompson."

Parker placed the plastic bag back in the Styrofoam container, removed the gloves, and produced two documents. "Are these the affidavits?"

Richards scanned the papers. "Yes, sir."

"Please summarize for the court. What do these documents tell us?"

"Smith and Thompson swear that the curette was used in a D&C procedure on Bretta Jean Wright—performed by her father, Dr. Joseph Wright—and that the blood and tissue samples on the curette prove that this was an abortion."

"A fertilized embryo?"

"Dennis Smith called it a fetus."

"Taken from the womb of Bretta Wright on June 10?"

"Yes, sir."

Parker paused to let these facts sink in.

Jenny took my hand and held it tightly. Most of the time our conversations about the D&C had been focused on Bretta, on the solution to our daughter's problems as a rape victim. Now, here in the openness of the courtroom, with the frozen embryo displayed before us, I sensed that all those years of Catholic teaching came rushing back as an emotional force. It was classic conflict. I whispered in her ear, "Just a few more minutes."

District Attorney Parker carried the Styrofoam container and the affidavits back to the evidence table. Then he picked up a clipboard and studied it. I could feel static electricity in the room as we waited for his next question.

"Two weeks ago Joseph Wright came to you and asked that you send the curette and tissue samples to Austin for DNA testing."

Richards nodded, "Yes, sir, that's correct."

"Along with DNA samples from the defendants and from Bretta Wright?"

"Yes, sir."

Parker handed a letter to Richards. "And this document from the Austin CSI Lab reports the results of the DNA tests?"

"Yes, sir."

"I've underlined the significant part," Parker said. "Please read it aloud for the court."

Richards read. "DNA from the tissue match those of Bretta Wright and Oliver Mackenzie. They are the parents of this embryo."

The silence in the courtroom was deafening.

103

Thanksgiving Day, at home, 1109 Westbrook Terrace

It snowed. Not unheard of, but somewhat unusual for late November in Amarillo. Big white flakes drifted down as I sipped the last of my coffee and studied the front page of the *Amarillo Globe-News*.

I reread the headline—RAPISTS RECEIVE HEAVY SENTENCES—grateful that the article concentrated on the bad guys rather than on our family. The three photographs showed Oliver Mackenzie, Frank Underwood, and Hector Garcia. Mackenzie received life. Underwood and Garcia each got twenty-five years. There were no pictures of anyone named Wright.

Jenny pulled two pies from the oven—one pumpkin, one pecan. Both smelled wonderful. Fortunately, we have two ovens for special days like this, and the aroma of baked turkey blended with the pies.

"More?" Jenny asked as she held the coffee pot over my empty cup.

"Just a half, please," I replied.

She leaned over, one eye closed as if taking expert aim, and poured, what appeared to be, exactly a half cup. “How’s that?”

I chuckled, held my cup to eye level, and shook my head with disapproval. “Just a smidgen too much.”

“Criticism is everywhere,” she groused.

“Ain’t it the truth.”

She leaned over and kissed me.

“Speaking of critics, I’ve decided to become one,” I announced.

“Oh, really?”

“And Isaac ‘s agreed to be my agent.”

Jenny laughed. It was a *make-fun-of-my-husband* laugh. “Why would you need an agent?”

“To book my speaking engagements.”

Jenny gave me her look—the look of incredulity. “Joe Wright—giving speeches?”

“Stop laughing,” I said. “Isaac has three already lined up. If you behave yourself, I’ll take you along.”

“And where, exactly, are these speaking engagements?”

“Dallas on Wednesday, New York on Thursday, San Francisco on Friday.”

The look on her face was priceless. “Good grief, will you be speaking about abortion?”

“No, not exactly,” I said. “It’s about taking the issue out of the courts and letting the people decide.”

“And how do you propose to do that?”

“By suggesting people vote on it—state by state.”

“Hmm,” she said. “Wonder what that would do to the conflict between pro-life and pro-choice movements?”

“It just might settle it,” I replied. “Have you noticed how people become more tolerant of differing views when they’re involved in reconciliation decisions?"

Jenny chuckled, shook her head, and then left me to check on the turkey. A minute later she was still smiling—a big Cheshire Cat grin.

Bretta walked into the kitchen and took note of the grins. "Inside joke?" she asked.

"Mom and I were just discussing how we might ameliorate the battle between pro-life and pro-choice extremists," I said.

"When I think of a pro-life zealot, a certain name comes to mind," Bretta said. "Starts with an M."

"What about Dennis Smith?" I asked.

"What about him?"

"Well, it seems to me . . . the greatest irony of the past six months is Dennis's zeal. His effort—to document the infamous D&C—is what eventually nailed the rapists."

Bretta joined the circle of grins. "Little did he know—"

She walked over, sat on my lap, put her arms around me, and kissed me on the forehead.

Sitting there with my daughter close, those big, fluffy snowflakes visible through the kitchen window, a fire crackling in the fireplace, and the aroma of Thanksgiving dinner filling the room—I thought about how lucky I was to have such a wonderful family.

And then, a devious thought wormed its way out of my subconscious.

"Good old Dennis," I said. "Why don't we write him a thank you note?"

Credits

I first started writing *Overturn* eight years ago. The idea came from my son, Harvey, and from an article he found in *The Atlantic Monthly.* At that time, the South Dakota Legislature had just passed House Bill 1215—legislation that banned all abortions in the state. The article in *Atlantic Monthly* predicted that this South Dakota law would eventually reach the U.S. Supreme Court, where it would "overturn" Roe v. Wade.

With the passage of time, we can now see, that didn't happen. The people of South Dakota circulated petitions calling for a vote of the people. The vote was held in 2006, and the law was rescinded. Apparently, the South Dakota Legislature misjudged their constituents.

In a story like this, the 800 pound gorilla is character motivation—it's the essential ingredient. Get it right and you have a potential spellbinder. Get it wrong and you have a flop. Readers who have followed my writing will recognize that *Overturn* is my seventh novel, and you would think that, by now, I would have a well-developed writer's sensitivity about this critical component. I thought I did—until I found myself knee-deep in the confusing attitudes about abortion. It's not like other issues. It's emotional as well as intellectual, and this mix causes people to hedge their views. So, writers have to work extra hard to get it right. The crucial scene in *Overturn* comes in chapter nine when Bretta takes a coat hanger and tries to self-abort herself. It's the pivotal event to which everything else in the story is linked. And I have fellow writer Paul Fry and his wife Nancy to thank for this scene. It's a biggie. It makes possible an imperative motivation for all the leading characters. Thank you Paul and Nancy.

Critique groups are needed for feedback in story development, especially for a novel with such fundamental, and sharply divided, issues as "pro-choice" and "pro-life." I was lucky to have Stan Cosby, Bettie Haller, Pam Kessler, Bob McGinnis, Janda Raker, and Nan Rinella, a wonderful group of skilled writers who were almost equally divided on abortion. We met at the church on Tuesday afternoons and debated my fairness in treating both sides of the conflict. If you, as a reader, feel that I have crafted a story that treats both viewpoints equally, then we should thank my critique group. They did their best to keep me honest.

Special thanks to Paula Silici, the lady with the blue pencil. Paula edited the South Dakota version back in 2007 and made hundreds of suggestions. And then, seven years later, she went through it again in 2014 to further tighten the Texas version. Thanks, Paula, for your many, many helpful ideas and suggestions.

This is a story that contains an enormous amount of professional detail in two areas: medical treatment and law enforcement. I was fortunate to have expert help from Robert Gross, M.D. for the former and from Joel Richardson, Randall County's award-winning Sheriff, for the latter. Thanks Bob and Joel—I couldn't have written this story without you.

Thanks also to my granddaughter, Heather, for her suggestion about the reversal of Evelyn Jones. It's a pivotal point in the story, and, I think, helps to illustrate the "slippery slope" of the abortion debate. Thanks, Heather.

In closing, I must once again thank the folks at Denny's Restaurant in Amarillo. Most of *Overturn* was written there in the early morning hours with "white noise" and "aroma of breakfast" to feed the writer's muse. Special thanks again to Diane McGinnis, the world's best waitress, for 1,000 cups of coffee to keep the words coming.

Sometimes fiction imitates life at a higher level. So, to enrich the probability of this idyllic fantasy, I have set the story in Texas, which has a strong Republican (read conservative) legislature and would rank high as one of the most likely states to pass anti-abortion legislation. And I have included my son Harvey's suggestion about how our country might resolve the seemingly, unending, "pro-life/pro-choice" debate. It's presented in the closing scene. Hope you like it.

Harry
Canyon, Texas
Summer, 2014

Novels by Harry Haines:

Orphan

Texas Panic!

Collusion

The Cover-up at Ann Arbor

Offshore

Puppet Politics

Overturn

$26.95
ISBN 978-0-9834537-4-1
52695>
9 780983 453741